Aliens vs Dinosaurs
at the Beginning of Time

By Nick Delmedico and Nick Delmedico

Published by

halfabook.com

Copyright ©2001, 2013 by Nick Delmedico

Revised, Third Edition

Manufactured in the United States of America

Aliens versus Dinosaurs at the Beginning of Time

Young Adult Fiction RL5

Cover illustration: Chad Barbour
Back cover by Aaron Arter
Interior illustrations: by Nick Delmedico, Rod Gonzales

ISBN   978-1-58884-003-5

ALIENS VS. DINOSAURS

at the beginning of time

by Nick Delmedico   & Nick Delmedico

Aliens vs. Dinosaurs at the Beginning of Time
Prologue: Selection Day, 65 million BC

There was a roar, a beastly sound that came forth with such resonance that it shook stone as it echoed off the walls of the deep canyon. The roar carried with it the power and presence of the King, the leader of the dinosaurs, who accepted the challenge for dominance of the herd. It carried with it his spirit, the thrill of the hunt, and the alpha male assurance that this battle would leave only one survivor.

The King roared again, taking up his position in front of a menacing tyrannosaur much like himself, only bigger. This did not disturb King Rex, it only strengthened his resolve. He knew a fight was not won with physical power alone, that it was actually won in the mind. He sized up the brute that stood before him.

Cavernjaw, as he was called, was almost half again the size of Rex, and Rex was a big dinosaur by standards. Cavernjaw was decorated with scars, signs that he had survived many battles. His claws were dagger sharp, mounted on huge feet attached to powerful legs that he continued to move nervously back and forth. His short, tiny hands clasped and unclasped in a maniacal fashion. His tail swayed as he teetered to balance himself. He opened his mouth, snarling and displaying his sharp, pointed teeth. He let out a bellow of his own but it sounded weak beside the King's voice.

Rex roared again, his voice shaking with power. They were in the center of a large canyon, a natural arena with small openings at both ends. The sound was amplified by the rock. He cantered in front of Cavernjaw, roaring again. The blast from his breath brushed past the skin of the larger dinosaur carrying the sound of his challenge to the crowd assembled on the surrounding cliffs. Here sat all manner of dinosaurs, large and small, posturing to see the drama that was about to unfold.

Rex let out another roar. "Let it begin," he yelled in the rough language of the dinosaurs. Not all the dinosaurs understood the language, but they knew the meaning. It was the time of the first season of the full moon, the time once a year when a worthy competitor could challenge the

King for the right to lead the herd. Smaller battles between beta males had finally produced this champion. Cavernjaw was well qualified to be here. The challenge had been duly issued and now accepted by the reigning King. A fight to the death was about to begin.

It was the way of the dinosaurs, the ritual of dominance. If no one challenges there is no fight, but that has never happened. In one respect, it is a necessary test. The dinosaurs demand certain qualities in their leadership, and one of them is the ritual of the death fight. It is the old ways, the way of the beast, and a way to acknowledge that dinosaurs, despite their long evolution, are still very much prey to primal instincts. It is also a public spectacle, something for the citizens to talk about, to glorify their leader and worship the King as a hero.

Cavernjaw made the first move. Towering over Rex he snapped downward with his jaws, barely missing the King's back. Rex pivoted on his thick legs, ducking and twirling as Cavernjaw continued to relentlessly snap at him. Saliva dripped from his teeth, spraying across Rex's back.

Large flying dinosaurs called Pterodactyl, circled overhead watching the action. They had sharp eyes, riding the currents of air on their wings while staying focused on the sights below. On the canyon ridge spectators passed comments as they also looked on in awe.

"I think this one's strong enough to beat him," said a stenonychosaurus, his bird-like body trembling. "We're witnessing the end of King Rex."

"I don't know," said a triceratops, shaking his head plate and twisting his horns around. "The challenge match is still young and Rex always has a few tricks left in him. He's a thinker as much as a fighter."

"He's clever, all right," said a nearby velociraptor, tapping his claws on a rock. "But Cavernjaw definitely has the advantage."

There was a roar of pain from the canyon as Cavernjaw's teeth graced the side of Rex's leg. Small, red lines were now etched in his skin across his thigh. Rex backed away and twisted, looking at the wounded leg. He let out another wail, this one a cry of anger. He narrowed his eyes at Cavernjaw, sniffing him for information, sensing the smell of fear, perhaps sickness, or perhaps even the blood fever.

"And now you will learn why they call me Cavernjaw," said the dinosaur, opening his mouth so wide that it could easily swallow Rex's entire head. He pointed his head skyward in display, his mouth open, showing the crowd his weapons. Mixed sounds came from the rim wall. Rex backed away slowly, his eyes fixed on Cavernjaw.

Above the Queen looked on, surrounded by her handmaidens and attendants. She was a stunning tyrannosaurus rex with deep, passive eyes. She tried to keep an air of dignity about her as she observed this horrible event. She closed her eyes, refusing to watch at times, suppressing the urge to use her psychic powers. She dared not interfere. Instead she thought of other things. She remembered all the good things she and Rex had been able to accomplish. Together they were bringing order to the dinosaur world. To think that all this could be undone with one brutal fight.

She could shut her eyes but not her ears. She could hear everything around her. There were sounds in favor of Rex and those that spoke for Cavernjaw. Behind her a handmaiden whispered to another beside her. "If Cavernjaw wins, he will have the right to take the queen as his own."

"Or immediately put her to death," replied her friend.

An old Spinosaurus overheard them. "Quiet, you imbeciles. Show some respect! Don't you think the Queen knows that?"

Down in the arena Cavernjaw was swiping again, Rex barely avoiding his jaws. Again and again Rex was able to duck beneath the massive battering ram of a head. The large dinosaur looked annoyed and angry and he retreated for a moment, twisting his neck to loosen it from the effort. Rex studied him closely, evaluating his opponent for weaknesses. Sometimes the weakness was not in the body, but lodged somewhere in the spirit. Cavernjaw's anger betrayed his lack of control, his swipes were becoming more aggressive and random. It was making him weaker, draining him of energy and power.

Rex thought about his own position. The scars on his leg had widened. No longer were they slim lines, the centers were opening, bursting and glistening with something painful underneath. Rex focused. He must not lose his own self control. He took a deep breath as both dinosaurs backed away and rested.

Cavernjaw looked up into the cliffs, staring at some distant point. It was not the first time Rex had noticed him glance in that direction. Rex wanted to look but he dared not take his eyes off his opponent. He tried to use his peripheral vision, seeing both Cavernjaw and what Cavernjaw was looking at. What was so interesting up there?

Of course, though Rex. Oafs like Cavernjaw have massive bodies but they often lack in brains. They give their power over to others, acting as cronies for a more organized foe. Cavernjaw must be looking to his master for instructions. He's telling his master that his tactic of death swipes is not working. What do I try now, master? Look at him! I can see the look of confusion on his face lying just beneath his anger.

Rex roared, drawing Cavernjaw's attention away from the cliff. "Let's get on with it," he growled.

Cavernjaw again began his pattern of swiping and swaying, trying to hack at his opponent as if he were a giant scythe. Rex kept ducking just below the teeth. He took a few minor hits, the teeth creating lines of red that crossed over his back. Rex continued to duck, teetering like a log hung on a cliff, flexing his legs and lowering his body just out of reach of the gaping maw of Cavernjaw. Rex studied his swiping pattern. He had to be getting dizzy moving his head like that. His neck must be hurting.

Rex was correct. Cavernjaw stopped for a moment to shake his neck out. He lifted his head skyward again, his eye again seeking that unknown master on the high cliff.

Rex didn't hesitate. While the giant was distracted he rolled forward, swiping Cavernjaw's leg with his tail. The small red lines on Rex's leg broke open, dripping blood across his thigh. Cavernjaw toppled to the ground, his huge claws grasping the air. Rex moved in low, between the legs and beneath the claws. He opened his mouth wide and bit down into the fallen dinosaur's belly. He tore through the skin easily, tasting first the blood, then the organs as pieces of them shredded in his mouth. He opened his jaws wider, breathing the scent in through his nose and plunging his head deeper into the open wound. He swirled his head, the teeth cutting everything they touched and filling his mouth with new, more exotic tastes.

Cavernjaw let out a scream, a high pitched animal wail that hushed the crowd. Rex bit down again, chewing but never raising his head from the wound. He sucked in the juices of his enemy, a sweet nectar that tasted of success. He could suck the life out of Cavernjaw right now if he chose to. The two lay motionless together, the crowd silent in disbelief. Rex took one last taste and pulled back, moving away from the fallen dinosaur with amazing speed. His mouth oozed with blood, pieces of flesh and glistening innards that dripped to the ground.

Cavernjaw whimpered and shivered. Although he appeared finished, Rex did not take his eye off him. He continued to back away, chewing the soft parts of his enemy and spitting the hardened flesh on the ground at his feet.

"Finish him," yelled some of the crowd, beginning to chant the words in rhythm. "Finish him," they yelled in unison.

Rex roared, a sound full of anger and wrath. He stared at them, moving his vision to make eye contact with all he could see. His action silenced them, the chant dying to a single voice that quickly extinguished. The only sound heard was Cavernjaw's whimper, echoing off the walls of the canyon. It was a whisper, magnified by the rock, falling on the ears of every dinosaur assembled. Rex stared at them all, seeing the look of submission in them, asserting that he was truly leader of the pack, the King of the Dinosaurs.

As his eyes swept over the crowd, Rex noted their reactions. Some looked down toward the ground instantly, a sign of respect. Some stared at him eye to eye, daring not to consider themselves as equals, yet glaring with the reserved look of challenge, telling the King that next year he may face one of them as an opponent. He especially noted the looks of defiance where he scanned the area Cavernjaw had found so interesting. He wondered which one held the puppet strings of his poor fallen enemy.

His eyes found the Queen, his beloved Helena. Reading the relief in her, he smiled with satisfaction. It was his right of victory to kill her and choose a new mate should he so desire. Leaders of the past have done so, often to serve their own passions, but Rex had better aspirations. The subjects needed their Queen as much as they needed him. She was progressive, uniting the dinosaurs by teaching them a common language, and she had special talents few could imagine. Most of all she loved him and made him feel whole and complete. They ruled together and his subjects were better for it.

Cavernjaw groaned again, the gaping wound in his belly bursting with ooze and tattered, ragged organs. He rolled over and stood up weakly, looking at Rex for a moment before turning away. He limped towards the narrow passage leading out of the canyon. The guards at the exit stood ready. It was also the Kings right to order Cavernjaw executed and they were waiting for word to maul and tear the defeated dinosaur apart.

"Let him go!" yelled Rex. "Let him find somewhere to die with dignity. Let his body be food for the earth and for the lesser creatures. It's better than being fodder for this public spectacle." There were some nods of agreement. "Cavernjaw was a worthy opponent, and I salute him." Rex turned, his eyes following Cavernjaw off the field of honor. As everyone watched Cavernjaw, the King's eyes darted upward towards the area where Cavernjaw had been focused. His true threat laid there, a more worthy opponent, one who hunted with wiles and cunning. This one used minions to distract and test Rex, always watching and plotting from the sidelines. Rex thought about it. At one time all you needed to lead dinosaurs was brute force, but this was new territory. Dinosaurs were definitely evolving, but into what?

Rex stood alone in the center of the arena. He let out a roar again, the sound of victory and celebration, and a smile curled his lips when he was finished. All was right with the world. Cheers and roars went up everywhere and crowds began to disburse. Many headed towards the mystic pond, a place where naturally bubbly water was filled with microorganisms that made a dinosaur feel inebriated and light headed. In past victories Rex and Helena had celebrated with them, but now he preferred quiet time with his family.

The Elite Guard, a special component of handpicked dinosaurs, escorted the King back to his palace. They joined up with the Queen and it pleased Rex that they walked home together. The path went across high ledges with magnificent views of lush jungles and green valleysElite Guard. It followed wide rivers which they eventually crossed, getting wet up to their waists as they waded to the other side. It passed beneath a canopy of green and through a forest filled with wonder. They met many communities of dinosaurs, loyal subjects who wanted to catch a glimpse of their King and Queen. Some spoke words of congratulation; others thanked them for all they had done to make the kingdom safe from predators. Once they stopped for an insistent ankylosaurus, a low, armored dinosaur with short legs and a large, bony club at the end of its tail. Their spit is known to have great healing power and this one was quite concerned about the King. He said he could smell the infection and insisted on licking the gashes on Rex's thigh and back. Rex obliged him, bending down so the stout ankylosaurus could reach his battle wounds with his long leathery tongue. He then thanked him for his help and concern, inviting him to walk beside him and join him in a victory celebration at the Palace.

The royal procession finally arrived at the Palace, a hollow mountain that was a focal point of the Kingdom. They passed between giant rock gates and inside the entrance, through a labyrinth of caves. They climbed many levels into a giant room, half open to the light by a terrace outside. This was a perch fit to view a Kingdom. Two natural stone formations at one end of the room were the traditional sitting rocks of the King and Queen, giving it the name of the throne room. This was a room large enough to accommodate the stewards of government; the dinosaurs that composed the extended body of leadership.

The Elite Guard took up positions at the entrances of the room as it slowly filled with dinosaur dignitaries. Some spread out onto the terrace where food had been placed for snacking. Stenonychosaurus, intelligent dinosaurs with tiny hands that could grasp objects, moved through the room with large leaves filled with an assortment of food to choose from. Graceful, perfectly counterbalanced on two legs by a long, pointed tail, their long necks would twist through the crowd, passing between the guests as easily as a plesiosaurus passing through water. One stepped forward, offering a leaf full of tasty selections to the King and Queen.

Many faces in the room looked to the King with thanks. They all seemed grateful that Rex had remained in power. Everywhere dinosaurs were happy. It would lead you to believe that all was right with the world, that everyone was in agreement, but Rex knew that it was not so. There was still the unseen enemy, the one behind the fools like Cavernjaw. Rex felt the cold eye of this clever one watching him even now from a distance, testing him for weakness.

No matter. It was time for Rex to give his speech. The room was full, the guests well fed, and it was traditional to say a few words. It was a political speech by nature, and he had thought a lot about what he wanted to say, but in the end his words always came from his heart.

"Fellow dinosaurs, I thank you all for joining me in celebration on this Day of the Challenge. First, let me assure you that I have not elected to kill the Queen and feast on her innards, much as our ancestors did when they celebrated."

There was nervous laughter. "Our ancestors might have done that, but those were ancient times, and these are new times. At sunrise this morning I was unsure of what would become of our land. As I faced my opponent I thought of how we must also face the challenges ahead of us. We must overcome our differences. I know some of you don't agree with our progressive policies, but sooner or later we must evolve. We rule this planet, and we can fight each other like we have for the last one hundred and forty million years, or we can make a conscious effort to change the way things are."

There were nods of agreement around the room. Triceratops agreed with raptors who agreed with spinosaurus who agreed with stenonychosaurus and so on. Rex nodded, the final agreement, and he continued with his speech. "Tonight, as sunset approaches, I can tell you that things will move forward as usual here at the Palace. Tomorrow will be just another day. The Queen will continue conducting school and I will be here holding court. Our efforts to further our way of life will continue. Tonight, dinosaurs will be able to sleep outside under the stars with no fear of predation. Thanks to our flying friends who patrol our skies and carry our messages to the far part of our realms, our words will continue to spread." He paused to acknowledge the flying dinosaurs that were present in the room, the pterodactyl and the pteronodon. "Thanks to the vigilance of our Elite Guard and our concerned citizens, we live in a society where dinosaurs are safe from rogue packs of carnivores feasting on the innocent." He made eye contact with some of the guards around the room, then some of the leading citizens and heads of the big dinosaur families.

Even as he said those words, Rex paused, pondering his unknown foe. Despite his doubts, he had to send forth a message of hope to his people. "Have no fear. We will fight all our enemies and survive. I will, with all my powers and even my life, protect us from evil in this world. For I am your King and this is my job. Join with me and together we will work to maintain peace and safety among the land. Let us move through this time of change and advance our civilization out of the darkness that enslaved our ancestors."

There were roars of agreement this time. Thunderous applause, the flapping of leathery wings outside on the terrace from proud pterodactyl and pteronodon. There were triceratops pounding their hooves, and the tapping of claws against the stone floors. There was celebration in the Palace tonight.

"We have found a way to provide for all. We eat no more game than is necessary, take no more than the jungle provides, and waste nothing in our excess. We live in a land of peace and prosperity. With that, I bid you all good night. Enjoy the food, sleep here tonight, and rest well. I know with your help, the challenges that lay ahead will be met. They will be overcome, and the immortal power of the dinosaur spirit will endure. Sleep well tonight, my friends. For tomorrow is a new day in the history of the dinosaurs, the continued age of King Rex and Queen Helena."

There were cheers, chants of "Long live the King," and "Long live the Queen!" The royal couple stood side by side and waved to everyone in the room. Princess Natalie joined them and they left past a posted guard and into a dark tunnel.

At the end of the night, Rex lay in his bed nest with his loved ones, including a dedicated ankylosaurus that insisted on remaining awake to wet the King's wounds with his healing spittle.

"I'm glad you were victorious," said the Queen, nuzzling Rex gently as she settled into sleep.

"Me, too," said Rex, joking with her. "Otherwise you would be either dead or laying here with another."

"Death would be preferable to being with another," she said. "You are my life mate and my King." She nuzzled closer to him, the space between them melting into nothingness.

"You know I wouldn't want that," he said.

"What would you want?" she asked.

"I would want you to continue to help our people evolve. So many look up to you. You give the small dinosaurs hope. Look at how much they contribute to our society. Their labors give us many of the comforts we enjoy."

"And we give them peace in return," said the Queen. "We all have our price to pay. We all have an interest in our futures."

"What would have happened to me?" asked Natalie, their young daughter. She was at that tender age where innocence begins to flee, replaced slowly by the realities of the world.

"Maybe nothing," said the Queen. "Don't worry about it."

Helena still preferred to treat her as a child, but her Father knew better. "You may have been killed," he said.

"Rex," said the Queen. "No."

"Please, my darling. Natalie already knew that was a possibility, didn't you?" he asked. Natalie nodded somberly. "Then you also knew you might be spared, with the stipulation that you would become part of the new royal family. Correct?" Natalie nodded again. "And you also knew that the victor could murder your mother and choose you as his new Queen, didn't you?"

Helena was silent as she watched Natalie nod again. Rex looked at her and she heard his thoughts say, "See? I'm right about Natalie, aren't I?" Helena considered his opinion. Perhaps her daughter had grown up. Maybe it was time to stop looking at her like a child. She stared at the Princess again, but saw only a scared young girl. "Where did you hear such things?" she asked.

"Kids talk," said Natalie. "We listen. We know some of the oral histories."

"Sometimes the information is not correct," said the Queen. "You should ask your Father or me to verify it. You know we'd be happy to talk to you about any subject."

Natalie thought about answering. There might be some things you don't want to talk to your parents about, she thought. Instead she said "I just can't imagine being part of any other family." She looked in her mother's eye and knew Helena had heard her thoughts. She smiled sadly yet knowingly. Indeed, the Princess was growing up.

"You know I would want you to go on no matter what," said Rex. "You're a Princess, and yes, one day you could become a Queen. You must always endure. Survive no matter what."

"I feel so safe with you Father," she said.

"There is nothing I can't protect you from, my darling," said Rex. He had proven that today by defeating the mightiest of the dinosaurs. He closed his eyes as the ankylosaurus gently licked his wounds.

Helena had other thoughts as she drifted to sleep. She thought of how naive her husband's comments had been. How could you protect your daughter from ideas? From the world? Yes, even from the loss of innocence?

And could there be other threats, new dangers yet unimagined? Things that even the King could not overcome?

Chapter 1: The Beginning of Time

The young triceratops lowered his front legs, dropping his horn close to the ground. Though inexperienced, he knew the weakest part of the tyrannosaurus rex was his soft underbelly. He knew this but he had never tested it in battle. Mustering his courage, he pushed forward with his hind legs, ramming his horn forward towards his opponent.

The young rex was quick, instinctively twisting to the side to avoid being impaled. The horn managed to graze his skin making a gash on his inner thigh that started to bleed. He let out a scream, more from rage than pain. This was not his first fight with a triceratops. He knew his opponent's weaknesses and matched them against his strengths. Rex had powerful jaws and long teeth designed to rip through the toughest hide. If he could just maneuver his teeth around those horns.

He twisted to the side, moving to his left, balancing carefully on his two legs, trying to snap his jaws past the horns and beyond the giant bone plate on which the horns rested. He faked moving to one side. The triceratops made a move in that direction, exposing his side and giving his opponent the opening he needed. The rex brought his jaws down on the soft side of the triceratops, close to its back, driving his teeth deep into the flesh.

The triceratops screamed. He rolled onto his side, trying to pull the rex down to the ground where he could stomp on him, but the rex would not let go. Still gripping tightly, he twisted, his teeth cutting a small circle in his opponent's back. As he rolled on his side, the meat gave way, ripping a hunk of flesh out of the triceratops.

The rex spit the leathery piece of dinosaur out of his mouth, roaring a threat. The triceratops accepted, snarling back at him. He snapped his parrot like beak, normally used to crush plants into an edible pulp. He looked at the rex, imagining he was just another tree that needed pulping. He lunged forward, biting the knee of the tyrannosaurus. Now the rex let out a scream. Blood gushed from his leg and he backed away. The triceratops heaved forward thrusting his horns into his opponent's stomach. The rex let out an ear splitting roar that shook leaves in nearby trees.

Off to the side, two young T-rexes stared at the scene. Nate, the young male, had a grin on his face, excited at seeing another fight to the death. It was anybody's game now and he went through a series of mental calculations on what moves he would try against the triceratops. One thing was certain, the rex was in trouble. Blood spit from the open wounds on his leg, gushing in rhythms that ticked away the moments of his life. The triceratops stared at the piece of meat from his back laying on the ground. He licked it, as if that would ease the pain he felt from the open wound on his back. There was a rivulet of blood that ran from the hole and down his leg. This fight had to be ended soon or death would be the only winner. Nate has his money on the rex, betting that he wouldn't run from the fight.

The young female t-rex standing beside Nate had a completely different reaction to the fight. She looked on in disgust, shaking her head from side to side as if she were tired of the whole thing. She let out a gasp seeing the dinosaurs clash again, wondering why they didn't withdraw from the lethal combat.

"Brother versus brother," she said. "I don't know if I can put up with it, Nate."

Nate answered without looking at her, his eyes fixed on the fight. "It's the way it has been since the beginning of time Natalie. We have always lived this way."

"Not when I'm queen," she said. "We should spend time teaching our young, not fighting one another."

Natalie turned her back to the fight and began to walk away, down a trail through the thick jungle. Nate stared until he realized she was gone. He turned and followed her down the trail.

"It's the mating season now," said Nate, catching up to her.

A loud scream came from behind them. They both cringed and came to a stop.

"Does the mating season have to be so brutal?" she said.

"It's not so much mating as it is maturing," said Nate. He smiled, thrusting his leg out and drawing her attention to three deep gashes on his leg. They were fresh, not quite healed, running red, deep, and wide across his thigh.

"Oh, yes. Those scars on your thigh that you're so proud of," she said sarcastically. "Very mature."

"They are mature," he countered. "They're signs of my manhood. I got them with my father when he took me hunting."

"Well, if that's the price of maturity then I'll stay immature, thank you."

"Now you're really being immature," said Nate. "This is your father's empire, the empire you will inherit one day. And despite what you believe, the world is a brutal place."

"I know," she said. "Everyone tells me it's a jungle out there. Thanks to my father, we're safe from most of the dangers in the world."

Nate became enthusiastic at the mention of the King. "When I grow up I want to be just like him. He always does what's right, no matter how hard."

"My father is special," she said. "We've talked a lot about his plans. We want to bring a new age to the dinosaurs. We've had millions of years of evolution and haven't improved much. We need to take a bold step forward."

"He's awesome," said Nate. "He has psychic dinosaurs that can talk to anyone."

"You mean my mother," corrected Natalie. "She has the psychic ability, not my father. My aunts do, too. They all help father because they believe in him. He's trying to develop a common language. With that, we can all understand each other."

"Why would I want to talk to a dilophosaurus? Or a compy for that matter?" asked Nate.

They heard another roar from the fight behind them.

"I'd settle for a triceratops talking to a tyrannosaurus rex right now," said Natalie.

"But triceratops and t-rex can already understand each other," said Nate.

"Well, you're right," admitted Natalie. "Obviously talking to each other is not the same as understanding each other."

"It wouldn't matter anyway. Predators will always fight each other, either for mates, food, or for territory."

Natalie continued as if not hearing him. "Mother has been working on the language problem. There are many sounds we have in common, and this is the basis of her language. She has already taught the palace staff the basics. We will evolve despite your attitude, Nate. A lot of others are beginning to use the common tongue as well. And nobody has to be psychic to communicate."

"Are you psychic?" asked Nate.

Before she could answer they were interrupted by a scream of terror.

"That didn't sound like fighting," said Natalie.

"No, it didn't," agreed Nate. They heard another horrifying scream. They both turned and ran back towards the clearing. There were more screams, beginning to come from the jungle all around them.

When they reached the clearing they couldn't believe what they saw. In the middle was a strange, silver object, round and flat, almost like a river stone, except much larger. The two dinosaurs were no longer fighting each other. Instead they beat their bodies against the object, smearing it with dinosaur blood. A lightning bolt shot out from the object, striking the tyrannosaurus rex. He screamed in pain. The triceratops rammed the object hard, but was exhausted from the fight. His horns glanced off the side of the thing and his breath heaved with the effort.

Nate and Natalie looked up. The sky was filled with the strange silver objects. One of them hovered overhead and shot a bolt at Nate. He jumped back in surprise. More appeared overhead, with more lightning bolts. Dinosaur screams were everywhere. Nate heard a new sound, getting louder. He had heard it before, the thunderous sound of hooves steadily growing louder.

"It's a stampede," yelled Nate.

"We have to get to father," said Natalie. "He's not far away."

The stampede came into view, adults and children all running towards them, knocking down trees and tearing the jungle to pieces.

"Looks like a lot of us are headed to the Palace."

They turned and ran together, joining the stampede. The flying stones appeared over them and rays begin to strike around them. As they ran, they were joined by more dinosaurs. Natalie tried to organize and direct them to keep the crowd from giving in to blind panic.

"Come on!" she urged. "Hurry. There's safety ahead in the Palace."

She saw a baby brontosaurus nearby get hit with a red ray. This was something different than the lightning bolts. The baby bronto let out a wail as the ray formed a red, transparent bag around him. He screamed in fear, struggling for his footing as the bag began to shake and slowly lift off the ground.

His mother moved faster than any brontosaurus Natalie had ever seen. She charged the ray, throwing herself over the bag and breaking the beam. She screamed in pain, but the bag dissolved and her baby was free. He ran to re-join the stampede, followed closely by his mother. She limped, and there was a scar on her back where the ray had struck her. She was weak and slow to follow the herd, but she continued to roar and protect the children.

Two stones moved in close above her. She extended her long neck and snapped her jaws at them. They quickly moved off, hovering just out of range. A velociraptor ran up her back and leaped from her neck onto one of the stones. It wobbled and became unstable, tilting to one side. The raptor started to slide off but held on to something with his claws. It threw the thing off balance. It plummeted down towards the jungle, crashing through the treetops. The raptor jumped off just as a stout tree branch ripped a gash in the side of the flying stone.

It was hollow. There were things inside, two legged creatures with green, leathery skin and large eyes. One of them fell through the hole, dropping to the ground with an odd sounding scream. The stone continued downward, hitting another branch and catching fire. There were crunching sounds as it ripped through the canopy of leaves before it disappeared into the thick jungle. There was an explosion and flames shot out from the wreckage. The jungle was suddenly on fire, causing more panic among the dinosaurs.

The second stone hovered above the mother brontosaurus and glowed red. It moved towards the crash. It floated near the velociraptor, shooting lightning bolts at him until he disappeared into the safety of jungle. The mother brontosaurus bellowed, joined by other dinosaurs in a roar of victory, but it was fleeting.

She turned away, her victory roar becoming a scream. Her baby was trapped again, calling for her from inside a red-ray bag beginning to lift off the ground. She ran to save him. All about her dinosaur children continued to scurry to safety, yelling and screaming as they ran. Behind them the fire from the crash grew larger, flames crackling skyward as the jungle burned.

The mother bronto was weak, her movements were slow and painful. Her breath was labored and she limped. A black scar on her back steamed as a clot formed over another wound she had sustained. The bag containing her baby shook and began to rise. She ran as it was carried out of her reach, tethered to a flying stone by a red beam as it lifted skyward.

She wailed, looking upward and then dropping to the ground in emotional agony. The velociraptor stopped to comfort her. There was no time. Beside them, a fleeing compy slammed into a transparent wall that became a red, transparent bag around him. It lifted up and out of sight. The sky was full of stones. With great effort and the encouragement of several raptors, the mother brontosaurus stood up. She roared in anger at the stones. One hovered nearby and shot lightning bolts at her. She screamed in defiance.

Nate heard her and stopped running. It was a horrible sound, one he had not heard any dinosaur make. It was the sound of pain resonating in her long neck. He turned and looked at the wounded mother brontosaurus. It made him angry to see a mother separated from her child, there was something evil in it. Three stones circled above her, pelting her with rays and blasts from strange weapons. They reminded Nate of a pack of predators who had singled out the weakest of the herd, hounding the poor animal until they gave up under the torment. She screamed. As he gazed in amazement, a bag formed around a baby stegosaurus near him.

"I can't let this happen again," he said. Gritting his teeth he rammed full force against the bag. It started to lift off the ground. He leaped up, his tail flailing upward like a whip. It sliced through the beam, freeing the baby stegosaurus. He gave Nate a grateful look and scurried off.

A stone appeared over him, shooting lightning bolts at him. His leg burned and a wound appeared next to the distinctive gash of scars on his thigh.

"Hey!" he yelled. "Not my scar!" He ran off, merging with the herd, a quick glance back over his shoulder to see if he was being pursued.

The battle raged everywhere. Dinosaurs fought off flying stones and protected the mother brontosaurus as they moved her along. More and more, transparent bags formed around many of the baby dinosaurs. The mother bronto was exhausted and she stopped under a jungle canopy to rest for a moment. An ankylosaurus, the small armored dinosaur, came forward and licked her wounds while the other dinosaurs continued to fight. A red bag fell to the ground, smashing beside her and freeing a baby dinosaur.

She smiled, but she was tired. She rolled on to her side, laying her head down and looking up into the sky. It was filled with stones, many of them dangling bags beneath them as they flew out of sight. Flying dinosaurs, pteronodons and pterodactyls, were fighting the stones. She saw a pteronodon hit by a yellow lightning bolt from one of the stones. It dropped, falling limp and lifeless, hitting the ground beside her with a loud splat.

She wailed again, lowering her head in exhaustion. The fight raged about her but she didn't care. Her baby was gone, as was her will to live, and all about her seemed so empty.

Chapter 2: The Fortress

King Rex's palace was a huge labyrinth of caves carved in sheer rock, with features of both a fortress and a palace. It was a mountain riddled with tunnels. On one side of the mountain there was an opening, a large cavern, faced with two natural rock pillars on each side. From inside this cavern there were tunnels leading to other points within the palace. A ramp led to the cavern and served as the main entrance, but there were also ground level entrances and tunnels.

The King's Elite Guard, a special cadre of handpicked soldiers, stood watch over the entrance. Higher up the mountain there were balconies, terraces and dark recesses in the rocks. Towards the top there were pillars of rock that rose like minarets. There were stone spires that pointed skyward like the towers of a castle. Vegetation spilled out from crevices and ledges, adorning it like a palace should be.

There were many rooms and corridors in the palace. Deep in the lair was the King's bed-nest and private quarters where his family slept. There were barracks for the Elite Guard, dormitories, and chambers that served as meeting halls. There were living spaces and cool caves for food storage. There was even a latrine. Most of all, there was shelter for the fleeing dinosaurs. High above on one of the larger balconies that adjoined his throne room, King Rex looked down at the scene before him, his Generals standing silently behind him.

Dinosaurs, mostly women and children, stampeded towards the palace pursued by strange flying stones. Deadly rays blasted flying dinosaurs from the sky. On the ground, his troops were pelted mercilessly. Children were being carried away in red bags. He could see his best men fighting valiantly despite being cornered and blasted by the stones. Casualties were beginning to mount.

There were pockets of fire and smoke coming from the jungle. In one dark clearing he saw the charred bodies of dinosaurs that had been trapped by the flames. In the distance he saw a fallen brontosaurus. His eyes narrowed, his ear turning to catch the faint cries of her agony. The weight of it all fell heavy on his heart. He bowed slightly with pain, his head lowering towards the ground. Behind him one of his General's eyes flared with anger, another's with fear. Rex struggled to take it all in, but the scene was too fantastic. His world was falling apart.

Below, the King's Elite Guard formed a protective gauntlet that channeled the stampede towards the palace entrance. The herd thundered up the ramp that led to the opening. Into this hole poured hundreds of dinosaurs seeking refuge: children, families, stragglers, and old ones. Just inside the entrance they were greeted by duck billed dinosaurs, house servants who quickly directed them to safety deep within the palace.

"This way, this way," said one. "Slow down, please."

"Calm down," said another. "You're in King Rex's house. You're under his protection now."

"You're safe," said a third. "No need to panic any longer."

They directed them down various corridors towards receiving areas where other dinosaurs waited to give them further instructions.

"Move along," said the head duckbill. "Orderly, now. Children go left, families down this hall. Someone at the end of the hall will help you. Move along, please."

Despite what the duckbills said, the hoard was slow to change speed. Outside, Nate and Natalie avoided the ramp and moved towards a side entrance. They were quickly blocked by Cassius who was Captain of the King's Elite Guard and also Nate's dad.

"Don't bother your father," he said to Natalie. "He is meeting with his generals. He has sent me here to watch for you and see to your safety."

"We can take care of ourselves, Dad," said Nate. "Didn't you see us rescue that baby stegosaurus?" Nate stuck his leg out so Cassius could examine his latest scar.

His father looked down and smiled. "Yes, I know you can take care of yourself," he said. "I saw that brave rescue. Three scars of manhood were not enough, I see?"

"I'm ready to serve at your side, Father," he said.

Natalie grew impatient and interrupted them. "What is going on, Cassius? Do you see what's happening here?" she asked.

All three turned towards the battle. A pack of raptors had teamed up with a herd of brontosaurus, leaping from their backs and necks, trying to pull down a squad of low flying stones. Large dinosaurs were using their tails to fling rocks like artillery at the stones. One huge dinosaur scooped up piles of rock with his mouth and spit them out like a volcano blast. Several flying stones were hit. One tumbled from the sky, creatures falling like bugs out of an old log. Another burst into flames, the red, transparent bag beneath it dissolving as it fell. The small, baby dinosaur began to drop from the sky. A swift pteronodon rescued it from certain death, grabbing it in its claws and putting it gently on the ground.

The battle was not the focus of Natalie's attention. It was the growing number of stones rising towards the clouds that now had little red bags in tow, each one containing a terrified baby dinosaur. Over the sound of battle she could hear cries, growls, and wailing. It was a haunting sound, a chorus of youthful voices in desperation.

"They're stealing the children! Why?" she asked. "I must see my Father."

"I told you he is busy Princess," said Cassius.

"We have to find out where they are taking the children," she said.

"The pterodactyl will tell us," he said. "Look how high they are flying to pursue them."

They looked skyward where they saw pterodactyls trying to fight their way through a blockade of stones. They were protecting a fleet of fleeing ships towing bags. Lightning bolts shot out from the stones in the blockade, burning the pterodactyl. There were screeches and one unlucky pterodactyl fell limply to the ground.

"Look," she said. "They're no match for the shiny skinned flyers. Look how high they go! Where are they taking them?"

At the main entrance to the Palace the crowd of refugees had dwindled to a few stragglers. High above on a ledge, a brachiosaurus took a deep breath and forced air through the vents on his head, sounding like the blast of a horn. It continued in regular intervals like a warning klaxon.

"You father's signal," said Cassius, drawing to attention. He turned to his men, the Elite Guard who stood nearby in perfect formation as the gauntlet of protection. "You twelve, come with me," he said, splitting them in half. "The rest of you form a perimeter and guard the entrance to the palace. Protect the palace at all costs."

"Yes sir!" answered a lieutenant.

"Take me with you, Dad," said Nate. "I'm ready to serve at your side."

Cassius thought about the request for a moment. "I have something better in mind," he said. His voice suddenly became official sounding, clear and commanding. "Nate, because of your bravery in battle and for saving the baby stegosaurus I am giving you a field commission and appointing you to the rank of Protector to the Royal Family."

"Are you serious?" asked Nate.

"I was never more serious," he said. "Nate, you are now a Protector of the Royal Family, just like me. Your first assignment will be to protect the Royal Princess, Natalie."

Natalie frowned. "Oh, great. So now I'm saddled with him at my side? Cassius, playing soldier is fun but you still haven't answered my question. Why are they stealing the children? And where are they taking them?"

Cassius came to attention again as he focused on the klaxon sounding from above. His twelve selected men stood at attention, waiting for him. "Your father will know what to do," he said. "That's why he's calling for us now."

"Then why can't we go, too?" pleaded Natalie.

"This is business, Princess," he answered. "The business of war. Stay safe with the other children for now. Your father will send for you later."

Cassius turned and left. When he was out of sight, she muttered after him, "In case you haven't noticed lately, I'm not a child."

Natalie stared at the fighting in the distance. The battle looked hopeless to her. Everywhere she turned, dinosaurs were losing. The flying dinosaurs were making a noble but futile attempt to catch the flying stones. She doubted they could succeed in following them for long. Everywhere she heard wails and cries of defeat from baby and adult dinosaurs alike.

Nate watched for a while. "Come on, Natalie," he finally said. "Let's get inside the Palace where it's safe."

Natalie could not help but voice her question again. "Where are they taking the children?"

"Your father will find out," said Nate. "Let's get inside."

Natalie shook her head. "He doesn't know. Nobody knows where they are taking them. Nobody but..."

Nate waited for an answer but none came. "Nobody but who?" he asked. She remained silent, thinking. "What, Natalie? What?" asked Nate.

Her face lit with understanding and her eyes narrowed in determination. "I know, Nate. I know how to find out where they are taking them."

She took off running towards the battle. Nate watched her for a minute, then took off after her, muttering to himself.

"Watch over her, you said, Dad. Protector of the Royal Family. What did you get me into?"

Chapter 3: A Senseless Act

The throne room was a huge chamber with a smooth floor. One side was open to the balcony where the battle raged in the distance. Rex stepped inside from the balcony and into the throne room followed by his Generals. The room was crowded with dignitaries and concerned members of the royal court who stayed respectfully in the viewing area. Rex acknowledged them, then moved slowly towards his throne at the opposite end of the hall. The room began to fill as the emergency klaxon continued to summon the local leaders to the King's presence. Cassius entered from a side tunnel, catching his attention.

The Captain of the Guard stopped silently just inside, sensing a certain heaviness in the air. He motioned to his men and they took up positions along the walls at the entrances. Rex nodded to one of his Generals who gave the order to silence the brachiosaurus. The klaxon stopped and all eyes and ears fell on the King. The quiet was broken only by the distant sounds of battle drifting in from the outside.

Rex paced the floor in front of his throne, a natural stone bench that rose sharply from the floor. Two of the Elite Guard stood at attention against the wall behind him. The Queen sat passively nearby on her throne watching him through patient eyes. He had seen those eyes before and knew she was not actually looking at him. She was in a psychic trance, in touch with everything around her on a deep level that few could understand. Others had to turn and look at the battle, but she saw the events outside the Palace unfolding in her mind's eye. She couldn't explain how it happened. Sometimes she would hear a sound that would bring forth a picture in her mind. Other times, a muscle would spasm and she would suddenly see an image that she knew was real and happening. Sometimes it was a feeling, vague and unfocused until it solidified into something tangible.

The King leaned in close to her, peering into her empty unfocused eyes. He could almost hear the cries of young, trapped dinosaurs. He could hear distant roars, sounds of strange flying things as they crashed, raptors screeching, and screams in a language he had never heard. He couldn't tell if they were coming from outside the Palace or from inside the Queen. He studied her, imagining he could almost see what she must be seeing. The seeing became a feeling and the sounds became cries of anguish, dinosaur tears and wails for the loss of loved ones. The Queen shut her eyes and the sounds stopped.

"What did you feel, Helena?" asked Rex, speaking softly as he leaned closer to her.

Her voice was hollow and contracted. "Such pain!" she said.

"Why are they doing this?" Rex asked. He waited for an answer, studying her closely. He saw a tear form in the corner of her eye, growing larger until it expanded and broke free. She remained steely and he turned away from her.

"This is maddening," he said. "Let's go out there and fight."

The Elite Guard snapped to attention, beginning to fall in place beside him.

The Queen spoke. "Wait! Don't go."

"But they're stealing the children," he said. "How can I not go?" He moved towards the troops. A nervous Sergeant caught his eye.

"Tell us what to do, Sire," said the Sergeant. "Give the order and I will fight."

"What would you do, Sergeant?" asked Rex.

He stumbled over his words, trying to respond to the King's question. "I'm not sure, Sire," he finally said. "Just tell me and I'll do it. I'm ready."

Rex smiled. With loyal followers like this he could not help but win this fight. But his smile faded as he thought of the fallen soldiers he had seen outside his Palace. He moved back to the Queen and looked in her eye. Something in her face took his anger away. He turned towards the Sergeant.

"It's not the time to fight, my brave friend," he said. "It's time to use our heads."

Rex begins to pace, thinking out loud.

"But how can we outwit this flying foe?" he continued. "Our kind puts on a good fight, but we can't beat their air power. They move out of reach of our best flyers. How do we find out where they're taking the children? We must find a way to follow them."

One of the Generals stepped forward. "But how sire? As you said, they go higher than our best flyers."

Rex smiled, a clever idea beginning to form in his brain. He called for his best man. "Captain of the Guard!"

Cassius stepped forward and snapped to attention. "Sire!" he said.

"I need you to capture one of those things." Cassius stood poised, waiting to be dismissed, but Rex signaled him to wait. "No," he continued. "Capture as many as you can. Spread the word. Tell our soldiers not to destroy them. We will need them intact so we can learn the secret of flying without wings. It may be the only way we may ever see our children again."

"I go now, Sire," said Cassius. He made eye contact with several of the guards, including the eager Sergeant, who smiled. They understood each other without spoken words. The King also nodded and Cassius turned, his men falling into formation behind him. They exited through a nearby passageway, their footsteps echoing through the tunnel. Rex thought about how many of his messages went unspoken, how a simple nod could communicate exactly what he intended. Perhaps the Queen was not the only one who possessed psychic abilities.

He would have liked to consider this further, but the problem before him demanded his full attention. He continued to pace and think out loud again. "Flying without wings," he said, more to himself than to anyone around him. He looked towards his Generals for support. "Flying without wings," he said. "We must find the answer to this mystery."

They looked at him, bewildered. Before they could answer, Rex spoke. "But mastering this secret would be meaningless unless we knew where they were taking the children," he said. "Where are they taking the children?" he asked himself.

A spinosaurus entered, clutching a strange, green prisoner between his teeth. He dropped him in front of Rex. The green prisoner scuttled in terror but there was nowhere to run. He was surrounded by dinosaurs in all directions. They circled in close around him, staring at him with a mix of emotions he could not decipher. He cringed in pain, oozing green blood from deep gashes in his flesh. He spoke in some unrecognizable tongue, making high pitched squeals and gibberish.

The Queen stood up from her throne, moving forward to crane her head above the green prisoner. He appeared calmer and his speech grew softer until it stopped. She stared deeply at him for a moment and nodded her head. She answered him in what sounded like his speech, gibberish and squeaks. A murmur of astonishment erupted throughout the room. The Queen silenced them and began to speak.

"He is frightened and hurt," she said. "His body cries in so much pain that I am having difficulty reading his mind."

One of the guards turned to another standing beside him. "How does she do that?" he asked.

"I've seen her do it before," he replied.

"Yes, I have, too," said another. "But how does it work on things like that?"

Rex silenced them with a stare.

The Queen continued. "He thinks we are vicious animals, out to destroy him."

"How is that possible?" asked Rex. "They attacked us! We have no gripe with them. Tell him we are peaceful and mean him no harm. Tell him!"

The Queen moved closer to the green prisoner and hummed. A strange silence descended upon the throne room.

The green prisoner gibbered again in some unrecognizable language.

The Queen nodded and looked sideways. An ankylosaurus lumbered forward. The green prisoner backed away but the Queen assured him it was okay. The ankylosaurus licked the green prisoner's wounds and he was soothed. The Queen continued to hum as everyone looked on in fascination. For all intents, the Queen and the green prisoner appeared to be communicating through hums and body language.

The Palace shook and the sounds of an explosion echoed through the corridors.

"They grow closer to the Palace," said Rex. "How dare they attack my home."

"I thought the battle was over and they were leaving," said one of the Generals.

Rex turned to the Queen. "Hurry, my love. Unlock the secret."

There was another explosion from outside. Rex stepped through an archway and out onto the balcony. As he stared at the carnage, his jaw dropped in astonishment.

The jungle was on fire. Smoke and flames shot up from points in all directions. In a nearby clearing he saw two dead dinosaurs lying next to a crashed flying stone. The grounds around the Palace were riddled with scorch marks where lightning bolts had pummeled the ground. There were bodies of strange ones as well as dinosaurs lying still and quiet. Some had been crushed. He saw two dinosaur legs sticking out from under a crashed silver stone. It was surrounded by bodies, as if the stone had exploded on impact and spewed broken creatures in all directions.

Above, the sky was growing dark with smoke from the fires. Flying dinosaurs looped and screeched as they moved between the flying stones. Lightning from the deadly rays reflected off the clouds. Higher up, he could see more flying dinosaurs trying to desperately pursue a group of stones that were trailing red bags, each one containing a trapped baby dinosaur. He watched as they rose out of sight, becoming pin points of silver until they were lost somewhere up in the sky.

He lowered his head, looking at the palace grounds again. Several stones were holding back a squad of his men, keeping them away from something he could not quite make out. A pteranodon attacked one of the floating ships, ramming his body against the side in an attempt to bring it down. He saw a red ray from another stone shoot out and surround the pteranodon, forming a bag around him. The bag slowly collapsed, crushing the trapped dinosaur into an unrecognizable pulp. The beam and the bag dissolved, raining blood and misshapen body parts down on the soldiers fighting on the ground below. It was then he noticed messy piles of debris everywhere, pulps of lifeless meat that had eluded his eyes until now.

He could hear Cassius snarl as his men tried to leap upward and bring down a low flying stone. It was trailing a red bag. They desperately attempted to throw themselves into the red beam, hoping to break the tether that held a small tyrannosaurus rex trapped within the walls of that bag. His eyes narrowed into slits as he spotted something horrific. Inside the red bag he saw his daughter, Natalie, and he suddenly understood why his men were fighting so hard.

On the ground, in the center of a skirmish, a second bag containing Nate shuddered and began to slowly lift. Cassius and the guards chased after it but they were too late. The bag rose quickly as fighting craft moved between the stone and the ground. Lightning bolts shot out and he could hear the cries of his men.

The bags rose up through the clouds. Flying dinosaurs tried to stop the craft but they were thwarted and harassed by other stones. Lightning bolts shot out and one of the dinosaurs dropped from the sky wailing.

Rex turned, his eyes glowing with rage. He stared at the green prisoner, his eyes a curtain of red. Without warning he lashed out and snatched the green prisoner in his jaws. The Queen cried out as Rex bit down, cutting the green prisoner in half. He chewed a piece for a few gnaws before spitting it out against the palace wall. The body hit with a thud before slipping to the ground in a misshapen pile.

The Elite Guard and the Queen stepped back in horror. The hall was filled with gasps and murmurs.

Rex realized what he had done. His face fell blank for a moment, then turned to shame.

"Your majesty!" said a guard in surprise.

"He did nothing wrong," said another.

"Yes," said a third. "I've wanted to do the same thing ever since they brought that thing in here."

"Did he taste good sire?" asked a dimetrodon.

A few guards laughed, but a look from Rex silenced them. The shame flashed to anger for a moment. He looked at the green carcass still trembling in the corner and realized again what he had done. He was angry with himself.

"I'm sorry," he said. "I know I said not to kill the green one. I just… lost control of myself for a moment. I won't let it happen again. A King should live beyond such passions. Otherwise the green ones are right and we truly are no more than vicious monsters."

The Queen gasped and they all turned to look at her. She spoke from within a trance, her voice again distant and hollow. "Natalie," she whispered.

Chapter 4: Speaking Without Words

Everyone in the throne room was silent knowing that the Queen demanded full concentration. Her face grew tense and a small furrow formed in the center of her forehead. Her head turned, her eyes closed, and she began to speak to Natalie across space through her psychic abilities. The bond between mother and daughter could not be broken, even through the void of space.

"Natalie," she said, calling her daughter in a quiet voice as if she were sitting nearby.

Natalie felt her mother's presence and despite the coldness of space she was filled with her warmth and love. The feeling drew her closer to her mother. She knew that if she answered and spoke with an inner voice that her mother had trained her to use, that somehow her words would be heard. She drew a deep breath and calmed herself. There was nothing else to do. She was trapped in a small red bag floating in the middle of nowhere.

When she looked down she could see her home far below. At first it scared her, like looking over the edge of a high cliff, but then it fascinated her. The jungle lost its clear definition, the trees and ground merged into a single blob of undefined green as she was lifted skyward. Looking up, she could trace the glowing red tether and see it end at the center of a flying stone. The craft turned and banked and she felt the pull of gravity as it shifted beneath her. The ship angled and began to accelerate. Soon she felt dizzy, like she was falling in every direction at once. She drew another deep breath, wondering how she could breathe within the small confines of the red bag. There was so much she didn't understand.

Her thoughts were interrupted as she heard her mother's voice again. At first it was a feeling that her mother wanted her. The feeling became an image of her mother that spoke to her, not through her ears but with a voice inside her head.

"Natalie," she heard, as clear as if she were being called from the next room.

"Mother?" she answered, questioning her sanity. Was this dizziness and disorientation making her go mad as well?

"I hear you," said her mother's voice.

There was comfort in the sound of that voice, but Natalie sensed something else. She knew she had disobeyed Cassius and ran off when she should have stayed with the children. She knew she had hurt her mother.

"Mother. I'm sorry. It was the only way," she said.

But the Queen was not angry. "Your Father and I are proud of you," she said. "So proud. You solved a big problem for us."

"What do you mean?" asked Natalie.

"You figured it out," said the Queen. "Now we will learn where they are taking the children."

Natalie understood. "Yes! I see. We can talk with our minds, just like you taught me."

"I will be with you," said the Queen. "But there may be times when our gifts fail us. You must be strong."

"I will," she said. "And Father?"

"He is already planning your rescue," said the Queen.

She was comforted. "Thank you, Mother."

"Be patient," said the Queen. "We are working on a solution."

"I will try," promised Natalie. "I wish I knew where they were taking us. It's dark, and cold."

"You are not alone," said the Queen. "Nate is with you. Talk to him."

Natalie looked down where she could see Nate far below, also trapped in a red bag. "Poor Nate," she said. "He came after me. Why didn't he just stay?"

"He's a brave boy," said the Queen.

"Why did he do it?" asked Natalie.

"He cares about you, Natalie," said the Queen. "Trust him."

"I do," said Natalie.

"Remember you are royal blood," said the Queen. "The children will look to you for guidance and leadership. You must be brave. I don't know what you're going to face, but don't forget that you are a Princess."

In the throne room, the dinosaurs could see signs of strain in the Queen. Her body twitched and her head began to bob slightly as if she were drifting off to sleep and trying to stay awake. Natalie could feel the stress as well. "Mother, you're fading," she said.

The Queen's words became labored and Rex moved closer to her. He wanted to rest his hand on her shoulder and comfort her but he did not know what to do. Would he break her concentration and sever the connection? Before he could act, the Queen spoke again.

"We must rest, now," she said. "Conserve your strength. Don't fight captivity. There is nothing you can do about it for now. Fill your mind with calm. Keep your center, your balance."

"Mother?" called Natalie, her voice edged with panic.

"I love you, sweetheart," said the Queen. "But I feel you slipping, too. Rest. Rest. We will talk later."

"Mother?" called Natalie, but there was no answer.

On Earth, the Queen began to swoon. Rex reached out to support her and keep her upright on her throne.

"Are you all right, Dear?" he asked.

The Queen took a moment to compose herself. "Yes," she said. "It was Natalie. She says not to worry. She figured out how to tell us where they are taking the children."

Rex smiled at this news.

The Queen opened her eyes.

"She's clever," she said. "Just like her father."

Rex was all at once sad and proud. He looked down at the torn alien's body.

"What a fool I have been," he said. "But the past cannot be undone. I don't have time to regret this, but I must stop it from happening again. No one deserves to die because of a mistake."

He peeked outside, surveying the devastation again, then he turned to address his audience.

"The sky appears to be clear of them for the moment," he said. "This is not a time for anger, this is a time for thinking. Let the word go out. There will be no more fighting. Do not harm another greenie or destroy any of their flying stones. Bring them to me."

There were numerous cries of assent from within the room. The generals nodded in agreement. Rex nodded as well, then looked at the Queen.

"We'll find her," she said. She turned her head skyward, as if she could see Natalie through the layers of rock that stood above her. "She will tell us where and when to come to her."

"I know you are right," said Rex. He looked at her, grateful for her help, grateful for the news of his daughter. His mate was an incredible woman and he felt foolish beside her. "How can I have this great strength, and then be filled with such weakness?"

The Queen smiled. "To have one without the other is impossible. It is the price of mortality."

"You are so wise, my darling," said Rex. "It is times like these that test the depth of our love. You have never let me down. I fear I will need you at my side."

"There is no place else for me."

Rex nuzzled her and smiled. Despite the events of the day, he felt hopeful.

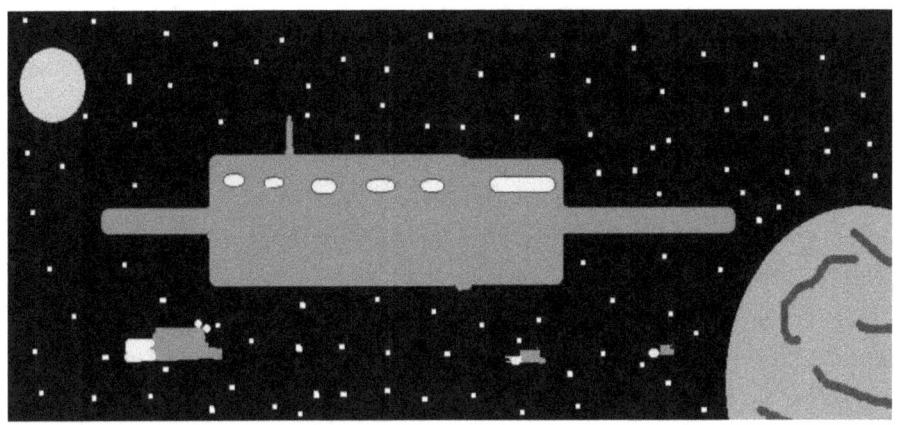

Chapter 5: Journey of the Red Bags

Natalie floated through the night in her transparent red bag tethered behind a flying stone, part of a larger group of flying stones. The bag was not much larger than she was. The fleet had tightened the formation and she could see hundreds of dinosaurs that shared her fate. She studied the bags. They varied in size based on the dinosaur, but none of them provided any room for their prisoners to move about. They seemed to take the shape of the dinosaur that it contained. As tired as she was, there was no place to lie down and nap. Besides, space debris, what appeared to be dust and bits of rock, occasionally pelted the sides of the bags, startling her every time she tried to doze off.

She thought about what her mother had said. She was royal blood, and the children knew she was their princess. Her mother was right. They would naturally look to her for leadership. Thinking about the current situation, there was not much she could do except try to keep their hopes up until her father rescued them.

"This is not my father's empire," she said to herself, remembering what Nate had said. Her voice was swallowed by the bag, like talking into a pile of moss in her nest bed. They were far from the palace, and this dark void was not part of her father's empire. She really was out here on her own.

She surveyed the ragged group. They ranged in all ages, from newly hatched nestlings who cried for food, to pensive adolescents who hid their fear beneath firm masks. They were prisoners of war, taken hostage by an enemy they had never seen before.

She saw many different kinds of dinosaurs including triceratops, brontosaurus, raptors, and flying dinosaurs like pteranodons and pterodactyls. There were other tyrannosaurs besides her and Nate and even a young allosaurus. There were saltopus and spinosaurus and odd dinosaurs that Natalie had never seen. The only thing missing were aquatic dinosaurs, water breathers like megalneusaurus and plesiosaur. Based on this wide variety, she concluded the area around the palace was not the only place on her world that was attacked.

The size of the fleet was astounding. In all directions there were stones towing bags. Natalie could not get an accurate count of how many there were. Behind the fleet trailed another group of stones, not quite as large or as numerous as the ones carrying the bags. These were the fighters that had been forming blockades and attacking the adults who were trying to rescue the children. She had seen a lot of stoness destroyed by the adults and she wondered how many of them had been in the original fleet that attacked them. Many of them looked damaged, scarred with gashes and battered with dents. Trailing far behind this main body she could see stragglers, moving slowly and looking like wounded dinosaurs cut out from the safety of the herd.

She was glad that the one carrying Nate was nearby. It was comforting to know that he was there, going through this awful experience with her. When she thought about it, Nate really was her closest friend and more than a Protector of the Royal Family.

Nate caught her looking at him. He was tired of struggling to get out of the bag. At one point he realized that if he did manage to break out, where would go? He'd just be left behind and would have to run to catch up to them. Dejected, he had settled in for the flight. "Any idea where they are taking us?" he asked Natalie.

She could hear Nate with her ears and she wondered how it was possible. She wondered if it was the same magic that allowed her to breathe when she knew there was no air. "It's so dark out," she said, answering Nate. "I really can't see anything."

"We've already flown higher than the moon," he said.

Natalie looked back at their world. It was slowly shrinking, becoming smaller than the moon. Everything looked different here. She felt so open and vulnerable. Where was the jungle to protect them?

Time passed slowly, or so it seemed. Every second spent inside the red bag seemed like an hour. But in actuality, time passed quickly for the fleet. The stones were traveling at a speed that warped time. While they experienced a relatively short trip, weeks went by on their home world.

"I miss our parents already," she said.

Nate focused ahead, seeing another orb growing in size. "I think we're headed towards that moon up ahead," he said.

"I don't think that's another moon," said Natalie. "It looks like another world. It's green and blue like ours."

The stones dove into the atmosphere. As they moved closer, details of the alien planet came into focus. It looked a lot like theirs, with clouds, mountains, and green jungles filled with lush vegetation. Long, wide canals were visible, filled with deep blue water. Strange craft, similar in shape and color to the stones, scuttled across the waves like leaves floating across a swift river.

The fleet got closer to the land. She could see roads, cities, and parklands. The sun reflected across the water, dancing off the waves. Flocks of low flying animals, like pteranodons, only fluffier, moved gracefully across the water. Clouds in the far distant horizon shrouded the mountains in a misty cloak. It was a paradise and in her heart she felt welcomed by the planet. How could these people be so evil when they lived in such a beautiful place?

Then she thought about how she had seen dinosaurs fighting each other back on her home world, and it was a beautiful place. In fact, she and Nate had witnessed a terrible fight just before the attack of the stones. Could Nate be right? Is fighting an inevitable part of life?

A large group of ships, none of which carried baby dinosaurs, broke off from the main fleet and disappeared over the horizon. The other ones towing bags continued down towards a magnificent city. They banked around buildings that looked like nothing the dinosaurs had ever seen or imagined. How could rock be shaped like this?

On the other side of the city they came to a flat area that was part of a huge plain extending towards the distant mountains. There was a lake nearby, dotted with boats. They flew over fields with stones parked in formations and many low, flat buildings. There were roads and lots of empty space and finally a remote field with only a few buildings nearby.

It was the end of the road leading from the city. The edge of the field was fenced off and Natalie could see crowds of creatures gathered around a stage. On top of the stage was another stage, a raised dais, decorated with colorful banners. The stage was crowded with dignitaries, the creatures she had seen falling from the stones. They had come to welcome home the victorious fleet.

The ship lowered the bag containing Natalie into a fenced area not far from the dais. Several other dinosaurs were already there, still trapped inside red bags. There were green creatures nearby with strange, hand held devices. They pointed the devices at the bags and somehow broke the connection to the stones. The stones flew off once they were free of their cargo. Using the devices, the beings on the ground could levitate the bags and stack them.

There was a podium on the dais. An important one stood behind it talking, his voice amplified by some strange device. He would speak in a series of high pitched squeaks and gibberish for a short burst, then pause while the crowd cheered and clapped. Fireworks went off in the distance. When the dinosaurs heard the sounds of the fireworks they were frightened and they stirred restlessly inside their bags.

Natalie closed her eyes and concentrated. "Mother, can you hear me?" she asked with her inner voice.

No answer came.

The one at the podium continued talking in the unrecognizable tongue. He was obviously the leader of these people. He had the look of authority that her father had, but he somehow seemed to lack her father's compassion. His talk seemed stilted and forced, not from the heart.

Stones continued to hover over the fenced areas as creatures with devices released the bags from their tethers. Red bags filled with dinosaurs were thrown about like freight in a warehouse, no consideration for the living cargo they held. They didn't care that they were piled with no real organization.

Natalie sensed the agitation among her subjects. They were tired and they wanted to get out of these prisons. Their legs ached to run free and their necks yearned to stretch upward. Winged dinosaurs really felt helpless.

Natalie studied their movements. She could tell a lot about her subjects by observing them, and it was something that didn't require psychic gifts, just common sense. Some of the trapped dinosaurs pushed helplessly against the sides of their tiny prisons, hoping the next push would find a weakness in the bag that would free them. These were the ones who still had hope. They would eagerly help her, if she could only come up with a plan.

Some were poised in fear, pushed backwards into the corner of their bag, not knowing what would happen to them. They would need comfort. She would have to be like a mother to them and reassure them. Still others lay lethargic at the bottom of their cages, as if they had given up all will to live. Somehow, she would have to give these lost ones a sense of hope.

The leader-alien at the podium finished his speech and the crowd roared in approval. More fireworks went off. Stones flew overhead in formation emitting bursts of color and light. Generals and dignitaries in brightly decorated clothes shook hands and congratulated each other. Admirals in dress uniforms were smiling as the one who gave the speech passed out medals and plaques.

"Mother, can you hear me?" asked Natalie again. "Please."

Natalie got no response. Flying stones continued to pass overhead in formation. The creatures began to move the bags with the hand held devices. They levitated them into a corral where they dissolved them, ending the journey of the red bags. As the dinosaurs were released one by one, alien guards motioned to them, indicating they should move to an exit at the other end of the corral. From there, the baby dinosaurs were herded into a fenced walkway leading away. A curious crowd of aliens pushed against the fences on both sides, trying to get a glimpse of the captives.

"I want to go home," cried a baby brontosaurus.

"What are we doing here?" asked a sacred ankylosaurus.

"Let us go!" demanded a small raptor, snarling in defiance.

One alien gibbered a response. Whenever the dinosaurs spoke, all the aliens heard was a roar. It was a shame they couldn't understand each other. Then again, maybe there was a way to figure out what they were saying. As she walked between the fences, she began to observe them with the same eye for detail that she had just used on her subjects.

An alien mother held her child protectively and gibbered fearfully, shielding her children's eyes and turning their heads away. An angry man next to her alternately shook his fist and cried. Another alien beside him pointed his finger in accusation.

The faces in the crowd astounded Natalie and she was overwhelmed with feelings. Aliens seemed to have all manner of reaction to the dinosaurs. She saw signs of terror, looks of confidence, disgust, and satisfaction. She heard fearful gibberish, boastful sounds, anger and doubt.

Nate was finally released from his bag. He quickly caught up to Natalie and took up a position at her side. He was, after all, a Protector of the Royal Family.

Natalie began to realize something as she continued staring into the faces of the aliens. "I can almost understand them, Nate," she said.

They continued their slow walk towards a low, flat building a short distance from the Starport where they had landed. Natalie could almost see through the aliens when she stared at them, her vision becoming clearer. A dream-like trance clouded her mind with subtle messages that she called to heart. They were filled with sadness, fear, curiosity, anger, all kinds of reactions, but what she saw the most as she scanned the crowd was fear.

Then she saw a sad alien in the crowd. She stopped for a moment and stared at him, caught by some strange impulse of her emotions. She was drawn to him for some reason. Their eyes met, and there was an exchange in that look. The alien knew that she was an intelligent creature, just as she knew the same about him. They had gazed upon each other as equals.

A tear seemed to form in the alien's eye, he looked so sad, regretful, as if in deep pain. She empathized with him, her face mirroring the same sad emotion as him. They nodded knowingly to each other, and an unspoken understanding passed silently between them.

An alien guard jabbed Natalie with a long stick, urging her to move on. She twisted, screaming with pain. Nate roared and started to charge the guard. Several aliens ran forward, armed with similar weapons. One of them jabbed Nate with a stick. He let out a loud, menacing roar and nearby aliens cringed in fear.

"Stop, Nate," commanded Natalie.

Nate roared again, a boastful sign. Upon hearing the ferocious growls, some aliens ran away and cowered, covering their ears. Parents scuttled their children away to safety. A few brave alien guards rushed forward brandishing their painsticks, short club like devices that induce pain wherever they touch flesh.

A young raptor joined Nate in defiance. There was a weakness in a section of fence that he had spotted. While the guards were focused on Nate, he burst from the ranks of the procession. He hit the fence strong, tearing a hole in it large enough for him to wiggle through.

Aliens screamed and ran at the sight of him. Guards rushed forward, surrounding the raptor. It only made him angrier and like a cornered beast he fought ferociously. He turned in a circle, sniffing the air as he did. One guard smelled particularly weak and he leapt on top of him. The guard toppled backwards and the raptor stepped on him, slicing him open with the powerful talons on his feet.

Guards went crazy. They started chasing the raptor. He tore through the crowd, parting the throng of aliens like a herd of prey. He jumped, sailing ahead of the guards in front of him, landing in the center of a dense crowd.

Soldiers arrived. They formed a perimeter, slowly cornering the raptor against the side of a building. Two trucks with mounted guns stood behind the soldiers, their turrets turning to focus on the trapped animal. The raptor screamed, a cry of insolence, taunting the guards and the soldiers to try and stop him.

Nate heard the cry. He looked at the small hole in the fence and judged the size. If he hit it hard enough, his head low to the ground, he might be able to open it wide enough to squeeze the rest of his body through. He postured for the charge.

"No, Nate," yelled Natalie.

There was a sound of thunder, clapping twice in quick succession, like nothing the dinosaurs had ever heard before. Smoke filled the air around the raptor, but when it cleared, there was nothing there. A smear of blood stained the wall and there was a crater in the ground where he had been standing. The turret of the gun trucks swiveled again, this time pointing at Nate.

"Stop, Nate! It's no use," shouted Natalie.

"I'm a Protector of the Royal Family," said Nate. "It's why I'm here."

"Then protect me," said Natalie. "Just don't get yourself killed in the process." She looked ahead at the sinister, low, flat building. She felt cold inside.

"I need you Nate," she said. "Please. The worst battle may be ahead of us."

Nate looked at the building. He moved alongside of Natalie and calmed down. Aliens threatened them all with painsticks and weapons, urging the dinosaurs to move forward.

He moved on, following Natalie glumly. "What did they just do to that raptor?" he asked.

"I don't know," said Natalie.

"They pointed those things at him and made him disappear in a boom of smoke," said Nate. "How could they do that?"

"I don't know, Nate," said Natalie. She had been thinking about something different, trying to make sense of her earlier observations.

"How could they do that?" asked Nate again.

"I don't know," answered Natalie forcefully. "How could they trap us in bags? How could they shoot lightning? How could they fly without wings?" She was frustrated with him. "I don't know."

He sensed she was not in the mood to talk. He focused on the guards instead, eyeing them carefully. He saw one that looked especially threatening and could not resist making a comment. "Not today, buddy, but someday," he said.

The guard gibbered threateningly, waving a painstick before Nate.

"Yeah," said Nate. "You and the stone you flew in on."

"It's all a misunderstanding," said Natalie. "They were misled into thinking we were a threat, that we would one day come and attack them. I saw it when I looked into the eye of that sad alien."

"That's a joke," said Nate. "Like there's something we'd want here." He made a low growl as he passed an alien guard who looked particularly threatening.

"I think they're under some kind of group mind influence, a kind of frenzy," said Natalie. "It's fear. You know the way a flock of prey moves together when it tries to avoid a predator?"

"Okay," said Nate. "So where's the predator? I don't see anything circling for the kill."

"Nate! They think we're the predator," said Natalie.

"That's insane," he said. "Although I kind of wonder what they would taste like."

"Stop it," said Natalie. "Just look at them for a moment. Close your eyes. Listen to them. Can't you smell the fear on them?"

"Of course I can," said Nate. "I know they're afraid of me." He roared and a few aliens jumped back. "See?"

"Stop joking Nate," said Natalie. "The problem goes deeper than that. They don't know us. It's not just our speech, it's our customs, our culture, our families. They know nothing about us. They're just afraid."

"My father has taught me about the different types of fears. I know this one, fear of the unknown, right? I've felt it before, usually in dark places where my senses fail me."

"Exactly," said Natalie. "Look at the angry ones in the crowd, the way they hide their fear behind that anger."

Nate looked at her nervously, wondering where she was getting all this information. Was she psychic like her mother? Then again, maybe he wasn't using all his senses either. He sniffed the air, deep draughts of alien air. It smelled a little like cornered prey. He smelled the children, but something more. Maybe fear smelled the same whether it was alien or dinosaur game. "Yeah. I smell it."

"Now, do you see the sad ones?" she asked.

These were obvious to Nate.

"Then there are some who direct their anger at each other. Look at that group over there."

They passed a band of alien protestors. They gibbered not at the dinosaurs, but at the crowd. They held banners with strange writing. One protestor was talking to another who was listening intently. Guards looked angrily at the protestors but quickly turned their attention back to the dinosaurs.

"See? They don't agree with each others," she said. "They're angry about something."

"How do you know these things?" asked Nate.

"I don't know," she said. "The same way that I know you hide your nervousness behind humor."

"But you know me, Natalie," said Nate. "I'm your friend. You never met these people. How do you know these things?"

"I just do," said Natalie. "I don't know how. I see it in their faces. Look at them! Can't you see it, too?"

"You're spooking me out," said Nate.

"I can't explain it, Nate. Something is happening to me. Can't you see it? I don't think they all fear and hate us. Look, Nate, that guard over there. He doesn't look happy to be here, jabbing us with sticks."

Nate turned and saw a sad alien guard. "I don't see anything," he said. "Maybe you are psychic."

"Maybe I am," she said, wondering if Nate was right. "Mother said the ability might come to me one day." Natalie looked up at the sky, then at the low, flat building ahead. "Mother! Where are you when I need you the most. I can picture you now. Your smile, your deep, knowing eyes. Help me if you can."

She looked up into the sky, a big, billowy cloud catching her attention. A strong wind seemed to grab it, twisting the shape into a familiar image. A bit fuzzy on the edges, but it looked almost like her mother. A wave of light headedness swept over her and she heard her mother's voice say, "I am with you, in your heart and in your mind, Natalie. I hear you. Thinking deeply of me has opened the link between us."

"Mother?" questioned Natalie.

"Quiet," replied the Queen. "I have much to tell you. Listen to me. Still your inner voice like I taught you. Remember. You can't hear anything while your inner voice is babbling."

"Yes, Mother." Natalie took a deep breath and closed her eyes for a second. Nate sensed something happening and looked oddly at her.

"What's going on?" he asked. "Are you talking to your mother?"

"Shhh! Quiet," she demanded. "You're distracting me. She turned her thoughts inward again and asked, "Mother, why do you take so much upon yourself?"

"Because I can," said the Queen. "You can, too, my dear. You are about the same age I was when I became aware of my powers. I am afraid you will have to mature in a hurry. A lot will be asked of you soon."

"What do you mean?" asked Natalie.

"Your subjects," said the queen. "Look at them."

Natalie opened her eyes to what was around her. There was sadness in the eyes of the captive baby dinosaurs. A baby pteronodon was shackled to a weight he dragged, a small triceratops sported a broken horn, and an Iguanodon limped in pain, a burn scar on his back. Alien guards herded the dinosaurs towards the entrance of the low building by jabbing them with painsticks. One jabbed Natalie, yelling harshly at her in the strange alien language. It broke her concentration.

Nate growled at him and he was jabbed with a painstick from another guard.

"Stop," said Natalie. "Don't test them. They are looking for a chance to hurt us."

Nate obeyed.

They moved towards the low, flat building, into the entrance and through corridors that were mostly underground. There was a huge room filled with cages. The baby dinosaurs were put one by one into the cages. A few were taken through an ominous set of doors at the opposite end of the huge room.

Natalie followed directions, having lost touch with her mother. They put her in a cage. Nate started to protest again, but a look from Natalie stopped him from getting out of control. He hated it when she was right. He knew it wasn't time to fight but somehow he couldn't help himself. He accepted his fate and moved into a cage not far from Natalie.

Their cages were larger than the red bags they had travelled in. Dinosaurs continued to file into the room and the cages slowly filled. Each cage locked with a loud click, a sound of finality and defeat that began to fill Natalie with despair. Maybe it was wrong to accept this without a fight. Maybe Nate was right to resist.

The activity continued. Occasionally they would hear the sound of a painstick making contact with one of the resistant dinosaurs, followed by a roar. Some of her subjects were slow to accept their new accommodations. The baby pteranodon just wanted to fly. His wings were stiff and the weight chained to his leg was uncomfortable. The aliens had attached it too tightly and it was painful for him to walk. He slowly entered his cage, and when the door slammed shut he started immediately to try to chew the chain off his ankle.

The rest were slowly settled in and a bright light came on above them. Guards patrolled everywhere and at all levels, armed with painsticks. A speaker blared an authoritative announcement and some of the guards shouted out to each other in their unrecognizable language. Natalie couldn't tell what was going on. She couldn't see much from her cage and the room was large, filled with aisles and aisles of prisoners. It had taken a long time and a lot of work to lock up all the children.

There was a loud hum that quickly subsided, then the sounds of machinery followed by more authoritative gibberish from the loudspeakers.

Natalie grew nervous. "Mother, what is happening?" she asked. "I feel you slipping."

There was no answer.

"Mother! Mother?" she called again.

At the far end of the room the ominous doors shuddered and closed with a loud clang. There were dinosaur screams of intense pain coming from behind the door, muffled by the thickness, but still loud enough to disturb the caged dinosaurs. The children became agitated and cried out. Guards jabbed them with painsticks and there were more roars and cries but they soon quieted down. The screams of intense pain continued, and in the silence enforced by the painsticks, the dinosaurs began to withdraw. Isolated in their cages, unable to huddle together, to share each other's warmth and closeness, the ranks of the hopeless dinosaurs grew.

Natalie had the answer to her question. The long journey was over. This is where they were taking the children.

It only raised more questions. How could her father ever hope to find her here, especially if she couldn't contact her mother? How could she keep up hope under these conditions?

A muffled wail came from behind the ominous doors, but it was the awful silence that followed that was more nerve racking.

And Natalie thought of a final question on her mind, a question they were all asking now: What went on behind those doors?

Chapter 6: Holdouts

There was a commotion outside the throne room, loud enough to draw attention away from the debate between the dinosaur dignitaries. Rex turned to see what all the excitement was about. Before he could react, Cassius burst into the room, flanked by the eager sergeant and two of his top men, Brutus and Antilles. It got quiet in the throne room. All you could hear was the heavy breathing from Cassius and his men.

"You have news of my daughter?" asked Rex, his eyes narrowing into slits.

"We have another problem." Cassius reported to the King.

"What's the problem?" asked Rex.

"Fighting in the jungle. There are some holdouts on both sides who refuse to give up the battle."

"They must," said Rex. "I have ordered it." He turned to his court, his advisors and generals. "We all want that, don't we?" There were nods of agreement. "At least we agree on that."

"Perhaps your presence on the battlefield," said Cassius. "It may quell the thirst for blood."

"Yes," said Rex. "And convince them I'm serious about peace. Take me there." He turned to the Queen. "I hesitate to put you in danger, my dear, but I may need your skills on the field."

"Then you'll have them. Give me a moment to prepare," she said.

"I can't give you what I don't have," said Rex. "Time is critical. If I go quickly I may be able to prevent more senseless murders." He turned away for a moment. "Cassius!" he called.

The Captain of the Guard moved forward. "Yes, sire."

"I trust you with my most precious possessions and you never let me down," he said.

Cassius cringed at the King's compliment. He looked away. "Not so," he muttered.

"What?" asked the King. "What do you mean?"

Cassius looked sad. "The Princess," he said.

Rex dropped his jaw. "Do you think you were responsible for the Princess being captured?"

Cassius hesitated. "It was my job to protect her. You assigned me personally."

"I understand they took your son as well," said Rex.

"The last thing I told him to do was protect her, watch over her," said Cassius.

"Then she is in good hands. Nate's a fine young rex. Look, you need to put this behind you, Captain. We don't have time for the luxury of regret," said Rex. "The Princess is a headstrong little one, but I encourage that. I could not be more proud of her actions. She is truly my daughter. If only I had taught her to hunt as you taught Nate."

Cassius laughed, thinking of the Princess. "Nate says he tried. She has no taste for the hunt."

"Not so, my friend," said Rex. "She hunts like her mother. They hunt knowledge the way we hunt meat."

Cassius became sad thinking about the missing children. Rex placed his hand on his most loyal subject and personal friend. Cassius raised his head and looked Rex in the eye. "Nate," he said weakly.

"I know," said Rex. Both could see the other's loss, and they bonded again as brothers who shared a common pain. They had done so much together in the past, and Rex could not imagine his life without Cassius at his side. He might as well lose the Queen as well. There was enough of a hole with Natalie missing.

"Look," said Rex. "Let's continue this later. Right now I have an important mission for you. The Queen needs some time. I can't spare it. You know the situation. I will go to the battle on a full run. Give me some of your best, your fastest fighters. You follow behind with the Queen and anyone else who wants to help. Raise an army of reinforcements and be prepared for anything."

"Good plan," said Cassius. He turned to his men and smiled at the Sergeant, who immediately stepped forward and took a position beside Rex. With a few quick eye movements and a nod, the Elite Guard broke into two groups, one which fell into formation behind the sergeant.

"I know some of you have just run a long way," said Rex to his team, "But I need you to run again."

"We never tire of the hunt, your majesty," said the Sergeant. There were nods and shouts of approval from the guards around him.

"Then let's go," said Rex. He nodded to the Queen, then to Cassius. He turned toward the Sergeant, but his men were already thundering down a corridor towards the exit of the palace. Rex smiled, determined to catch up to the Sergeant who was surely at the front of this pack. He thundered down the hallway after them.

The Queen turned to Cassius. "I need only a moment," she said, exiting through a door into a nearby antechamber.

Cassius turned to his remaining men and surveyed them carefully. Many of his best men were missing. He had watched in horror as they fell in battle against the flying stones. In fairness, he had also seen many of the strange craft downed and destroyed in the process. Like all good leaders, in times like these he looked within the ranks for the ones who would replace the fallen.

"You, come with me," he motioned to Scarback, one of his trusted Elite Guard. Scarback immediately stood beside him. He singled out another. "Polonius," he called.

Another battle scared trooper stepped forward. "Yes, sir," said Polonius, snapping to attention.

"Take the rest of these men. Check the Palace security. See if the sentries need relief. See if the spotters have seen any sign of the silver things in the sky. Tell the fliers to stay on patrol. We want a report of anything trying to escape. Are the raptors still combing the jungle to locate survivors?"

"I don't know, Sir," said Polonius.

"Then find out, trooper," said Cassius sternly. Then he tempered his words with kindness, something he had learned from his King. "I have seen your leadership on the battlefield, Polonius. I need those skills now. This war is not over yet, and until it is the palace remains in danger. I must prepare to escort the Queen on a mission. As much as I know you would like to go, I need you here. Greylord used to attend to the safety of the palace but he fell in battle against the flying ones. You were his best and now I need you to be my best." He became official. "In my absence the palace is yours, soldier."

"Yes, sir," said Polonius.

"I will organize the Queen's party and meet you outside the entrance to the palace in short order for a report. Check the barracks and recruit anyone you can. Your priority is to secure the palace, but we also need to raise the army. We need reinforcements for both."

"Yes, Sir," said Polonius.

"Gather intelligence for me," said Cassius. "Find out what's happening. Send a few men into the jungle to meet up with the raptors. The King will demand a detailed report when he returns."

Cassius dismissed him, then turned away and went into the antechamber, followed closely by Scarback. The Queen had assembled a small cadre of aliens and dinosaurs. Cassius recognized several of the Queen's sisters among the group.

"We are just about ready," said the Queen. She nodded to some of the alien creatures, humming in strange tones that had become her way of communicating with them. Some of them broke off from the main herd, stepping around Cassius and into the throne room. They were followed closely by some of the Queen's sisters. The rest gathered around a strange assortment of instruments and gadgets assembled in the antechamber. Cassius realized that he had been so busy giving orders that he had not been aware of all the activity in the room. There were objects of all sizes and shapes, from tiny hand-held things to large egg shaped equipment that glowed with light. Dinosaurs and aliens had been assembled into teams, all working diligently around collections of these objects.

Cassius saw more creatures enter the room from an adjoining chamber. He peeked through the doorway and spied groups of aliens and dinosaurs in what looked like a meeting hall. There were animated discussions going on. The communication barrier was eroding between the aliens and the dinosaurs. Cassius thought he heard the aliens speaking the language of the palace staff. He listened carefully and caught a few bits of the conversation. He saw an Ornithomimus teaching the aliens the palace language. One of the Queen's sisters joined the instructor, standing in front of the group, and the two of them continued teaching the class together.

There was a mixed group gathered around a pile of rocks and equipment. Dinosaurs with digging claws were nodding in agreement. Cassius heard them discuss a plan for acquiring more of the rock. The aliens said they would need huge amounts of it. Was there a place nearby where they could store it until needed?

Two Psittacosaurus, dinosaurs with tiny, useful hands, filed past Cassius carrying a large, square box. They placed it next to a group of aliens in the antechamber who immediately became excited and animated. At least there was lots of gibbering and squeaking.

He saw one of his men standing on guard at the other end of the assembly hall. They nodded at each other and Cassius smiled back at him, showing he was pleased with the arrangement. The guard went back to scanning the room, his eyes moving from side to side and his head bobbing in all directions.

Cassius wondered how they had been able to accomplish so much in such a short time. Everyone seemed so busy on all sorts of tasks. How had they been able to organize an effort this massive? Had he been gone in the jungle that long?

He suddenly had the thought that the Queen was ready. When he turned, she was looking right at him. She smiled and he accompanied her to the adjoining throne room which had become the impromptu staging area for her entourage. The size of the group caught him by surprise, and Cassius hoped that Polonius was able to gather more guards to help protect the Queen's party. Her group was an army in its own right.

"We will assemble outside at the entrance," said the Queen, in words Cassius knew were heard by alien and dinosaur alike. Groups began to file out together, and Cassius signaled Scarback to stay at the front of the line and guide them out of the palace.

Cassius would not leave the Queen's side. Rex had trusted him with his most precious possession, and once again the Captain of the Elite Guard felt the burden of his duty. After all, he had tasked young Nate with the same responsibility, and after thinking about it, he did not want to disappoint his son. And when he thought about that, he realized that he and Rex were not alone, that many of the Royal Court, jungle dwellers and cave huddlers alike, had lost children in the battle. More was at stake here than the lives of his own children.

With a renewed sense of urgency, he ushered the Queen's party out of the room.

Chapter 7: Rex Meets Pilot

Rex and his team moved quickly through the jungle. Two of the Elite guard headed the force, roaring to dinosaurs ahead of them to get out of the way. The Sergeant was next in line with Rex beside him. Following them was the rest of the Elite Guard, their minds keen on the hunt. Millions of years of predatory genes, primitive thoughts that centered on survival, were now awakened in the pack of running animals. They snarled and roared as they ran, the sound of their fearsome war cry could be heard for miles around.

As they thundered through the jungle they passed groups of dinosaurs, both small and large, who cheered them onward. Some fell in behind them because they were fathers and brothers who had lost their loved ones. Some were mothers and sisters who were ready to fight and die to return their children and siblings. Some fell in behind them for no other reason that they caught the scent of the hunt on the breeze as the King's party passed by.

"Slow down," said the King. "Your Sergeant looks a little tired." He turned to the Sergeant and smiled, who also broke into a grin. The dinosaurs ahead of them changed their pace from a full run to a trot, chuckling at the King's remark.

"Can you smell it Sergeant?" asked Rex.

"What?" asked the Sergeant, sniffing the air deeply. He didn't smell anything interesting, just normal jungle scents.

"We approach the battle," said Rex. "I smell the fear, the excitement, and mostly the blood."

"Yes, Sir," replied the Sergeant. As bold as he was, he wished that the Captain of the Guard were here instead of him. He knew Rex needed someone more experienced at his side and he felt unworthy. But he wasn't going to let the King down. He sniffed the air again and he thought he smelled it. He smiled at Rex and they both understood.

Ahead, they could hear the battle, roars from dinosaurs in pain, high pitched squeals, lightning bolts and the general sounds of chaos. At Rex's order, they assembled at the edge of a clearing, using the cover of jungle to stay hidden. Rex assessed the situation before revealing his position.

They saw a low flying stone hovering over a group of dinosaurs. Several other stones were on the ground, one so badly damaged that it was burst open like a piece of squashed fruit. Alien creatures were cowering inside, fighting back a team of raptors that tried to work their way through a hole torn in the side.

Suddenly the whole thing lurched, struck on the side by a charging triceratops. Squeals and screams echoed through the hole. Rex was sure the Sergeant smelled the fear now. Aliens in a nearby grounded ship tried to draw fire from the dinosaurs to give their comrades time to escape. Lightning bolts and rays hissed out from holes in the side of the grounded stone.

"Come out and fight," yelled a dark tyrannosaur, his jaws eagerly waiting for anything to emerge from the hole. "Ram it again," he yelled to the triceratops. The horned lizard shook his bony head and backed up, preparing for another charge.

Rex saw the problem at once. The dark tyrannosaur was not unknown to the King. He had encountered this beast on more than one occasion. They called him Roughstone, his name given because his skin was like rock. He had tried to challenge Rex numerous times for the leadership of the herd, but he was never good enough. Although Rex had defeated him time and time again, he still managed to cause trouble, always emerging in moments of crisis, hoping Rex would make a mistake so he could make his move to dominate the herd. Perhaps he was the intelligence behind Cavernjaw.

"Oh, no," said the Sergeant.

"What is it?" asked Rex.

"I know that Tyrannosaur," said the Sergeant.

"Roughstone?" asked Rex.

"No," replied the Sergeant. "The one behind him." The Sergeant pointed to a pale green dinosaur with a short, nubby tail. "His name is Snubtail."

"Good name for him," said Rex.

The triceratops had moved far enough away to prepare for another run. He lowered his head for the charge.

"Belay that," yelled Rex. "Stop that charge." At the sound of the King's voice, the triceratops froze. Roughstone turned as well. Rex stepped out of the protective cover of the jungle. His guards slowly emerged to stand behind him. "Roughstone! I ordered an end to all hostilities, or didn't you hear that?" yelled Rex.

"What?" yelled Roughstone. "You want us to spare this scum? Do you hear that, my friends?" he said to all the dinosaurs in the clearing. "Whose side are you on, Rex? Ours or theirs?"

"I just want to get the children back," said Rex.

"So now you've brokered a deal with these devils," said Roughstone. "What did you offer them in return for your daughter? Control of the herd?"

There were murmurs among the dinosaurs. The green creatures became quiet, sensing something was going on.

"She allowed herself to be captured willingly," said Rex. He was saddened at the thought. "She wanted to find out where they were taking the children."

"How like you, Rex," said Roughstone. "You turn her capture into something noble and good."

"It's the truth," he said.

"So you say," said Roughstone.

"Our plan for rescuing the children depends upon peace. We must rebuild the fleet together," said Rex.

"Why?" snarled Roughstone. "So you can help all your friends get home?"

"Partially," said Rex. "These beings have families as well. Did you ever think that they would like to see them again? We're really not that different from them, Roughstone. We all have families we'd like to be reunited with. If you stopped fighting them long enough, maybe talk to them, you would find out these things."

Roughtone was silent, so Rex continued.

"Since we have a common goal, we've teamed up to help each other. They want to get back home as badly as we want to get our children back."

Inside the stones the creatures held their breath. The dinosaurs had stopped attacking them. They began to jibber quietly to each other. Just like the dinosaurs, they had two different opinions. One group wanted to take advantage of the calm to escape while another thought it would be a good time for a surprise counterattack. One brave soul thought it was time for a truce.

He jabbered to his companions, reminding them that he was the Pilot, the one in charge of the downed spacecraft. He explained that even though it was damaged and unable to fly, he was still in charge. He ordered them to be silent and trust him. He had a plan.

Pilot watched Rex and Roughstone growl and posture against each other. It reminded him of many of the open debates he had seen in the Presidential Palace back on his home planet. He knew that the two powerful dinosaurs were discussing the situation. Whatever was being said, for the moment no one was fighting. As the talk continued, more dinosaurs came out of the jungle to take up positions behind Rex. Some of the dinosaurs that had been fighting for Roughstone also moved behind Rex.

"Come back here you cowards," yelled Snubtail. He didn't like the idea of anyone switching allegiance.

"Shut up, Snubtail," yelled the Sergeant. "Let them make up their own mind."

"I don't go by that name anymore, or haven't you heard," he snarled. "They call me Razorclaw now."

"You can change your name but you can't change your reputation for trouble," yelled the Sergeant.

"Laugh now," said Snubtail. "You'll find out why I'm called Razorclaw soon enough." He held up his hand, displaying sharp claws that glistened in the sunlight.

Despite the posturing, more dinosaurs continued to move away from Roughstone. The crowd behind him began to dwindle. The presence of the King had an effect on Roughstone's warriors. Some shifted their allegiance by moving behind Rex, others took the opportunity to wander away from the battlefield and disappear into the jungle. Few stood behind their former leader now.

Pilot heard his own crew debating their options from behind him. There was talk of attacking, firing upon the dinosaurs while they were distracted. Some spoke of running for the nearby ship, anything was better than waiting in this old broken heap to be crushed in the next charge. Another asked what had happened to the ships that were hovering over them. Some just spoke of home, making all kinds of promises about what they would do or how good they would be if only they could make it back to their planet safely.

There were so many ideas, but Pilot felt that somebody had to act. He too wondered what happened to the ship that was hovering over them. He decided to risk taking a peek outside before doing anything. Slowly he emerged from the hole in the broken ship, turning his head skyward to see what was happening. The light was bright overhead, brighter than the sun on his planet. His eyes were watering as he emerged from the darkness of the broken ship. When he looked upward, he saw nothing but clear sky overhead.

One of Roughstone's men, a raptor, spotted Pilot and made a sudden move towards him. Pilot dropped to the ground in fear while aliens inside the downed ship raised weapons and took aim. Pilot tried to yell to them, telling them not to shoot. He didn't want to begin fighting again before the drama between the dinosaurs played out.

Rex saw the raptor and acted quickly. Keeping one eye on Roughstone, he pivoted his body and swatted away the raptor with his tail before the beast could maul Pilot. The raptor flew in the air and landed somewhere in the jungle. Rex heard the rustle of leaves which told him the raptor was okay. He heard the rustle move deeper into the jungle. Obviously, the raptor had enough for today.

Roughstone looked like he was going to lunge at Rex, but all it took was a menacing growl from the King to make him stop and think. Roughstone froze. The army behind Rex took another step forward, narrowing their eyes at Roughstone.

The creatures in the ships were amazed. Why did Rex protect Pilot? Before they could find an answer, they heard a sound overhead. The hovering ship was suddenly there again. It glowed yellow and let out a horrible whirring sound.

Pilot knew what was happening. He had learned about this last desperate strategy when he was a young officer at flight school. Failure was sometimes not an option for his people, and they often did strange things in the name of victory. In this case, the whirring sound and the yellow glow were a signal that the ship was about to sacrifice itself by crashing into the enemy.

Pilot sensed that not all the dinosaurs in the clearing were his enemy. Rex had certainly proven himself friendly by protecting him. Pilot thought that the creatures in the hovering saucer were about to make a mistake, but there was no way to tell them.

The saucer flew high into the air and glowed yellow again. Then it began to plummet downward in a crash course towards Rex. Rex and the other dinosaurs were unaware of what was about to happen. They were so busy facing off to each other that they did not look up.

Pilot ran in front of Rex and began gesticulating wildly. Rex couldn't understand what he was trying to say, but something in the alien's desperate look made him take note. Pilot kept pointing skyward and tugging at Rex's leg. When Rex bent down to look, he broke eye contact with his enemy. That's when Roughstone made his move. The dark tyrannosaur lunged forward, his jaws opening wide to grab at Rex's neck. Razorclaw, as he liked to be called, joined his evil boss in the charge.

A pachyrhinosaurus noticed what was happening. He looked upward and saw the flying stone coming down fast. He knew that there were seconds left to act. "Move!" he yelled. "Now!" He pushed aside dinosaurs as he ran forward towards the King.

The Sergeant was focused on Roughstone and Snubtail (he refused to call him Razorclaw), his only concern was for the safety of his King. He saw what Roughstone was doing. With the King distracted, the dark tyrannosaur was already making his move. The Sergeant saw the jaws open, the legs uncoil, Roughstone lunging forward towards Rex. He didn't wait to see what would be next. He leaped in between Rex and Roughstone, surprising Rex with the swiftness of his actions.

Before Rex could turn, he was struck in the side by the pachyrhinosaurus. The bone headed dinosaur rammed into Rex pushing him out of the way. "Protect the King," he yelled. "Death comes from the sky."

Everyone seemed to look skyward at once, just in time to see the saucer plummeting towards them at breakneck speed.

The Sergeant pushed Rex aside, the pachyrhinosaurus connecting not a moment sooner. Rex was off balance and he was easily knocked back into the jungle. Roughstone's jaws came down on the Sergeant. He screamed as the teeth tore into his flesh. He tried to twist around to bite back but at that moment the stone hit the ground next to them. There was an explosion. Pieces of metal flew everywhere. The Sergeant fell to the ground, Roughstone clamped firmly to his back.

"No!" yelled Razorclaw, a look of horror frozen on his face.

A piece of hot metal cut through the Sergeant's thigh. Pilot was right next to him as he and Roughstone came crashing down on top him. Chunks of metal whizzed by them, one small piece cutting into Pilot's leg. He fell forward as the dinosaurs crashed beside him. The massive body of the Sergeant shielded him from a second explosion as the stone blew into a thousand tiny fragments. The clearing became an inferno. The last thing Pilot saw was the grounded ship enveloped in flames. His men were coming out, their bodies on fire, screaming in agony. Dinosaurs were screaming as well. He thought of how foolish the suicide attack had been. It seemed they had killed as many friends as they had foes. He suddenly felt weak, full of regret for the way things played out.

"Why?" he said, the sound coming out like sad, astonished gibberish to the dinosaurs that heard him. "Why?"

Without waiting for an answer, he slumped forward, the pain in his leg becoming too much to deal with as he slipped into unconsciousness.

Razorclaw stood mesmerized, staring at the mutilated body of the Sergeant. He looked as if he was going to cry, but instead he hardened his face. He cursed the fates that did this.

"What's wrong?" he heard someone ask.

Razorclaw ran. He ran headlong into the jungle. He screamed so loud that crowds parted to let him by.

"What's wrong?" he heard someone else ask.

He continued to run, fleeing like a child running from danger.

Chapter 8: The Hero of Glade Rock

As the Queen's party approached the scene, they were warned about what to expect. Runners carried the news of the devastation in all directions, summoning help. Ankylosaurus, the medical dinosaurs of the cadre, swarmed over the field applying their saliva balms and leaves to the wounded heroes. Jungle fires were being extinguished by a steady procession of brontosaurus carrying gullets of water from the river to spit on the flames. Triceratops helped clean up the battlefield by removing carcasses to a special holding area where they could await final disposition. Rites were being administered to the dying and comfort to the living.

The Queen had an ominous feeling even before the runners arrived. "Hurry Cassius," she urged her escort. "I sense that the King needs us."

"Double-time," yelled Cassius. His men picked up the pace, urging the Queen's sisters to quicken their step as well. Ahead they could see columns of smoke as they neared the clearing, but nothing prepared them for the devastation they saw.

Bodies were everywhere, aliens and dinosaurs alike, spewed on the ground like so many fallen leaves in the wake of a windstorm. Some were moaning but many were silent and still. The Queen moved quickly to her husband's side, not waiting to be told. Rex was stunned, but he was alive.

"They tried to kill us all," he said. "Even their own people."

"Shhh," she silenced him. "Rest. You've been wounded." She placed her hand on his shoulder and applied healing energy to his body.

Rex looked down. Blood poured from an open gash in his underbelly as he tried to stand up.

"Medical dinos," called the Queen. "Quickly. Your King needs you." She urged him to lie down, pressing her hand on his shoulder. Several Ankylosaurus came to the King's side and began treatment. Rex began to feel better.

"Thank you," he said.

"I'm proud to help you," said one Ankylosaurus. "One of your men saved my son from abduction. I owe you a life."

"You owe me nothing, my friend," said Rex. "We have all paid in blood for this war." He rolled over on his side to allow the medical dinosaurs to inspect him for other wounds.

Cassius had been busy giving orders, taking command and directing the cleanup effort. That done, he focused on his second priority, the safety of his King.

"Cassius," said Rex, spying his old friend.

"I should have been here with you," said the Captain of the Guard. "What happened?"

"It was Roughstone," said Rex.

"Roughstone?" said Cassius, surprised to hear that name. "General Roughstone?"

Rex was angry. "Don't call him that. I stripped him of that title when he went renegade."

"Roughstone did all this?" asked Cassius.

"He challenged me again. While he postured, the alien holdouts attacked us."

"What?" said Cassius. "I'll slaughter every last one of them for this."

"No!" urged the King. "Remember the plan. We came here to end this war and form an alliance. Murder is a poor way to reward an ally."

"How can you trust them now?" asked Cassius.

"Cassius," said the King. "Just as there are those among us who would wage war, so it is with them. We must find the peacemakers and enlist them in our cause. At the same time we must be wary. They may have their own versions of Roughstone who hide among them."

"How can we tell the good ones from the bad?" asked Cassius.

"There was one that warned me," said Rex, beginning a thought. "He was right beside me."

"There's nothing beside you except this big piece of metal," said Cassius.

Rex groaned, shifting position.

"Lie still," commanded the Queen.

"In a moment, dear," he said, struggling to turn around. His head was close to the ground and he could see something under the metal. It looked like...

He suddenly realized what it was. He wedged his head under the metal using it like a lever.

"Here, let me help you," said Cassius, lending a hand. Together they lifted the large piece of metal up and thrust it aside. Pilot lay there, still and quiet, his tattered uniform even more ragged after the suicide attack. Before Rex could do anything, another alien rushed to Pilot's side, gibbering fanatically.

"Must be his friend," said Cassius.

"This is one of the good ones," said Rex. "And I'm betting the friend is, too." He spoke to the medics that were helping him. "I'm okay now," he said. "Help him." The ankylosaurus dutifully did the King's bidding and began licking Pilot.

"Bring me leaves and healing wood bark," he called between licks. A duckbill quickly arrived with the needed medicine.

Rex collapsed from the effort of standing. His leg bled again.

"Slow down," said Cassius. "Sit and rest for a minute." Rex knew the Captain of the Guard was right. He lay down on the ground again.

"He tried to prevent this," Rex said to Cassius. "He left the safety of his stone to warn me. He tried to pull me out of harm's way but he didn't have the strength to move me."

"How did you survive?"

"It was the Sergeant," said Rex. "The Sergeant!" said Rex, turning to look for the loyal soldier. Cassius scanned the battlefield. He didn't have to look far. Lying nearby on his side, he recognized the Sergeant's back by a pattern of scars and a knot on his head. He ran to his side.

Rex saw the horror in Cassius' face as he moved in front of the Sergeant. Rex tried to twist and see but the Queen urged him to lie still while an ankylosaurus finished ministering to him.

There was a bite mark on the Sergeant's side close to his stomach, but that's not what killed him. A sharp piece of metal from one of the flying stones was lodged through his heart. It had entered the side opposite the bite mark and pierced completely through him. The Sergeant had tried to knock it out by ramming himself against the ground. His effort had only deepened the wound and he eventually bled out from the hole in his chest.

"He's dead," said Cassius.

A tear came to Rex's eye. Another good one lost, a faithful friend and fighting companion. He had grown to like the Sergeant, had even made plans to advance him in rank and move him into his command. More plans that would never be carried out.

"He died in the line of duty protecting me from Roughstone and Snubtail," said Rex.

"Snubtail was here?" asked Cassius.

"He sided with Roughstone," said Rex.

"Where is he now?" asked Cassius.

"He ran away screaming like a little compy," said one of the Elite Guard.

"He got scared when Roughstone failed in his attack on the King," said another. "The Sergeant took the bite instead."

"It wasn't Roughstone," said a different eyewitness. "The sight of the Sergeant's body made Snubtail ill."

"You're right. That was it," said a third. "It wasn't Roughstone's defeat that made him run. Snubtail ran after seeing the Sergeant and I know why." They all looked at him. "You didn't know?" he asked in surprise. "Snubtail was the Sergeant's brother."

There was silence as everyone thought about it.

Cassius surveyed the battle field again. "I don't see Roughstone here. I'll check among the casualties."

"Don't bother," said Rex. "I asked. He's nowhere to be found."

"The coward," sneered Cassius. "Just like him to cause trouble and run."

"We need to be vigilant, but Roughstone is the least of our worries," said Rex.

"How can you say that?" asked Cassius.

"Like you said. He's a coward. He attacked me only after I was distracted. If not for quick actions of the Sergeant, it would be me lying there with a bite in my side and a spear through my heart. He exemplifies all that is good in us, reminding me of what we stand for."

"Unlike our enemy," said Cassius. "I understand they purposely destroyed a stone in this clearing hoping to kill a great number of us."

"True," said Rex. "I don't understand that logic. It is one thing to sacrifice your life to protect a friend, another to sacrifice your life to kill an enemy. I don't understand it."

"We value life," said the Queen. "And I sense that they do as well, but they have different ideas of what honor and sacrifice mean. It's important we learn these things."

Rex tried to get up. He groaned with the effort. Cassius tried to support him but he waved the Captain of the Guard off. Only when he began to teeter did Rex allow anyone to help him. His teeth clenched with pain, he started to limp towards Pilot.

The alien was still unconscious. Ankylosaurus had done all they could and he was wrapped with leaves. Pilot's alien friend was at his side holding his hand in comfort. The alien looked up at Rex and said something unintelligible. Rex looked over at the Sergeant. "I know," he said to the alien, answering him as if he understood the strange words. "I'm sorry."

The alien said something else, the words coming out sad and empty. He stood up and walked over to Rex and touched him gently. Rex could not help but be moved. As painful as it was, he leaned over and laid his hand on the alien's shoulder. The gesture was not lost on other aliens that were standing a cautious distance away.

Finally he stood and turned to his men. "Let's clean up this mess and get back to the palace," he said. "Take this one to the infirmary." He pointed to Pilot. "Take all the wounded to the infirmary, friend and foe alike. Let's heal the wounded and then sort this out."

He looked over at the Sergeant. "For the unlucky ones no longer with us, a hero's grave. Let us honor what they have done. We will build our alliance on their sacrifice."

"Strange how death humbles us all in the end, friend and enemy alike," said Cassius. "We share more in common now. I wonder what it must feel like to know your countrymen are willing to kill at all costs to achieve victory. I don't mind them taking their own life, but I don't want them taking mine, especially without asking me. It goes against all natural law."

"Don't be so quick to judge," said Rex. "They may find some of our practices just as barbaric. You're right about death humbling us all, but it has also joined us together," said Rex. He looked at the Sergeant, then Pilot and his friend. "We would do well to honor this place."

Rex limped over to a tall rock near the center of the clearing. He turned and demanded everyone's attention.

"Let us remember what happened here. Let all of us, alien and dinosaur alike, remember what we have lost, and what we have gained today. Let all hostilities cease once and for all. Let there be no more blood. We will bury our dead together at this rock in the center of this glade, and with it our hatred."

Chapter 9: The Room of No Return

Natalie struggled to concentrate. The prison was damp and dark. Her cage was too small to be comfortable. She was exhausted and needed to sleep, but constant noise and activity kept her awake.

Some of the smaller children had managed to sleep. For a long time they cried as babies do, mewling for their mothers. Natalie longed to comfort them, knowing that they needed the warmth of an adult. She and Nate were probably the oldest ones and the closest thing to an adult, but they were locked tightly inside their cages and just as helpless as everyone else. She wondered if any of the captured dinosaurs were small enough to slip through the prison bars. Not likely, she decided.

"Mother," she said, trying again to unlock her mind. "I can't hear you mother, but maybe you can hear me." She took a deep breath, trying to send out waves of thought that would communicate with the Queen.

"We're in some kind of underground prison, Mother," she whispered. "I don't know how Father will find us. They have us locked up in cages. Every now and then they come out of their safe places and walk among the cages, looking at us with great curiosity. I hate those times. They always stop in front of one of the cages and talk for a while. I'm beginning to understand them, Mother. Not every word, but I can sense their intentions, their thoughts. In the end, it's always the same. After talking, they unlock the cage and take the poor occupant away. At the other end of this prison is a set of double doors, large and forbidding. They always take them in there. No one comes back. The cage stays empty. I don't know what happens in that room, but I don't want to think about it."

"Mother can you hear me? I'm scared. I don't know what to do. Please tell Father to hurry."

Chapter 10: The Busy Palace

Rex greeted his generals as they entered the throne room. There were aliens standing among them, friends that had been made during the uneasy alliance that the King demanded. Many did not trust the aliens but Rex knew that the key to rescuing the children lie in fixing the flying stones and launching them towards the alien planet. The alien leaders that were stranded on Earth felt that they had little choice in the matter if they ever wanted to get home. Some of them felt remorse. They were told by their leaders that the dinosaurs were ferocious beasts, incapable of anything but violence. That is what they had seen through telescopes, dinosaurs fighting each other, hunting each other for food. If the aliens ever hoped to colonize the Earth, they would have to deal with the dinosaurs.

Their leaders taught them to fear the dinosaurs. They used many compelling arguments and came to very logical conclusions, except they were based on false assumptions. Now, the aliens stranded on Earth realized how foolish this thinking had been. They had firsthand experience working with the dinosaurs. Many of them had gone to classes in the palace where they were taught to speak the dinosaur language.

The Queen had been correct all along. The key to growth and understanding is communication. She had long ago initiated a dialog among her own people. Now she was doing the same between dinosaurs and aliens. She treated them as she would any of her beloved subjects. When she looked in their hearts, she saw the same things she saw in her own people: hope, fear, hunger, good, bad, anger, love, devotion, and friendship.

It was exciting to see the cooperation. Rex saw the value in a joint project that brought the two cultures together in a common goal. He immediately set in motion a plan to fix the damaged space ships that remained on Earth. He relied on the Queen's ability to communicate with the aliens to tell them of his plan to rescue the children. Many of the aliens wanted to bring the truth back to their world and tell their people there was nothing to fear from Earth, that they were welcome here.

With teams in place rebuilding the fleet, Rex turned his attention to Natalie. For this he relied solely on the Queen, and lately her efforts had been disappointing.

"I've lost her," said the Queen.

Rex's greatest fear always came to mind when she said this. He couldn't help but ask. "Is she dead?"

"No," said the Queen.

"Do you still know where she is?" asked Rex "She told you, didn't she?"

"I saw it again," said the Queen. "It is far from here."

"There is no such place for me," said Rex.

"She traveled through the darkness of night for weeks," said the Queen.

"Was it painful to her?" he asked.

"She had no knowledge of it," said the Queen. "To her, not much time passed. While we here have aged weeks, maybe months, she has aged days. It was hard to contact her. I fear I have lost her for good."

"Don't worry, dear," assured Rex. "She's not lost as long as I can find her. All I need is transport to their planet."

The room was busy these days. There were many discussions, many things to plan. Stenonychosaurus were working with aliens to determine how to transport the huge amounts of supplies they would need for this campaign. They calculated the size of the force and had estimated the amount of food required to keep them fed for a couple of months. Could they haul it in red bags outside the ships like the children? Could they adapt alien flying technology and build supply ships?

One team led by Phaedra, one of the Queen's sisters, was testing some of the aliens for psychic ability.

Pilot entered the throne room, wearing distinctive decorations, but his uniform was torn and ragged. Marfu, another alien and his close friend, was with him. Marfu had been trained to speak the dinosaur language. He spoke directly to the Queen, talking in the language of the court.

"My friend Pilot was hoping to see King," he said. "He just got out of infirmary. He wants to thank him for saving life. He would have died under metal if King had not lifted the debris off of him."

Rex spotted Pilot and excused himself from the General. He pushed back through the crowds to join the Queen and the two aliens. "I remember you," he said to Pilot. "You were the one who warned me about the suicide attack."

"Yes," said Marfu, translating for his friend.

"I found him just in time," said Rex. "Lucky the Ankylosaurus could reverse the damage by wrapping him in special leaves."

"The aliens seem to heal quickly," said one of the Generals.

The Queen interrupted them. "He comes with a warning for you. He says not all the surviving aliens feel the way he does. Some still harbor distrust. They may be plotting to sabotage your mission. He fears for your safety."

"Thank him for the warning," said Rex. "This is twice he has helped me. I will be on guard against treachery, both alien and dinosaur."

Rex whispered to the Queen. "I know there are some in my own rank who would try to take advantage of this situation. I intend to guard against that as well. I have already arranged for your protection while I'm gone."

"We risk much to help them," said the Queen.

"It's for the children, not them, that I do this," said Rex.

"As to you, we have given each other the greatest gifts that two beings can exchange. To that, I can only add my friendship." He stepped forward and extended his hand.

Rex saw a kindred spirit in Pilot, someone who shared the same goals and values. He also saw a new friend, always a pleasant surprise when he wasn't looking for one. He took Pilot's hand and raised it high.

"No one can refuse a gift of friendship" said Pilot. "All I can offer in return is my own friendship."

"I'll do more than that," said Rex. "You have protected my life, a task usually reserved for an elite group. To further show my gratitude, I award you the rank of Protector of the Royal Family, which makes you an official member of my Elite Guard."

Pilot was overwhelmed. Rex called to Cassius, the Captain of the Guard. "He's one of you, Cassius. Treat him as such. I want him assigned to my court, to be at my side as a valuable member of my team."

"How?" began Pilot.

"Because I am the King," said Rex. "And I decree it. As a member of the Elite Guard, you are now entitled to live here in the Palace, to come and go as you please, and more importantly, to take a special place in shaping this alliance."

"What do you mean?" asked Pilot.

"Don't think I haven't noticed how you behave around your men, how they behave around you," said Rex. "You obviously have rank in your army as well. Don't you see the value of having title in both camps?"

"I do, but why me?" asked Pilot.

"Because your people need you, just as mine need me. I know that I ask a lot of your friendship, but this is a time when I need friends most of all. Please accept this honor."

Pilot did not need to answer. He smiled, as did Cassius, and a cheer went up in the hall. The combination of high pitched alien squeals and dinosaur growls resonated throughout the palace. Rex gave a friendly nod to Pilot and motioned for him to accompany him onto the balcony. As they stepped outside, a crowd formed behind him. Rex realized that his entourage was getting rather large and more diverse, but he needed all kinds of experts these days. There were aliens and dinosaurs of all shapes, ages, and sizes. The elite guard, sworn royal protectors of the clan, were always nearby, but now there were old dinosaurs, senior planners, and other dinosaur dignitaries. There was even an ankylosaurus serving as a full time medical officer. And now, finally, an alien.

Rex walked to the edge of the balcony where a large brontosaurus was craning his neck up to his level. Behind him Rex could see a huge shipyard where dinosaurs and aliens were working together to repair flying stones. Many of them looked ready and flight worthy. Large experimental ships, arc-like and massive, made of native materials, were being assembled in a field in the distance.

"Boss Bronto," said Rex with a smile. "How goes the progress here?"

"Come down and see for yourself," said the massive dinosaur. "The crews are working hard. They are feverish to rescue the children."

Boss Bronto bent his neck to the ground and talked to Garlan, an alien advisor who was helping him with the reconstruction of the fleet. Then he looked off into the distance and opened his throat, making a tremendous roar. A team of triceratops hauling a ship roared in return, changing direction and moving the stone into a new position. He turned his attention back to Rex, but he was no longer on the balcony. Bronto looked below and saw the King and his entourage emerging from the main entrance. He went right to Boss Bronto, Pilot at his side. Helene, the Queen's sister, was working nearby with a group of alien engineers. She came over to join them too.

"I decided to take you up on your offer," said the King to Boss Bronto. "I like the view from the ground."

"Let me give you the tour. We have functional production areas, Your Majesty, based on the needs of the ships being repaired. That stone was being moved from the junkyard to the hull repair depot. That alien with it is Kram, one of their engineers. He thinks it is salvageable. It may not have full electronics, but he's sure he can get it to fly. Maybe we can use it to transport supplies."

Bronto pointed to another area where aliens were carrying electronic equipment into a ship under repair. Holes in the hull had been fixed using armored plates from a stegosaurus. "This team works on the internal repairs. They're mostly aliens since we don't understand their technology. We'll know if they are successful. We have tests scheduled tomorrow."

"Good," said Rex. "How is Helene, the Queen's sister, doing?" He smiled, touching his sister-in-law affectionately.

"She's a real help. Most of the aliens know our language, but there are times we just can't understand each other. Helene is really good about communicating the finer points. I don't think we have the words to describe some things we need to. I just wish we could talk more directly with the aliens."

"We're working on that problem," said the King. "Meanwhile, do your best."

"Helene has told me a lot about them, Your Majesty," said Boss Bronto. "She understands more than their language. The aliens are working hard, but for different reasons than us. They're afraid of being trapped here. Many see this joint effort as their only way home."

"But they wouldn't be trapped," said Rex. "They'd be welcome here. This would be their home, too. Tell them that," he said. He turned to Helene. "Tell them that, my dear."

Helene spoke in the alien tongue, her voice carrying far. The work stopped momentarily, the sound of reconstruction pausing to hear her words. When she was finished, there were a few cheers, a lot of murmuring, and then the sound of building again.

Pilot said something. He wished he knew the language better, but he was still learning. He spoke to the Helene who translated for Rex. "He thinks we're not as primitive as the aliens were led to believe."

"Civilization does not always mean machinery," said Rex. "We accomplish a lot when we work together and cooperate. Through that we come to know each other."

Everywhere he looked he saw the dinosaurs and the aliens working together to rebuild the ships. Brontosaurus were holding pieces in place while aliens made adjustments, a stegosaurus dragged pieces of a recovered ship from the jungle guided by aliens, and raptors acted as go-fers to ferry supplies to busy aliens working everywhere. "We would like to send a delegation to your world to discuss the release of the children and a cease of hostilities," said Rex. Helene patiently explained this to Pilot.

One of Rex's advisors stepped forward, also speaking to Helene. "Tell him that I would welcome the opportunity to meet his people and work with them. I would love to be an ambassador to their world. We have an abundance of food here. The jungle produces more than we need. The aliens have been eating it for some time and it seems to agree with them. Let me propose a gift of bounty in good faith."

Rex nodded approval. Helene translated again as Pilot said, "The food here is quite healthy. I think it is because you are closer to the sun than our planet. There is more energy in your food."

A loud scream broke the conversation.

"It came from the palace," said Boss Bronto, his head high in the air, looking towards the palace.

There was a shout from the balcony to summon Rex, but the King recognized the sound of the Queen screaming. The crowd parted as he rushed back towards the entrance of the Palace.

A guard met the King just outside the throne room. "Sire, the Queen has fainted," he said.

Rex brushed past him and went right to her side. She was not lying still and lifeless on the floor like someone who had fainted. Instead she was squirming in pain. He looked into her eyes, calling her name gently, but she was empty, vapid and distant.

If he could see into her soul he would have felt her pain. Deep in her vision, the Queen felt Natalie being jabbed with a painstick. She heard screams from behind the ominous doors. She felt claustrophobic and confined in small cages with dinosaur children. She felt lost and hopeless.

Rex called to her but she could not hear him from deep within her nightmare. She continued to squirm in pain.

He called for medical dinos, but there was nothing they could do. This was an affliction of the mind, something unique to the Queen, something they did not understand.

"We can't leave soon enough," said Rex.

Chapter 11: Prison Life

The prison was a rancid, lonely place, especially for creatures that had spent their entire life outdoors. It wasn't so much the cages as the lack of sky overhead. There was some kind of spiritual connection between the dinosaurs, the earth and the sky and that connection had been broken.

The cycle of night and day had been broken as well. Gone were the transitions of sunrise and sunset. These were replaced with bright lights that hummed when they were on. If only there were a moment's relief, the gentle shade of a wide, jungle leaf to block out the blinding light. Then, weary and begging for night, the lights would go off as sharply as they went on, plunging everyone into an uneasy darkness. No hum, just the occasional tread of alien footsteps across a metal catwalk high overhead. It was better to hear these sounds from overhead. When they were nearby at floor level, they were almost always followed by screams from one of the children as they were prodded with painsticks.

There were the ominous doors at the end of the room of cages, the entrance to the room of no return. The only sounds from there were cries of agony and pain, of unimaginable suffering, followed by quiet extinction. Natalie sometimes wished for that silence, an end to this madness. She had not heard from her mother in some time, and this added to her misery. Nate was becoming restless and adversarial with the aliens and when he was alone with her he was withdrawn. She wondered how long he could hold on to his sanity.

She laid in the darkness in her tiny cage, listening to the sounds of the night. She wondered if it really was night outside or if there were daylight and warm breezes just beyond the walls of the compound. She wondered if anyone was coming to rescue them, if her father had mastered the secret of flying. She wondered if this building had the power to hide them from their loved ones. It certainly seemed to affect her ability to sense her mother's presence and communicate with her.

There was a sound outside her cage. She stopped in mid breath and listened, but she couldn't hear over the pounding of her heart. There was another sound, this time louder and nearer.

"Princess," came a small voice.

She let herself breathe, taking in enough air to answer. "Yes," she said.

"We must escape this prison," said the voice. "If we don't, they will take us one by one into the next room."

"Who are you?" she asked. "This is not the first time I've heard you scuttling about at night."

"I am Dozer, and this is my brother Closer," said the voice. "We are full grown Compys. I'm sorry, Compsognathus. I don't think the aliens realize that we're adults."

"No, I don't think they realize that either," said Closer.

"If they did, they would probably destroy us," said Dozer.

"I would have to agree," said Closer.

Natalie thought about it. Compys were some of the smallest dinosaurs, smaller than any of the baby dinosaurs in captivity. With two strong legs that were twice the size of their arms, they could run fast and were balanced for speed. They were curious creatures, and she considered how they were well suited to explore the prison and gather information for her.

Dozer moved nearer to the Princess. "Have you noticed that no one comes back from that room?" he asked. His voice was solemn and sad.

"I've noticed," said Natalie.

"In my opinion it would be better to die trying to escape than to be taken into that room," said Dozer.

"It would be better," echoed Closer. "That is why we explore. They will kill us anyway."

"My father is coming to rescue us," said Natalie. "We must be patient."

"How can he find us?" asked Dozer. "You saw how far we came. You know we left our home world far behind."

"Yes, we did," said Closer. "We left it behind, traveling through the long night. We could have touched the stars if not for the walls of the red bag."

"By the time your father gets here there may be no one left to rescue," said Dozer.

"He is correct," said Closer. "My brother is often correct, but I can verify it. There are many empty cages."

"My father will find a way," said Natalie. This time when she said it, she didn't sound as convincing, even to herself. She thought about her father and asked herself what he would do in this situation. He always listened to his subjects, valued their opinion. It was one of his strengths as a leader. "Say we were to escape, where would we go? We know nothing about this place."

"We will spy for you," said Dozer. "I told you, the guards don't know we are adults."

"Because we are small they think we're children like you," said Closer. "There is a lot they don't know about us."

"Yes, like night is our day time," said Dozer. "We see better at night. Back home on our planet we sleep during the day to avoid the bright lights."

"I wish I could sleep," said Natalie.

"They don't know we can squeeze through these bars" said Dozer.

"They don't," repeated Closer.

"What else don't they know about us?" asked Dozer.

"They don't know that we know their secret," said Closer.

Dozer became silent. The life seemed to drain from his voice. "We already found another room that leads to a cave," he said hoarsely. "It could be a way out, but you have to go through that room." He pointed to the door of no return.

The conversation stopped. The compy brothers seemed unusually quiet and had little to say. Natalie wondered if she should press them further. "What goes on in that room?" she finally asked, her curiosity getting the best of her.

There was no answer, only more silence. Dozer and Closer looked at each other in the darkness, shaking their heads.

"Princess," said Dozer. "I heard that you allowed yourself to be captured. You chose to be with us, so help us now. To wait here in cages is certain death."

"My father..." she began to say. "My father," she repeated to herself, thinking again of what he would do.

"Yes," coaxed Dozer. "Your father?"

"My father always says to wait for the right opportunity to present itself," she said. "That opportunity is close at hand, I feel."

Dozer listened to Natalie.

"Don't fear," she continued. "I trust what you say. You're right. If we wait here they will take us one at a time. Together we stand a better chance. We will act when the time is right."

Dozer and Closer looked at each other and smiled. "Yes, your majesty," they said at once.

"Have faith, loyal spies," she said. "Pass the word. We must have hope, but be careful. Don't put yourself in danger."

"We'll try to follow your example," said Dozer.

"We will wait for your signal to act," said Closer.

They scurried off, their spirits lifted by the Princess' support.

Nate heard everything and spoke softly from a nearby cell. "Now we're talking," he said.

"Yes, we're talking," said Natalie. "Now stop talking, unless you want to get jabbed with one of those sticks."

"They don't hurt anymore," said Nate.

"I always said you were insensitive and unfeeling," said Natalie.

"This is no time for joking," said Nate

"I'm just trying to keep my spirits up," said Natalie. "You're not the only one who uses humor as a mask."

"Well, if making fun of me helps then I'm all for it," said Nate.

Natalie's fears could no longer stay hidden beneath a mask of humor. She was worried, but she had another mask to wear as well. The compys had called upon her as the Royal Princess. Her mother had been right. Leadership had been thrust upon her, and the safety of her subjects should be her main concern.

She considered what the compy brothers had suggested. How could they make a move against their captors when they were all confined in separate cages? Was her father really on the way or was he having trouble mounting a rescue? What happened in the room behind the ominous doors?

Nate noticed her silence. "What's up?" he asked. "My conversation doesn't amuse you anymore?"

Natalie couldn't hide her anxiety. "What are we going to do, Nate?" she asked.

"Just what you and our little friends suggested," said Nate. "Follow the plan. Look for the opportunity to escape. Like good predators, we're going to sit and observe. Stalk our prey."

"That's you, Nate. What am I going to do?" asked Natalie.

"What you've always done. Be the Princess," said Nate.

"I'm already the Princess, Nate," she said.

"Then that makes your job easy," he said smiling. "Real easy. Look at my job, though. Protector of the Royal Family, Member of the Elite Guard."

Natalie laughed. Humor wasn't just a mask to Nate, it was a way of life. "I'm glad you're here, my royal protector," she said, playing along with him.

"I'm not sure I want the job anymore," said Nate. "I liked it better when I was just your friend."

"Being my friend was never easy, was it, Nate?" she asked.

"You really want an answer?" he asked back.

Natalie thought about what he said. "I didn't mean to drag you into this, Nate," said Natalie. "You shouldn't have followed me into..."

The lights suddenly came on. Guards approached Natalie's cage with an alien scientist. They stopped and the scientist pointed to Natalie, gibbering in their strange language. The guards took up positions, activating their painsticks. They moved forward to open the cage, standing in front of Natalie's cage. One of them placed a key in the lock. Natalie backed away into the corner.

"No!" yelled Nate. He became enraged, roaring in defiance. He started banging against the cage. The guards laughed, thrusting their painsticks forward. Nate cringed on to the other side of the cage, retreating for a moment. The guards laughed louder, moving closer to the cage. Nate waited, then turned suddenly and thrust his tail through the bars of the cage. He was quick and he swept his tail low, knocking the guards off their feet. One of them screamed as he was accidentally struck with a loose painstick.

"Who's laughing now?" yelled Nate, his teeth salivating, looking every bit the predator.

Guards seemed to appear from out of nowhere. Nate was jabbed repeatedly with pain sticks. He seemed almost immune to them, fighting back with rage. Natalie yelled to calm him down but he was in the throes of a blood fever. All he could hear were the shouts of his enemies as they descended upon him with pain.

Guards continued to arrive, armed with more powerful weapons. Some brought strange, animal control devices, harnesses made of ropes and metal straps.

Natalie screamed. The scientist locked her cage and moved away from her, focusing on Nate. He spoke to the guards, indicating Nate. The guards came closer to Nate and one of them unlocked his cage.

"No!" screamed Natalie

The Scientist continued to gibber and point at Nate. They tried to wrap and bind Nate with the animal control devices and restraints. He resisted for a while, but there were too many of them. He was easily outnumbered and overpowered. The gibber of the scientist became more confident and smug. The scientist barked out a series of orders.

The guards wrangled Nate out of his cage, Natalie screaming all the time. The ominous doors opened and Natalie caught a glimpse of strange devices and odd colored lights in the dim shadows beyond the threshold. Natalie screamed louder.

"Nate! Nate!"

Natalie heard one last roar from Nate. The doors closed with an eerie metal bang, made even more poignant by the silence that followed. Guards appeared on the catwalks overhead, looking down over the scared dinosaur children.

The guards watched for a while, the sound of their footsteps on the catwalk above. Soon it was quiet again, except for the faint muffled screams coming from behind the door. One by one the guards disappeared until only a few remained. Then the lights went out again.

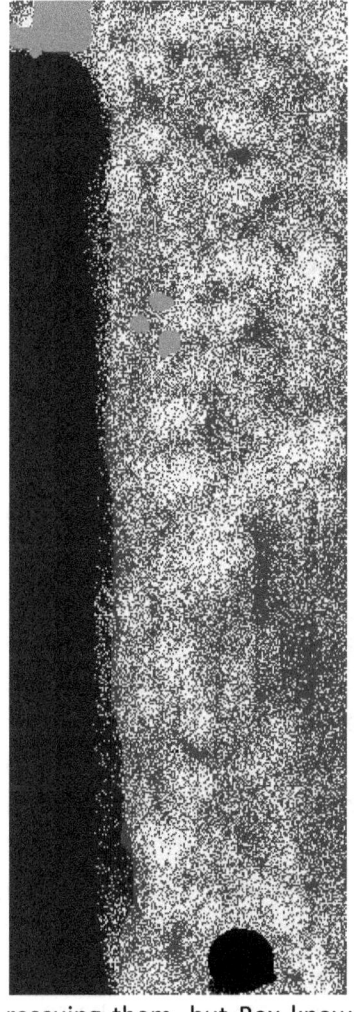

Chapter 12: A Pensive King

Rex paced back and forth across the throne room, the cave echoing with his footsteps. His advisors, aliens, and the Elite Guard gave him a wide berth, staying close to the walls. They had never seen their leader like this and they could not imagine how he was holding up under these conditions. Despite the massive reconstruction, reports were still coming in that he had lost many of his top soldiers to the alien attack. The scent of death still lay heavy on the land. The winds carried the faint smell of charred flesh, burning jungle, and rotting meat even to the lofty chambers of the palace.

His people were growing weary with the effort. They questioned the validity of the alliance he had formed with the aliens. They questioned the reconstruction of the fleet of ships as a way of getting the children back. Other ideas had surfaced as a way of rescuing them, but Rex knew they would not work. News of the Battle of Glade Rock had spread. True to the King's fears, his old adversary Roughstone had managed to survive the battle and had issued a public challenge to Rex, a death duel to wrest control of the leadership from the King.

"That's the last thing I need," he thought as he reached the opposite wall and turned to pace in the other direction. "A blood duel for control of the herd would serve no purpose but to divide my people even further."

So many things were going right, and so many things were going wrong. It had been weeks since the attack, and the rebuilding of the fleet was proceeding on schedule. He was making daily inspections of the progress. Pilot was an immense help to him and Rex had come to trust the alien without question. Saving his life had been a wise move, and so was sparing the other surviving aliens, despite the protests.

He knew it was the emotions born of grief, of losing their loved ones. He knew that well. He never stopped thinking of Natalie, his only child. He felt anger, fear, loss, and even anguish at times. He questioned his leadership and his motivations. Was his plan for the benefit of the people, or was it just a way to get his Natalie back? How selfish could a king afford to be?

He turned and paced again, all eyes in the room following his movements as they tried to guess the thoughts that swirled in his brain. The Queen was among them. Of anyone in the room, she knew the inmost thoughts of her husband, but he had become so dark and pensive lately that she was having difficulty reading his mind. She reminded herself often, saying, "He forgets that he was not the only one who lost a daughter," she reminded herself.

She reached out again with her mind and felt something dark and fearful. It was as if she had touched a poisoned spine bush in the jungle, its prickly thorns causing her to pull back. The King was sensitive to her. He felt it and stopped in mid pace to look at her. She flinched, gasping for air as if dying. There was a look of panic on her face and she twitched again.

"What is it?" asked Rex, rushing to her side. If anything brought him back from the edge of darkness it was his concern for her. The Elite Guard stood ready, stepping forward at the sounds of the Queen gasping. These dizzy spells of hers were on the rise. They seemed to come upon her whenever she attempted to contact Natalie.

The Queen felt heavy in his grasp and he shook her, as if he could dislodge the darkness that had engulfed her. He thought he saw her eyes begin to clear, the darkness wavered and for a moment he sensed his wife beside him again. She looked into his eyes.

"It's the children," she said.

He understood. "They need us," said Rex, turning to address everyone in the room. "They need adults. We've delayed this too long." He turned to his guard. "Signal the troops," he said. "We have to launch immediately."

"We're not ready yet," said Cassius.

"We'll follow the quick plan then," said Rex.

"We can't afford to be hasty," said Cassius. "Wait until we finish repairs. We need full capability and support."

"The quick plan!" demanded Rex. "We send an emissary, a small force to try to negotiate with their leaders. I still believe this is a misunderstanding that we can correct."

He motioned to Pilot who also nodded approvingly.

"They will kill you if you go," said Cassius. "And Pilot, Cedric, Marfu, even Garlan. Everyone who joined the alliance will be considered traitors by their own people."

Cedric spoke with the aid of one of the Queen's sisters. He could understand and speak some of the dinosaur language, but he wanted to be very clear on this matter. Penelope spoke, but the words were Cedric's.

"If it takes my death to correct this mistake, then so be it," he said. "I don't consider myself a traitor. This attack was a mistake. Once my people see this, we will be vindicated."

"I am not so quick to forfeit my life, Cedric," said Cassius.

"When it comes to our children, Cassius, we have no choice," said Rex. "Haven't you been to the infirmary? Have you seen the mothers who mourn for the loss of their children? Have you seen the ones who have no will to live?"

"I have a wife at home," Cassius reminded him. "She is among that group."

"And I'm not ignorant of the fact that your son is among the missing," said Rex.

"We feel your pain, Cassius," said the Queen.

Rex turned to the gallery. "Assemble the delegation. Prepare the fleet. We will launch everything that can fly."

"And what about those left behind?" asked one of the trusted advisors.

"Continue the reconstruction," said Rex. "Follow us with the rest of the fleet when you are done. Cassius, assemble your men. You're coming with me. Bring whoever you see fit. I don't anticipate trouble, but it is always better to negotiate from a position of strength."

Cassius nodded, motioning to some of the Elite Guard, including Scarback. "I'll see to the preparations," he said to Rex, exiting quickly with his men.

Chapter 13: We Need More Scientists

Nate was gone. They had taken him away. Many of the cages around Natalie lay empty and silent. Even the roars and cries from behind the ominous doors had subsided and the guards eventually became bored with tormenting the dinosaurs.

High above the prison floor in an observation room, the Warden looked down upon all this and smiled. He had done a good job of running this hell hole, and he expected to be rewarded for it someday. After all, the President had appointed him personally to this job. When all the dinosaurs were gone, there would be no purpose to this place, unless there were plans in the works for second expedition to collect more specimens.

"I must remember to ask the President when I see him again," he said.

"Sir?" questioned a guard standing nearby.

"Sorry," he said. "Just thinking out loud to myself."

"Yes, sir," replied the guard in a crisp voice. "I do that myself sometimes."

"Yes," replied the Warden with feigned interest. "I'm sure you do." He sat down behind his huge desk in his oversized comfortable chair, feeling the power it gave him. He opened a drawer full of buttons and pressed one of them. On a side wall a video monitor sprang to life, displaying an image of the President.

"I forgot he was giving a speech today," said the Warden.

"Yes, Sir," said the guard.

The Warden gave the guard a sideways glance.

"Yes, sir," said the guard sheepishly. "I'll be quiet so you can hear the President."

The Warden tweaked a knob in the desk drawer, increasing the volume on the monitor.

"This is a holy war," came the President's voice. "You are either with us or against us."

There were cheers.

"Don't despair," continued the President. "This war will be over soon. Our scientists are studying these creatures. They are using that knowledge to build a weapon so powerful that it will end this threat forever. We will not sacrifice our children to these beasts."

More cheers.

There was a noise outside the door to his office. The Warden looked at the guard who reacted. "Yes, sir. I'll go see what it is."

He left, returning momentarily with a group of scientists escorted by more guards.

"Great," murmured the Warden. "Visitors." He silenced the monitor, leaving the image of the President mouthing words.

Gorka, one of the scientists, stepped forward from the group. The Warden looked him over and judged him to be an inconsequential man, barely worthy of his precious time. He'd rather listen to the President's speech, but this was the duty of his office, listening to complaints and problems from whiny underlings. This will all change when the President gives him a new, more important assignment.

"These experiments are useless," said Gorka. "We have learned nothing new in the last two weeks and it is fruitless to continue them."

"You will continue the experiments as you were ordered," said the Warden.

"This is murder," said Gorka. "I will not be a part of it."

"As you wish," said the Warden. "Gorka, isn't it?" The Warden narrowed his eyes.

"Yes, sir," replied Gorka. "Dr. Gorka." The group around him became uneasy. Some stepped backwards, distancing themselves from Gorka slightly.

The Warden nodded and motioned to the guard. "Dr. Gorka has decided to switch sides," said the Warden. "Take him away. Lock him up with the others."

"Wait! That's not necessary," said Gorka.

The scientists around him cowered and moved further away. Gorka acted quickly to try to keep the group together. He turned and looked at one of his comrades for support. Some of the group nodded while others seemed to drift further away. He knew when he was beaten. He sensed that the Warden would never listen to his argument.

He turned and reluctantly addressed the scientists. "We shouldn't have bothered the Warden with our silly complaints," he said. "Let's get back to work."

The group began to shuffle towards the doorway. The Warden had a smug grin on his face.

Suddenly one of the scientists turned. "No," he said, trying to persuade everyone the argument was not over. "That's not why we came here. We wanted to be heard."

The Warden looked amused.

"These animals are intelligent," said the scientist. "They are made of the same materials as we are: amino acids, protein, DNA. They cry, feel and think like we do."

"Then perhaps you should join them," said the Warden, thinking for a moment. "Croton, isn't that your name?" He turned to his guard again. "Take this one away instead."

Guards moved forward, two of them taking up positions beside Croton. The remainder of the group became animated and uneasy. Gorka made a move to protest, then restrained himself. The President continued to mouth empty words on the monitor, making them all aware of the silence and tension that filled the room.

The Warden nodded and the guards started to move again. Gorka looked as if he were going to say something. The Warden held his hand up.

"Wait," he said to the guards "I may have some others for you."

Gorka looked at the outspoken scientist surrounded by guards, his only apparent backer. The rest cowered behind him, looking at the silent monitor as if interested. He drew a deep breath and summoned his courage.

"We should be learning to communicate with these beings rather than torturing them," said Gorka.

"Take this one, too," said the Warden. "Put him in a cage beside the beasts. See if they communicate."

"You're going too far," said Gorka.

"I am only following the President's orders," said the Warden. He made a flicking motion with his hand and turned towards the huddle of remaining scientists. The guards took Gorka and Croton away. The remaining scientists looked at each other and shuffled slowly out of the room.

The Warden called for his assistant.

"Better contact headquarters," he said. "We may need more scientists. Ones who think more like us."

The assistant looked at him oddly. "But it's a scientist's job to think objectively," he said.

"Then get soldiers," said the Warden. "I'm sick of these weaklings. I need someone who will follow orders."

The assistant started to say something, then considered his own fate.

"As you wish," he said, turning to leave the room.

Chapter 14: The Rescue Begins

"I'll be back before you know it," said Rex. "With Natalie, too."

Rex prepared to leave with the fleet. He nuzzled and kissed the Queen goodbye again, knowing it might be some time before he would see her.

"I must board the flagship soon," he said. "I'll miss you."

"I still think I should come along," said the Queen.

"I'd only worry about you," said Rex. "Knowing you are safe here will keep me from being distracted. Besides, at least one member of the royal family should stay behind and rule in my absence."

"Then take my sister Penelope with you," she said. "She will help you when you need it."

Rex nodded. "She has your abilities and your strength," he said. "I will take care of her."

"Some of my students wish to join crews in the other ships," said Penelope. "We offer our services as you see fit."

"I accept your offer," said Rex. "Welcome to the fleet."

"Come back safely to me," said the Queen, nuzzling him.

"I will," he promised. "And I will bring Natalie back." His goodbye to the Queen was not as private as he hoped. He opened his eyes from a passionate kiss and noticed all eyes were on him. They had been listening to his every word. The public often enjoyed this glimpse at the private life of royalty. It made their leaders real. "We'll bring them all back," he said to the crowd around him. "I will not rest until our families are whole again."

There were shouts of approval from the crowd. "Time to go!" he yelled.

There were more hasty goodbyes. The Queen was not the only one who had come to see her husband off. Cassius' wife was there, hopeful and optimistic as the Captain of the Guard gave her the same reassurances. Aliens and dinosaurs began boarding ships. A ship took off and hovered over a huge brontosaurus. A red beam lashed out that formed a bag around the behemoth.

"I was wondering how we could take some of the larger dinosaurs," said Rex.

"They won't be too uncomfortable," said Cedric. "Those bags shield them from radiation and they get fresh air pumped from the ship through the umbilical."

"We'll keep the big transports out of sight until we know it's safe to land," said one of the Generals.

Cedric nodded. "We have a cover story. We're going to say that we're survivors returning with a few of the larger specimens."

Rex nodded approval. He nuzzled the Queen one last time. Others did the same, seeing their loved ones off for what they felt might be the last time. Rex smiled at Pilot and the two of them walked together towards the flagship, followed by Cassius, Penelope, Cedric, Scarback, the General, a medical Ankylosaurus, dignitaries, and a squad of raptors.

The entrance to the flagship was framed by a gauntlet of Elite Guard who ceremoniously joined the end of the procession and followed them inside. The door was secured. There was a hum and the stone shuddered and rose, emitting beams of colored light. Ships began to rise everywhere, some holding huge dinosaurs. There was another brontosaurus, several brachiosaurus, even an oversized triceratops.

Mothers and wives hugged their children and husbands as more ships took off. All eyes looked skyward in hope as the fleet disappeared into the sky. There was some conversation, congratulations, and a few promises among the group that had been left behind. Mothers and children began to slip away. The rest stared at the sky, including the dinosaurs and aliens who had volunteered to stay behind and continue working on the rest of the damaged ship. They stared skyward, their eyes filled with hope. Finally Boss Bronto raised his neck above the crowd.

"Okay, folks," he said. "Nothing more to see here. Let's get back to work. The sooner we get finished, the sooner we can join them."

Chapter 15: New Friends

The lights went out in the prison, plunging the room into shadows. In the silence, Natalie heard sounds coming from Nate's cage. Could it be he was back? If he was, he didn't sound good. No matter how many times she spoke to him she got no answer. After a while she gave up hoping it was Nate and decided it must be a wounded child, a victim of what went on beyond the ominous doors.

She didn't know it was Gorka, the alien scientist. She had been resting when he had been placed in the cage by the guards. She called to him again but heard only strange sobbing noises in return. She wanted to comfort him, even if it wasn't Nate. Nobody deserved this fate and now that Nate was gone she was lonely for company. She didn't realize how much Nate had meant to her, but that is often true. You never know what you will miss until it's gone.

"There is nothing in the darkness that wasn't there, in the light, a moment ago," she said gently. The whimpering stopped for a moment, then continued.

There was a click in the darkness. She heard scampering and recognized the familiar sounds of her faithful spies, the Compy brothers. She wasn't surprised when Dozer and Closer appeared in front of her cage.

"We have a new skill," said Closer. "A way we can release you."

"We're getting good at picking locks," said Dozer. "But it still takes us a long time."

"I have sharpened my claw, Princess," said Closer. "It is time to release our people."

"What's that noise I keep hearing? Is Nate back in his cage?" she asked.

"It's one of them," said Dozer.

"They put him in a cage like the rest of us," said Closer.

"Why?" she asked.

"We don't know," said Dozer. "They just came and put him there in the darkness."

"He's just like us," said Closer. "Destined for the doors at the other end of the room."

"Maybe if we free him, he could help us escape," suggested Dozer.

Natalie thought about it. This might be the opportunity she had been waiting for.

"Is he okay?" she asked. "He doesn't sound well."

"I'll go check on him," said Closer.

While he was gone, Natalie discussed a plan with Dozer.

"You may be right," she said. "This may be the time to act. We need help to get out of here. The creature in that cage may know the quickest way to the exit."

"Do you think he will help us?" asked Dozer.

"I'm not sure," she said. "But it seems he's in the same situation that we are. It's worth a try. We could at least ask him."

"Never hurts to ask," said Closer, appearing out of nowhere.

"What did you learn?" asked Dozer.

"You were right. He's one of them," said Closer. "He doesn't look too good. He's all curled up in a ball in the corner like a newborn hatchling."

"Is he the one making the strange noises I hear?" asked the Princess.

"Yes. I think he's crying. He doesn't look too happy," said Closer.

"He doesn't sound happy," said Natalie.

"Who would be in these circumstances?" asked Dozer.

"True," said Closer. "True. None of us are happy."

"Have you tried talking to him?" asked Dozer.

"What do you mean?" asked Natalie.

"Talk to him," said Dozer.

"Like your mother does," said Closer.

"Yes," said Dozer.

Natalie was pained at the mention of her mother. "I'm not my mother," she said, feeling the inadequacy of her powers. She turned in her cage and lowered her head, thinking about the Queen with all she could muster. She concentrated, took deep breaths, and focused her thoughts on her mother.

She felt calmer, but she did not feel like her mother. Neither did she feel the presence of her mother. Her thoughts came back to her like an echo across a deep canyon. She was alone.

A dim light filtered in from above, but all she could see were shadows in front of her. She turned back toward the compys, defeated. "I'm not my mother," she said again. "I don't have her gifts."

"But you do," said Dozer.

"You must," insisted Closer. Desperation filled both their voices. Natalie could see it in them. She looked closely at them and thought she saw a blur form in front of them. In that blur was the image of the compys picking every lock in the prison. She also saw how long it would take, the compys revealing the plan's weakness to her as she looked into the blur.

The alien in the nearby cage let out a whimper. Natalie turned her attention away from the compys and towards the alien. She reached out to him, wanting to comfort him as she had the children.

As she reached out with her mind, she could see Gorka in the blur, curled in a ball in the corner of the cage. He had been abandoned by his own kind. He was worried about his friends; he thought he had failed them. He was afraid of what was going to happen to him, she could smell the fear leeching off his skin.

Something odd happened.

He could feel it! She knew he could feel her presence. He reacted to her invisible touch where his mind met hers. He relaxed a bit, uncurling from a ball in the corner. He told her that he wanted to get out of the cage, too. In a blur she saw the image of a switch. The switch was on the wall near the ominous doors at the other end of the room. An alien hand pulled the switch down and all the cages opened at once. If only they could reach that switch.

She suddenly knew what had to be done.

"Are you all right, Princess?" asked Dozer.

"The time is now, loyal friends," said Natalie. "There is a device on that wall over there, by the door of no return." She pressed a mental image of the switch into the minds of the compys.

"I know that thing," said Dozer.

"Yes," said Closer. "It looks like a smooth tree limb coming out of a crack in the rocks."

"Yes," urged Natalie. "You must pull that tree limb down. It can release all of us at once."

Compys, being night time creatures, see well in the dark. Dozer and Closer craned their necks and looked at the switch, then at each other.

"It's pretty high up," said Dozer. "I don't know."

"You can do it," said Natalie. "You must."

Dozer and Closer moved towards the switch. They leaped several times, falling short of reaching it. Closer even tried jumping on Dozer's back, using him as a platform to leap higher. The lights got a little brighter and two guards appeared, attracted by the noise they were making. The compys scurried out of sight before the guards could see them, retreating to a dark corner nearby. One stood by the door while the other walked down an aisle between the cages.

"We can't take them on," whispered Dozer to his brother.

"It wouldn't be a fair fight," said Closer. "They have weapons."

"We're too small," said Dozer.

"We need a distraction," said Closer.

"Yes. A way to get them away from here so we can try pulling the tree limb again."

They could see the guard standing near the switch and scanning the area. There was a muffled noise from behind the ominous doors. The guard turned around and looked at the door. He nodded to himself, thinking it must have been what he heard.

The second guard continued slowly down the aisle, staring into every cage as he went by. He passed close to Dozer and Closer and didn't see them. He focused on something else. He walked with purpose, coming finally to stop in front of Gorka's cage.

He spoke some alien gibberish, sounding boastful. Then he laughed, unmistakable in any language. There was the hum of a painstick. In a quick thrust, the guard jabbed his painstick into the cage.

Gorka screamed.

The sound made Natalie uneasy and she let out a low growl. The guard turned away from Gorka, facing Natalie and threatening her with the painstick.

Gorka yelled a stream of defiant gibberish. The guard stood transfixed, gibbering to Natalie as he paced in front of her cage.

The compys looked at each other in recognition.

"A distraction," whispered Dozer.

"Yes, I agree. A distraction. But he's going to hurt the Princess," said Closer. "We should help her."

"We should follow her orders and move the tree limb," said Dozer. "That would release everyone and then we can all help her."

"Oh," agreed Closer. "You're so clever."

They moved towards the switch. Natalie screamed from behind them as the guard jabbed her with a painstick. Closer cringed. There were more screams and roars as many of the dinosaurs became agitated. The guards focused on the distraction, unaware of the small dinosaurs lurking near the switch.

Dozer decided to make his move. Taking a last look at ground level, he ran to the top of a cage near the switch. He stood for a moment, looking slightly down at the switch, thinking about what he was about to try to do. It was a long way, definitely a challenge for the small dinosaur. He saw the guard terrorizing his brother with the painstick. Closer was quick, bobbing and darting around expertly. His brother had always been better at this game. Closer looked up, making eye contact and nodding to Dozer. He knew what Dozer was going to try.

"Can't think about it forever," said Dozer to himself. Leaping from the top, he sailed down until he landed on the switch. He started to slip off but managed to grab it with both claws and hang on. It would not budge. He tried swinging back and forth while clutching the switch but it still wouldn't move.

"Help!" yelled Dozer.

The guard didn't understand what Dozer said, but he heard him. He turned away from Closer and ran towards the switch, gibbering wildly and swinging his painstick from side to side. It made contact with Dozer and he let out a scream, but the tiny dinosaur did not let go of the switch. The guard swung again, hitting him harder with the painstick, trying to knock him off. Dozer screamed in agony. Dinosaurs in their cages became more agitated and roared in defiance, banging against the sides of their cages.

"They're in trouble," thought Natalie. "I shouldn't have ordered them to do this."

Closer heard his brother scream and he ran to the rescue.

The cruel guard who had been tormenting Gorka heard the commotion as well. He turned away from Gorka and headed towards the source of the noise. He saw Closer and started running to catch up with him, yelling in angry alien gibberish. The Compy was quick, adept at ducking and scurrying. It was a game to him, one he had played for life and death back on Earth where there were always large dinosaurs trying to make a snack out of him. The more the cruel guard tried to hit him, the more Closer eluded him. It just made the guard angrier.

Closer heard his brother scream again. He heard both guards gibbering excitedly. Then he heard the sound of the painstick making contact with something, something longer than a quick jab. It was a sickening sound, a searing hiss not unlike a volcanic steam vent. It sounded just like the time he had seen a member of his herd fall into a hot spring. He could almost remember the sound of the animal instantly cooking to death.

Dozer screamed in agony but he would not let go. To the guards it sounded like an animal wail. The guard had heard similar screams from many of the animals he had tormented. It was music to him, and he smirked. It took him back to his childhood when he tortured livestock on his uncle's farm. Cleaning stalls, bathing them, walking them, feeding them. He hated taking care of those animals, but his parents forced him work on the farm. He took out many of his frustrations on those helpless animals.

The cruel guard was distracted by the sound as he heard it again. This was a deep wail, loud and resonant; the kind that stirs gut-wrenching feelings. He stood still for a moment, startled at the sound. He had been staring out into space, remembering his youth, when he noticed something at the edge of his vision. He looked down and saw Closer directly in front of him. It startled him, but he gripped the painstick with both hands, raising it above his head. One strike downward and he would knock this renegade creature senseless with pain. He hoped the added force would break bones and cripple it, allowing him to apply the painstick slowly and with more focused intent.

Closer saw an opening. He ran between the cruel guard's legs and clawed up his back where he bit him on the neck. His two rows of sharp teeth clamped tightly, his jaw ached with the effort, but he held his mouth closed. The guard twisted and tried to push the small dinosaur off his back, twisting as he jabbed at Closer with the painstick. He accidently hit himself, sending him reeling in pain. Now it was the cruel guard who screamed. The alien yelps of pain sent waves of excitement and hope through the prisoners who were listening to the sounds of the battle. The cages rattled as dinosaurs tried to force their way out.

As the cruel guard twisted, he saw the switch with Dozer hanging on to it. He couldn't reach the dinosaur on his back, but he could take his anger out on the one on the switch. He took a violent swing at Dozer as he hung onto the switch.

The other guard saw Closer dangling by his teeth on his friend's back. He took a swat at it with his painstick.

Green blood was beginning to ooze from the cruel guard's back as Closer clamped his jaw tighter. He got a bad taste in his mouth. He saw the second guard coming out of the corner of his eye. He dug his claws into the cruel guard's back to secure his footing. He let loose with his teeth and scurried to the top of the guard's head where he leaped towards the switch. The cruel guard yelled as the other guard's painstick connected with his back right where the compy would have been. Worse, still, it hit the open wound left from Closer's bite, adding pain on top of pain. The cruel guard dropped to the floor in agony. The second guard tripped over him and fell on top of him. They struggled in a heap on the floor.

Closer sailed forward. The two compy brothers reached out to each other. Dozer had one claw firmly held to the switch, the other stretched out towards Closer. His brother twisted in mid air, reaching out towards the outstretched claw. Dozer swung a little, bracing for impact.

Closer's aim had been perfect. He hit his brother near his head, nearly knocking him off the switch. Dozer grabbed on with both claws to keep them both from sliding off. Before he could adjust his grip, the switch shifted underneath him, sliding downward until he lost balance.

They both fell to the floor, but they had done it. Even though they only weighed a few kilos each, their weight was enough to throw the switch.

A buzzer sounded and all the cages opened. Dinosaurs moved quickly as a platoon of guards entered the room. A melee ensued. Guards assembled on the catwalk above and aimed weapons downward. The Warden came out of his office in a panic. He called a Chamberlain to his side, spoke with him briefly, then dispatched him to personally inform the President of these events.

"Over there," yelled Natalie, motioning to nearby dinosaurs. "We have to move now."

An ankylosaurus rushed to the baby pterodactyl and clubbed the chain that was attached around his ankle. It shattered on the third strike. The baby pterodactyl flew upward and knocked two of the guards off the catwalk. They screamed on the way down, landing with a soft, meaty thud. The baby brontosaurus rushed forward and stepped on them, smashing one of their heads like an overripe piece of fruit. The Warden ran for the safety of his office. Without hesitation, the guards turned and fired at the pterodactyl. He flew higher and out of reach, distracting the Guards from the escaping dinosaurs below.

Natalie led the group towards the entrance. She had thought about it often in her cell, remembering in detail the path she had traveled from the starport to this building and to her cage. It was the only way out she knew for certain.

Her strategy was too obvious. One of the guards on the catwalk looked down, shouting and pointing as he drew attention to the dinosaurs. An alien guard rushed off the catwalk to a panel where he threw a switch. Heavy doors closed around the entrance to the low, flat building, sealing them in.

Gorka ran to Natalie's side and caught her attention. He pointed towards the ominous doors, indicating that they should go through there. Natalie nodded that she understood. She rallied the dinosaurs, herding them towards the doors.

"This way," she said. "Let's free our friends from torture."

A baby triceratops rammed the door, assisted by several small pachycephalosaurus. Natalie whispered words of hope to herself, optimistic of what they would find.

"Nate, please be okay," she said. She turned to the dinosaurs shouting, "Ram harder."

"I hate these doors," said the baby triceratops.

"The pain and fear they brought us," said one of the pachycephalosaurus.

They rammed together, joined by Natalie. Even Dozer and Closer added their shoulders to the effort.

The doors creaked as the dinosaurs continued to put all their combined strength into it. The thuds were deafening, echoing through the prison as they beat against the doors. There was the sound of twisting metal as the doors slowly gave in to the relentless pounding of the dinosaurs.

Guards fired their weapons down at them. Gorka fired back, armed with weapons he had taken from the fallen guards. Whenever the guards looked down, the baby pterodactyl would swoop down from above and knock them off the catwalk. The guards were confused, caught in the middle and fighting in two directions.

The pounding continued, drowning out shouts from the guards above. At last one of the doors failed, the hinge buckling as it was knocked inward. A few more rams and the door was opened wide.

"Quick," ordered Natalie. She didn't have to say it. The escapees poured through the opening without being told. Natalie let others pass before her, keeping a watchful eye for guards who might have regrouped for another attack. She motioned to the pterodactyl who stopped harassing the guards and joined the escape. He glided low to the ground, pulling his wings in tight as he sailed through the door and landed on the other side.

"Ahhh," he said. "Haven't done something like that in a while."

"All clear," yelled Natalie. Seeing no dinosaurs left behind, she turned, stepped over the door and entered the room.

Stopping in horror at what she saw.

Chapter 16: Inside the Room of Death

It was a dreary room, far different than anything they had imagined. There were sinks and steel tables and shelves. There were strange metal instruments, knives and clamps and shiny things that smelled of death. Looking closely at the shelves that lined the walls, the dinosaurs noticed jars and vats with body parts floating in different colored liquids. It was obvious they had been taken from the missing children. Where else would the aliens get these things?

To one side there was a long room lined with tables. Some of the tables had dinosaurs strapped to them. Some of them moved, struggling against their bonds. At the far end there was a group of scientists huddled around one of the tables. On it laid a squirming baby Saurolophus, one of the scientists holding a menacing instrument above the dinosaur. He had a distinctive crest, a large piece of bone sticking out the back of his head that seemed to interest the scientists. His tiny webbed hands were bound and his small, bird-like feet were strapped firmly to the table.

Behind this group were more alien scientists, these huddled around a helpless trachedon. One scientist held a large paddle in his hands, hissing with electrical charge. He touched the paddle to the trachedon and it screamed in agony.

Natalie cringed, frozen in awe and in fear. Before she could react, a triceratops pushed her aside and ran past her. Natalie saw the dinosaur move in a blur, his beak open. She had seen that beak snap through thick tree trunks and gnash vegetation into a ragged piece of pulp. Now she saw it close on a point somewhere between the paddle and the scientist.

There was an alien scream and the paddle fell to the floor, a piece of arm with a hand still grasping the handle. The scientists moved back, pressing closer to the wall. Dozer and Closer climbed on the table and began chewing through the straps, freeing the trachedon. Several dinosaurs helped lift him onto the back of the baby brontosaurus. Gorka helped secure it in place with straps.

"Hurry," yelled another dinosaur as he came through the broken doors. "I'm the last one." Behind him in the room of cages, guards were rallying for an assault. Gorka shouted and pointed. Dinosaurs quickly saw why he was excited. They pushed the doors shut in the face of the approaching guards. The broken hinge twisted and groaned, but the door pressed into place. Others started to help by shoving large objects against the doors hoping to barricade the guards out.

Natalie looked everywhere. "Nate! Nate! Are you here?" she shouted.

Gorka ran to her, shaking his head and tugging at her side. He pointed to the doors that the dinosaurs had just blocked. There were thuds and pounding coming from the other side. The doors seemed to move slightly. Cracks formed in the mantle above the doorway, dust beginning to stream down from above. Gorka drew her attention away from the doors, again pointing with urgency towards an exit on the opposite side of the room.

"I won't leave without Nate," said Natalie.

"Over here, Princess," came a cry from the pterodactyl.

They rushed to the far end of the room where the pterodactyl stood beside a lump of dinosaur flesh strapped to a table. Natalie stopped partway, fearful at what she would find. The lump was oddly still, the shape silent. There was no squirming, no rise and fall, no labored breath as she had expected.

She forced herself to move forward, enough to see if it really was Nate. He had a look of peaceful agony on his face, his face was twisted in pain but there was a look of calm in his eye. The ends of his mouth seemed to curl in a smirk, as if he had somehow managed to extract one last act of revenge against his tormentors.

Her eyes moved down from his face, across a chest scarred with incisions and strange burn marks. Down to his abdomen where the marks continued, finally down to his leg, where she looked for the distinctive marks that gave him such a sense of pride.

They were gone. In fact, the whole leg was gone. Lying nearby she saw it, a severed stump, bloody and ragged at one end where she saw three deep gashes and a burn mark from the ray of an alien ship.

"Nate!" she cried. "No!"

The thuds at the door became louder. It started to give. Faces of alien guards could be seen through cracks forming in the doors. The pile of debris that barricaded them in shifted with each thud. Dust streamed harder as the building shook under the strain.

Dozer saw the urgency of the situation. He jumped up on the table beside Nate, taking one last look at the Princess' friend and protector. He turned to her saying, "Nate is no longer with us, Highness."

Closer jumped up on the table. "It's only his shell," he said to Natalie. "Nate lives here now." He pointed to her heart. Natalie started to sob, but she understood.

"You are wise for such a small one," she said.

Closer blushed. Humility was one of his best virtues. "Thank you," he said. "But, really, size has nothing to do with brains."

"Size has nothing to do with a lot of things," said Dozer.

There were more thuds, louder, and the sounds of angry guards gibbering.

"We have to go," said the triceratops.

"Come on," said Dozer.

"He's dead, Princess. No time to mourn him," said Closer.

Gorka was at the other end of the experimentation room. He had a passkey he had taken from one of the fallen scientists. He used it to open a door. He waved to the others and they began to move towards the door.

"This way," said the baby bronto. "Quickly!"

Natalie was crying. "Nate," she said.

More thuds and angry shouts drove the rest of them toward the exit. Gorka spoke to Croton, who had also been caged with the dinosaurs. He nodded and went through the exit, motioning for the dinosaurs to follow.

"Come on," said the Pteronodon. "We can trust him."

The alien scientists had separated into two groups. One group huddled together cowering against the far wall. The others gathered near Gorka, wanting to join the escapees but uncertain about the dinosaurs. Gorka spoke with them as dinosaurs continued to file through the door.

"Come on, Princess," urged Dozer. "Please."

She looked away from Nate and down at the tiny dinosaur. She saw the worry and concern, wrapped around him in a fog of thoughts, clouds that her mind shaped into perceptions. She realized that Nate may be gone, but others had stepped forward to fill the role of her protector.

They escorted her to Gorka, who stood at the exit. Croton stood beside him gibbering and looking nervous. They joined the last of the stragglers and filed through the exit. As they looked back they saw a guard breach the doors across the room. Gorka put the passkey into a slot on the wall and the exit door slammed shut. The nervous alien hit it with his hand but nothing happened. Gorka shouted and he stood aside as a pachycephalosaurus whizzed by him and rammed into the locking mechanism. The sound of the impact echoed in the room as it smashed it to pieces.

"I hope that will hold them," said Closer.

"Yes, but where do we go now?" asked Dozer.

Chapter 17: Armada of Stragglers

The fleet of rescue ships approached the alien planet. From within the flagship, Rex stared out a porthole.

"You certainly have a beautiful world," said Rex.

"It's a lot like yours. It's even blue and green like yours," said Cedric. Rex was surprised at how well Cedric and Pilot were learning the dinosaur language, definitely faster than he was learning the alien's language.

"We have a lot in common," said Rex. "I have great hopes for this mission."

"You'll like our planet," said Pilot.

"I have no doubt," said Rex.

"I have enough doubt for the both of you," said Cassius. He had been listening in on the conversation. "I hope we do get a warm welcome, but just in case, I have some security measures to enforce."

"Your measures are in place," said Cedric. He pointed to a red sash on his arm. "We all wear the banner of red, the sign of our alliance. We all have been briefed on the plan. We will land at the starport and my people will disembark while you remain hidden. Once we pave the way, you can come out, be introduced, and we can begin the negotiations."

"Good," said Rex.

"Meanwhile, the rest of the fleet will drop the large dinosaurs off in a holding area near the starport," said Cassius, expanding details of the plan. "Some of our fleet will remain airborne to protect them if there's any trouble. We can use the same weapons on them as they did on us. And we can rescue anyone in trouble with the same capture bags that were used to steal our children."

"I'm anxious for peace," said Rex. "I want to get the children released as soon as possible." He turned to Penelope, the Queen's psychic sister, who stood next to him. "Do you sense anything yet?" he asked.

Penelope had been searching with her mind since they had entered space. Like his wife Helena, Rex seldom saw her rest. She had no contact with her sister, the Queen. It drained her spirits, and she was beginning to doubt the extent of her powers and her usefulness.

"I see nothing, your Majesty," she said. "All I get is an overwhelming sense of fear from this planet. I still haven't been able to contact the Queen."

"Don't despair," said Rex. "It's not your fault. There must be something in this void that blocks your ability to reach one another. It could be why the Queen lost touch with Natalie."

"I'll keep trying," she said.

"How close are we?" asked Cedric.

"We're beginning to decelerate, relative time is changing," said Pilot. We should be at the starport in less than an hour, but a day or so will pass for them."

"And there is still no word from the planet?" asked Cedric.

"Communications are still blocked by a solar storm," said Pilot.

"We'll have to go in blind then," said Rex. He turned again to Penelope. "You see, it's not just you, Penelope, all communications are blocked. Why don't you go in the other room and rest for now? I will need your talents later when we negotiate for the children."

"As you wish, your Majesty," said Penelope.

She left. Rex turned and stared at the planet again, thinking and considering everything he had heard. He went over the plan again in his head "Something doesn't feel right. I don't like going in blind," he said.

"I have twelve of the Elite Guard standing by in case there's trouble," said Cassius.

"Let's stick to pomp and ceremony, Cassius," said Rex. "I need your skills of statehood more than war."

"Yes, Sire," said Cassius.

Rex took a deep breath. "You may be right. I fear it may take both to bring this mission to a successful end," he said.

"Let's hope not," said Cassius.

"They must see us by now," said Pilot. "I wonder what they are thinking."

Chapter 18: The Underground

"Where do we go now?" asked Dozer.

They were in an underground room with dim lighting and no windows. There were lockers along one wall. Spelunking equipment, backpacks, ropes and lights, hung from hooks. Gorka and some of the renegade scientists busied themselves donning equipment and clothes. There were thuds against the door and shouts from guards on the other side. Natalie wondered how long this door would hold them back. The Pachycephalosaurus had disabled the lock, but the guards could still force their way in, and there was nothing in this room to use as a barricade.

The dinosaurs watched the scientists with great curiosity, wondering what they were doing. Despite the alien gibberish and strange activity, Natalie could tell that they were packing things they would need for their escape. Gorka pointed to another door, the only other exit to the room. He pressed a panel somewhere and the door slid open. Natalie understood as Gorka pointed towards the dark hole behind the open door. The dinosaurs looked uncertain until Natalie spoke.

"Trust him," she said. "Let's go."

They filed through the open door and into the darkness. Gorka planted an explosive device near the door that had been jammed by the pachycephalosaurus. The door was beginning to shudder as if it would fall at any moment. Voices on the other side of the door became more urgent, the thuds louder. He opened a locker and removed communication devices, stuffing them into a shoulder bag he took from a nearby hook. He indicated haste as he guided the last of the escapees through the exit.

An explosion rocked the cavern. Rocks fell and the exit was buried in rubble behind them. They were suddenly plunged into darkness.

"I guess we're not going back in that direction," said Dozer.

"Would you really want to?" asked Closer.

They heard uneasy sounds, mewls and sighs from some of the baby dinosaurs. The sounds came back in a hollow echo, adding a surreal tone to the eerie darkness.

"Well, I'm certainly not afraid of the dark, but some of us are," whispered Dozer.

It was true. Many of the baby dinosaurs were day dwellers, used to sunlight and open spaces. This was dark and confining, more so than the prison. The air was still and stifling with a strange odor of dirt. A hollow wind echoed in the distance. Natalie could feel the anxiety grow among her subjects.

"It's going to be okay," she said.

As if to support her words of confidence, light began to shine around them. It was not daylight, but at least they could see where they were. Gorka stood to one side with another alien scientist. They both held small lanterns.

"This way," he said in alien tongue, pointing towards a large dark opening. "We will guide you."

Natalie understood him. She saw pictures in her mind of Gorka and his friends walking ahead of them, leading the dinosaurs through a cave towards a brighter light.

"Let's go," she said.

The lanterns cast dim light on the walls revealing a large cavern with a high ceiling. Gorka pointed to a dark hole on the other side of the cavern and began walking toward it. The room was not unlike any of the passageways in the Palace back on Earth. It was dark and cool, the walls lined with patterns of textured rock. The strange odor took on an Earthy scent as she adjusted to the darkness and her surroundings. She joined Gorka as they stepped into the unknown together.

As the passage narrowed the rest fell in behind, a procession of scared children scattered between aliens bearing lanterns. Strange shadows passed on the walls. Footsteps and voices echoed through the cavern.

Dinosaurs whispered to each other and the sounds of faint conversations in alien languages echoed back at them. They passed dripping water.

They moved on, feeling better about putting distance between them and the prison, but still uneasy. Natalie did not feel uneasy. For her the cavern was filled with sadness. She wished Nate were here at her side. He would make her laugh again. She had forgotten how to laugh.

It must have been one of those times when she was unconsciously broadcasting her feelings. Dozer and Closer scurried up the column of dinosaurs from their position in the rear. A pterodactyl squawked as they ran past, startled by the sounds they made. They ran between the legs of a triceratops, ducking their heads to avoid the low hanging belly. Closer lingered next to a scientist holding a lantern, admiring the size of the shadow that mimicked his every move on a far wall. They finally caught up to Natalie, driven by an inner feeling that their Princess needed them.

They followed her in silence for a while, making sideward glances at each other, speaking without words as they had their whole life. A lot could be said with the twitch of a facial muscle or a down turned lip, especially between brothers who knew each other well. Dozer walked beside Natalie, studying her. He wanted to pierce through her black mood. It was not good for her. They all had a private pain to carry. They all knew someone who was taken into the room of no return. Dozer wanted to let the Princess know that she was not the only one burdened with this pain.

"Some of us didn't make it," said Dozer.

"A lot of us didn't make it," mumbled Natalie.

"You are not the only one who misses him, Princess," he said. "He was a friend to everyone, even the small."

Dozer thought he saw her lip curl into a smile for a moment, but he wasn't sure in the darkness.

"The Boy Protector would be proud of us for escaping," he said. "He was willing to sacrifice his life for our freedom." He looked up at her face in the darkness. He thought he saw a sparkle in her eye, but it could have just as easily been the lantern light reflecting off a tear on her cheek.

"What do we do now?" asked Closer.

"Keep moving," said Natalie. "This way."

They followed Gorka through a big cavern and then through a tight restriction. There was a narrow, dark corridor on the other side, long, quiet and cramped. At the end of that tunnel they entered a bright room with walls that glowed with light. The scientists turned off their lanterns and the dinosaurs noticed that the light came from glowing plants on the walls. Gorka donned a strange looking device that rested on his head. He spoke softly into a round ball that hung off the headgear and close to the side of his face.

"I've never seen anything like this," said the triceratops.

"Go ahead and eat," said Gorka.

"I'm hungry," said the triceratops. "Don't mind if I do." He bit into a green plant and chewed, and suddenly realized, "Hey, did you just say something to me?"

Gorka smiled, and Natalie couldn't help but smile back. His smile was full of happiness, success and hope. It was contagious. It had been a long time since she had smiled.

"This is an interesting development," said Closer.

"I wonder how those devices work," asked Dozer.

Gorka passed out some of the devices to his fellow scientists, muttering to them in alien language. The scientists begin tuning the devices, adjusting them carefully. Some of the scientists tried using the devices, fiddling with controls that the dinosaurs could not understand.

Finally one of them said, "This is a perfect example of bioluminescence." He scooped up a small hand full of the plants and pushed them into his mouth. As he munched, his mouth opened between bites, making him look like the flashing lights that decorated the starport.

"Bio-what?" asked the baby triceratops, joining him for a taste. He bit a small piece off with his beak, wondering what he must look like with his mouth lit up.

"Bioluminescence," said the scientist. "Tiny creatures that emit light."

"Croton here is one of our top biologists," said Gorka. "He studies living things and their environment."

"How do they live?" asked Dozer.

"They feed on plants that would not be here unless there was light," said Croton. "The creatures emit light that make the plant growth possible."

"Which came first?" asked Closer.

"We don't know," said Croton.

"All we know is they need each other," said Gorka. "One could not exist without the other."

"Kind of like us, now," remarked Natalie.

"Yes," said Gorka, as if reading Natalie's mind. "Go ahead and try some." He scooped some of it off the wall and ate it. "A mixture of plants and animals," he said. "It's quite nourishing."

Others began to sample the food.

"It's good!" said the Baby Brontosaurus. "Tastes like pond algae back home."

"At least we won't starve," said Natalie.

"Take only what you need," said Croton. "This is a fragile environment."

"Some of us need meat," said one of the carnivores.

"Like I explained," said Croton. "This is a mixture of plants and animals, so you are getting your meat."

They rested and drank from a nearby underwater stream. Some took the opportunity to sleep, Natalie included. Some could not sleep, their minds filled with visions of guards following them with painsticks.

As if to fuel that fear, there was a large rumbling and a boom that echoed through the caves. A pterodactyl screeched and startled dinosaurs roared. Croton jumped and hit his arm against the rock. No one was able to sleep now. The rumbling continued and there were shouts of panic.

"Calm down," commanded Natalie. The sound of rumbling mysteriously died out and the dinosaurs grew calmer.

"She has her mother's powers," whispered someone within the crowd. "She silenced it with a word." Natalie heard the comment but ignored it.

"Since we are all awake, I suggest we continue on to..." she looked towards Gorka. She didn't know where they were headed.

"Yes," said Gorka, standing up. "We have rested enough. We might as well move on. The further we go, the harder it will be for them to find us."

He walked over to Croton, who was sitting down and rubbing his arm. "Show me where it hurts," he said.

Natalie located the ankylosaurus quickly, wondering if baby saliva was different from the adult. She had only seen adult ankylosaurus healing wounds.

Gorka was about to wrap the arm in some kind of restraint when Natalie told him to wait. "There might be an easier way," she said. "Don't be afraid," she said to Croton. "My small friend here would like to try to help you." She motioned to the ankylosaurus who stepped forward and licked the alien scientist's arm.

At first he was repulsed, but with Gorka's hand on his shoulder for support Croton agreed to the procedure.

"Come on," said Gorka. "You're a scientist. Let's try an experiment."

"Okay for you to say," replied Croton. "You're not the subject of the study."

"If only we had some healing plants," said Closer.

"Why don't we try some of these?" said Dozer, scurrying over to the nearest wall. He scooped up a small amount of bioluminescent mass and quickly dabbed it on top of the saliva on Croton's arm.

"And something my mother said always works," said Natalie, coming over to put her arm on Croton's other shoulder. "Love." She imagined and felt healing energy, love, sympathy, call it what you want, flowing down her arm and into Croton. A smile crossed his face and Natalie and Gorka gently lifted him until he was standing. The rest gradually stood, preparing for the trudge ahead. It was obvious they were still tired.

"This way," motioned Gorka, pointing to a narrow corridor leading off to the side. Natalie wondered why he had chosen this one over all the other possible exits. She had noticed many similar looking corridors. What made this one special?

She really didn't know where they were headed. She looked over at Gorka, who still radiated hope and promise. She trusted him and that should be good enough, but as they filed into the narrow corridor, going deeper into darkness, she wondered if she could ever find her way back to the surface. And a worse thought still: If her father was on the way to rescue her, how would he ever find her now?

Chapter 19: Plenty of Empty Cages

The Capital City was the largest city on the planet and a showplace of alien technology. It rested gently on the planet's surface with clusters of buildings spaced between open areas. The aliens had discovered the secret of manufacturing strong building materials, allowing them to twist designs into abstract, yet functional shapes. There was a core set of buildings that consisted of massive towers interconnected with a lattice of walkways. From there, the city spread outward into smaller groups of buildings that eventually transitioned into gardens and farmland, then trees and steppes and terraces.

There was a straight, wide canal strewn with boats that ran close to the city. In the distance the canal flowed into a large lake framed by tall mountains. In another direction a major road led from the city to a smooth plain that held the starport, one of two on the entire planet. The road passed an armory with a field of gun trucks, all parked orderly in straight lines. A small ravine paralleled the road along one side. On the other side there were a few storage buildings, warehouses and such, but otherwise there was nothing but unbroken vistas of the surrounding hills and mountains.

At the end of this impressive scenery lay the starport. In contrast to the natural beauty of the planet stood this marvel of engineering and planning that took up almost as much space as the city. There were lookout towers with viewing decks atop buildings ringed with glass windows. Clusters of space ships in various sizes, parked every bit as orderly as the gun trucks, sat on fields ready for takeoff. There were huge open hangers containing more ships, some in various phases of construction.

The buildings surrounding the starport were exotic, designed to give visitors the impression of opulence. Most contained large rooms, making individuals feel small and insignificant when they walked through them. Foot traffic passed through a giant reception building and down a corridor where goods and people were equally treated like baggage, tagged and routed through various doors and corridors towards waiting ships.

There was another starport on the opposite side of the planet near the Capitol's sister city. Regular flights were available between the two starports and there was also a network of small landing strips to encourage commerce and traffic.

There were service vehicles, ground cars, and trams buzzing around the starport. Preparations were being made for a grand reception. A stage was being erected on a stage at the far side of the starport. A fleet of ships, the largest group of stragglers ever spotted, was on its way home. The President intended to welcome them personally at the starport when they landed. There would be speeches and displays of military might, flying formations, a convoy of gun trucks, and a parade for the returning heroes.

Beyond the starport and beyond these grand preparations the road narrowed and led to a low, flat building, the prison complex, built discretely off to the side and mostly underground. It was at the end of the road, as far away from the city as possible, a lonely building with its room of dinosaur atrocities, hidden in plain sight.

Traveling back along the same road, past the starport and closer to the city's core complex sat the President's mansion. It was one of the largest structures in the city. It had high towers and thick walls with flying buttresses and elegant details. There were balconies on all sides with views of the city, the starport, and the surrounding vistas.

The President sat high in the administrative wing of his palace where he did the bulk of his work and his thinking. He was surrounded by his top advisors and aides. He had speechwriters, generals, majordomos, and attendants. They sat in a meeting room, their attention fixed on a monitor that displayed a fleet of ships approaching the planet. Some of the ships were the oddest looking craft they had ever seen. They appeared to be made of native Earth materials.

"How clever," mumbled the President. "The survivors show a lot of ingenuity." He turned to a nearby aide. "Arrange for engineers at the debriefing," he said. "We can learn much from what they endured."

A ship crossed the monitor with a huge brontosaurus in a red bag. He drew their attention to it. "It appears they are bringing more specimens," he said. "Good. We need more subjects for our research."

A Chamberlain entered. "The Warden wishes to speak with you immediately, your honor," he said. "He has dispatched me from the prison to request your presence."

The President did not take his attention away from the monitor. "Don't bother me, Chamberlain," he said. "Can't you see I'm busy?" The Chamberlain stood silent, observing.

"They are probably one, maybe two days away," said one of the aides. "We can't predict the exact time of their landing. They are under the effects of time distortion because of their speed, but we are also experiencing heavy solar storms, blocking communication. Too many variables."

"Have all the arrangements been made?" asked the President.

"The population has been notified," said a second aide. "Families of the missing have been invited to join you on the podium."

The speechwriter stepped forward, his hand holding a small cube of data. "Here is your speech, sir," he said.

A General snapped to attention. "I have medals for the returning heroes," he said. "Ready with full honors and ceremony."

The President smiled. "Good," he said. "I want to stay at the starport lodge tonight. If they land at night, I want to be awakened!"

"Sir?" said the timid Chamberlain. "Might I suggest a visit to the Warden? At the prison? It's not far from the lodge where you'll be staying at the starport."

The President turned and looked at the Chamberlain as if he were insane. "Don't you see what I am doing, here?" he asked, speaking patiently, as if talking to a child. "This is a historic moment. The brave troops return victorious over the monsters of Earth. We owe them a parade and a celebration. I can't be bothered with the Warden and his prisoners right now."

The President lit up as if he had a brilliant idea. "Perhaps they have more prisoners inside the ships. Has anyone thought of that?"

"I hope so, sire," said the nervous Chamberlain.

"Did you say something about the Warden?" asked the President.

"He needs to speak with you," said the Chamberlain.

"But I will speak to him, loyal Chamberlain," said the President. "Right after the celebration."

An aide appeared at the doorway. "Your car is waiting to take you to the starport."

"Excellent," said the President. He turned to an aide. "Notify my entourage," he said. "We leave for the starport immediately." He turned back to the Chamberlain. "Return to the prison. Tell the Warden I am busy. I will speak to him later. I want to go to the prison after the celebration and inspect it personally. Tell him to prepare his facility for new prisoners. That should make him happy."

The room was suddenly ablaze with activity. The President gesticulated and pointed, barking out orders and making plans. He motioned to the door and the crowd followed him through the exit, leaving only the Chamberlain behind.

The Chamberlain pondered his orders, weighing the urgency of the prison break with the President's plan to welcome the heroes. He thought it might be wise to intervene, but he had heard tales of what happened to people who displeased their leader. He had a small taste of it when he made the simple suggestion to come to the prison. Nobody likes to be talked down to or treated like a child. He decided to follow the President's orders and return to the Warden with the news.

"I'll tell him to prepare for more specimens," said the Chamberlain to himself. "There certainly are plenty of empty cages."

Chapter 20: The Forever Caverns

Natalie followed Gorka down the narrow corridor. It twisted in all directions. They passed random side corridors, tunnels of darkness leading off towards the unknown. She wondered how Gorka knew which path to choose.

She dispatched Dozer and Closer to fall behind and watch for stragglers in the line. She didn't want any of the children to get separated and lost in this maze. The dinosaurs continued single file through the narrow hallways of stone. She had been in some of the dark parts of her father's palace, but it was never like this. Who knew how deep they were beneath the surface? It was a spooky procession, a march through shadows. It was hard to tell if the floor slanted upward or downward. She had lost all sense of direction.

The rock around them swallowed up the sounds of their footsteps. Occasionally there were open rooms where she could feel the emptiness of stale air above her, but always it continued into a procession down a dark, narrow corridor. There was no more bioluminescence, and whenever they tried to rest, the tight quarters only reminded them of the small cages they had left behind.

At one point she noticed that the walls had become round and smooth, looking artificial. It no longer bore the discoloration or the uneven smoothness of rock. This was something different. When had it changed? As if reading her thoughts, Gorka spoke up.

"This cavern is not natural," he said. "It was constructed long ago."

"Why?" asked Natalie.

"The Ancients knew many things we did not," continued Gorka. "They buried their secrets here in the depths of the planet to hide them from the surface dwellers."

"What kind of secrets?" asked Natalie.

"Marvels that we can only guess at," said Gorka. "Most of these caves were sealed in the last great quake. The ground shook and a giant volcano erupted. Many treasures were buried in the lava. My father was on the original expedition that explored this area."

"What did he learn about the Ancients?" asked Natalie.

"He learned enough," said Gorka.

"What do you mean?" asked Natalie.

"The Ancients hid their secrets for a reason," he said. "My father learned enough about the Ancients to respect their reasons."

"So he kept them hidden," said Natalie.

"Yes," said Gorka.

"And that made him unpopular, didn't it?" asked Natalie, sensing the images in Gorka's thoughts. She saw his father being persecuted and rejected by his peers. She felt the sadness.

"His friends thought he had gone mad when he reported this. Ancient civilizations that were more advanced than our own? It was unheard of. Our leaders taught us that we were the only life in the universe."

"That was before you discovered life on our planet," prompted Natalie.

"Oh, no," replied Gorka. "We had discovered life before you on another planet. Actually on a large moon that circled a great planet not far from this one. We kept it a secret as long as we could, but people found out eventually."

"What happened then?" asked Natalie.

"There was a horrible war, born of senseless fear," said Gorka.

"Sounds familiar," said Dozer.

"Did you take their children as well?" asked Closer.

Gorka ignored the comment and continued. "My father was discredited and ridiculed. He lost his friends. The only ones who believed in him were entrepreneurs and businessmen, motivated by greed and a desire to exploit the secrets he had discovered. Even then, I don't think they believed whole heartedly in the Ancients. My father had a few treasures he had recovered, things made of ornate metals and jewels. They were so unique that no one could place a value on them."

"Sounds beautiful," said Natalie. "Pretty things to wear."

"Oh, no," said Gorka. "It wasn't something to wear, it was a teaching machine."

"I'd love to use it," said Natalie. "Do you think it would work on me?"

"Most likely," said Gorka. "But nobody knows where it is now."

"Your father lost it?" asked Natalie.

"I think it was taken from him," said Gorka. "I'm not sure. Despite everyone trying to exploit his knowledge, he did not betray the location of the Ancients to anyone."

"Why didn't he exploit his discovery?" asked Natalie.

"My father wasn't like that," said Gorka. "He had principles."

"Just like my father," said Natalie.

"The Ancients studied the secrets of the mind," said Gorka. "They could move objects with the power of thought. We require complex machines to make our space ships fly. They could will it."

"What happened to them?" asked Dozer.

"We don't know. They could still be down here somewhere," said Gorka.

"The President was interested in the secrets of the Ancients until we were reassigned," said Croton.

"Reassigned? To what?" asked Natalie.

"To you," he said. "It was our task to study you with the same intensity we study anything else."

Croton looked downward. He was ashamed of what he had done. Gorka changed the subject. "I'm glad we didn't reveal the secrets of the Ancients," he said. "My father was right. Our people are not ready to wield this power."

They seemed to pass through the smooth tunnels forever. One cavern led to the next, gloomy darkness illuminated only by the glow of the lanterns. There were tight passages and even one place where the triceratops helped widen the tunnel so baby bronto could squeeze through. There were places where they stepped carefully, guided by Gorka over cliffs that seemed to fall into endless night.

They stopped to rest one more time. Gorka had a little food, survival rations that were stored in the backpacks. He promised there would be more food when they reached their destination.

"It's not far," he said.

The children were tired, and they rested a while, some of them sleeping, others unable to sleep, still feeling uneasy by the closed in walls and lack of sunlight. It was cold so they slept together for warmth. There was something comforting in sleeping together after being separated in small cages. They had forgotten what it was like to touch one another.

The next morning (who could tell morning anymore?) they began again. Gorka passed out the last of the rations.

"Tonight we will dine on fruit so tasty, it will numb your lips. We will bathe in rivers of clear, refreshing water."

Natalie did not know if Gorka was exaggerating, but his talk motivated everyone to begin the slow march again.

Dozer couldn't wait to see 'Gorka's Paradise,' as he called it. Still, it was hard to keep spirits high. Everything began to look alike. They stopped at a small pocket of bioluminescence where the scientists cautioned the dinosaurs about eating too much. It was a delicate balance and Croton explained that this community was in danger of disappearing. Natalie passed the word to the other dinosaurs and those that needed food ate sparsely. It provided some nourishment and a little distraction from the never ending darkness, but otherwise the short rest ended again with a dismal procession. One of the lanterns malfunctioned and went out, adding more gloom and darkness to an already depressing situation.

Finally, they sensed Gorka's excitement as they approached a dazzling light ahead.

"That's too bright to be bioluminescence," said Natalie. "What is it, the surface?"

"No," explained Gorka. "One of the marvels of the Ancients that we discovered. There are glowing spheres that emit light down here."

"We don't know what powers them, but we estimate they have been burning for centuries," said Croton.

"They're certainly bright," said Natalie, squinting her eyes. There were shapes ahead and movement in the light.

"Gaff," said Gorka, rushing toward the light. He was met by another alien and they began squeaking excitedly in their alien language, greeting each other.

Gaff noticed the dinosaurs behind Gorka and let out a yelp. Gorka calmed him, pressing his communication device into Gaff's hand. He reached into his shoulder bag and extracted another one, busily fumbling with it.

"Don't be alarmed," said Gorka. "These are my friends. They helped me escape."

"Escape?" said Gaff. "From what? Were you in prison?"

"It's a long story," said Gorka. "But where are my manners?" He brought Gaff over to Natalie and introduced them. "This is my friend Gaff. And Gaff, this is Princess Natalie."

Gaff bent to one knee and bowed his head as a sign of respect. "A Princess," he remarked.

"Oh, stop it," said Natalie, feeling a bit silly. They were a long way from courts and protocols. "We're all friends here."

"Yes we are," said Gaff. He stood and turned to Gorka. "Yes we are," he said again, embracing his friend. "So, what are you doing here? Are you here to stay?"

"We're hiding," said Gorka. "There are strange things happening on the surface. A second fleet returns from the dinosaur world."

"My father," said Natalie. "It has to be him. Why didn't you tell me about this sooner?"

"I didn't think it was important. There have been reports of stragglers for some time, damaged ships limping their way back home. Solar flares and storms keep us from contacting them at times. This was the largest group ever spotted, but they have been oddly silent. You'd think they would find a way to get a message to us."

"They could have dismantled their radios and used them for spare parts to rebuild their ships," suggested Gaff.

"It must be Father," said Natalie. "He's coming to rescue us. I must contact him."

It was urgent to her. She walked off to the side to be alone and concentrate. She slipped into a trance.

"Oh, my," said Gaff, noting her discomfort. "This is not good."

She slipped easily into a trance, despite her nervousness and anxiety. Instead of contacting her father, Natalie had a vision. She saw destruction, dinosaurs fighting aliens, brushfires, and a giant comet out of control. She heard cries of fear and desperation that shook her soul. It jerked her out of the trance violently and she started to shake like she was having a seizure.

Gorka saw her become pale and weak. He rushed to her side, calling for help from any nearby dinosaurs. He knew he wouldn't have the strength to support her should she collapse. The ankylosaurus waited nearby.

"What happened?" asked Gorka.

"I don't know," she said. "I had a vision. I didn't see anything clear enough to get an image."

"The Ancients put a psychic shield around this whole area," said Gaff. "To protect the city from mind probes."

"City?" asked the Baby Triceratops.

"Just over there," said Gaff. "Walk towards the light. Come on, I'll show you."

The weary herd followed Gaff as he led them away. Natalie felt weak and remained behind, shaken by her vision. Despite feeling weak, she closed her eyes and tried again.

"I'm sorry, mother," she said, trying until she exhausted herself. "My abilities fail me when I need them most."

Chapter 21: A Hero's Welcome

At the Starport on the surface of the alien planet, ships hovered overhead as crowds cheered below. The President sat behind a podium on a high dais. The ships came in low over the planet, flying in formation. High tech fireworks blasted in the sky, creating colored patterns even though it was daylight.

The crowd was packed with eager faces, hopeful and full of expectations. Pilot's wife, Preena, was in the crowd.

"My husband may be in one of these ships," she said to a woman beside her. "He's among the missing."

"I'm looking for my brother," replied the woman.

The crowd was full of such comments.

"Look how damaged some of the ships are!" said a tall alien, pointing to the sky. "It must have been quite a struggle."

"No wonder they took so long to get back," added someone beside him.

"They're so brave," remarked another in admiration.

An announcer stepped forward. "Returning heroes," he said, addressing the crowds and the ships above at the same time. "We have you on our scopes. You are clear to land at the starport near the capital where your victory celebration awaits."

A band played a fanfare, then started up a patriotic tune. Aliens in the crowd held their hands out in the planetary posture of respect.

In the flagship hovering above, Rex heard the announcer's voice crackle over the radio. The interference from the solar flares was still bad. Pilot reached for the microphone. Rex stopped his hand from picking it up.

"Don't tell him we are here with you," he said. "I don't want to cause trouble."

Pilot looked at Rex, keeping the microphone silent in his hand. "I know the plan," he said. "We will land and my men and I will leave the ship first. The President is likely to say a lot of words before turning the assembly over to us. At that time we can present our case to the people and introduce you."

"That sounds good," said Rex. "But will the people listen to you?"

"If my words are persuasive and well spoken, how can they not believe us? Besides, we are just reporting the truth," said Pilot.

Cassius cautioned them. "I have seen people prefer lies over the truth," he said.

"Yes, Cassius, but let's hope those days are behind us," said Rex. "Besides, we have Penelope to help us. She will clarify our message of peace."

"Your majesty," said Cassius. "We don't need Penelope to know that these people are afraid of us. What will they do when we emerge from the ships?"

Pilot spoke up. "If we demonstrate that we can talk to you, maybe they won't be afraid. People are only afraid of what they don't understand."

"True," said Rex. "But I still wonder if they be able to overcome that fear."

"We'll see," said Pilot. "Let's give it a chance. We've come this far."

Rex nodded in agreement, then looked to Cassius to concur with him. The Captain of the Guard shook his head solemnly, reluctantly at first, then with more confidence. Pilot wanted to reassure them both that things would be all right, but he wasn't sure. His people could be fickle at times. Nevertheless, he put these thoughts aside. This was no time to have regrets or doubts. They had been discussing this plan for a long time, they had practiced speaking, and it was finally time for action.

"Hang on everyone," said Pilot. "I'm going to take us down." He activated the microphone, asking for landing instructions in the alien language.

Rex spoke quietly aside to Penelope. "See if you can contact your students and sisters on the other ships. Let them know we have activated the plan."

The ships arranged themselves in a triangular pattern over the starport. The crowds applauded as the flagship broke free and hovered near the dais. The ships above emitted colored lights that brought more cheers from the crowd. In the background, two large transports made of earth materials were settling down in an open field. Other ships from the fleet were landing nearby, some toting large, red bags containing huge dinosaurs. Animal handlers moved quickly towards the area. Workers could not believe the size of some of the dinosaurs and some sought safety behind barricades and fences. Guards stepped forward, taking up positions, ready with painsticks and weapons should the need arise.

The flagship came down slowly over a large circle beside the dais. Pilot knew every eye in the crowd would be looking at him. The planetary news feeds would likely have their cameras running. This historic landing deserved perfect execution. The crowd grew quiet in anticipation; everyone could hear the low hum of the ship's engines as it approached. It settled gently on the planet's surface, not even disturbing the wind.

The door opened on the flagship and a ramp extended. Pilot emerged with some of his crew behind him, the rest waiting inside with the dinosaurs. Their clothes were still in tatters. The crowd gasped at the sight of them.

The President moved towards the bottom of the ramp, flanked by an admiral and a general. Pilot and the others walked slowly down the ramp to meet them. This was home, and with that realization, they felt the weight of all the weariness and trouble they had endured to come to this moment. There was joy in their steps, but also confidence. They had the attention of their entire world and they had the secret of a bold new alliance.

How would the people react to this news? Even now, the giant dinosaurs were being treated more like prisoners than like ambassadors. Could the alien people successfully replace fear with compassion and understanding? A lot depended on their willingness to let go of that fear.

"Welcome home returning heroes," said the President. He placed a medal around Pilot's neck. The crowd burst into deafening applause. The general and the admiral stepped forward with similar medals for others in Pilot's crew.

The President turned and waved to the crowd, Pilot at his side. The image appeared on huge monitors outside and in homes and offices across the alien world.

The President waved again, then stepped aside and motioned for the returning heroes to pass. Preena could no longer contain herself. She rushed towards Pilot from out of the crowd and threw her arms around him. Some of the others began to break free of the crowd, rushing forward to meet their loved ones.

"Welcome home," said Preena. As she embraced him, she became aware that this intimate moment was being shared across their world.

Behind them on a huge monitor was an image of them embracing. She didn't care, she was just happy to be with him again.

"I thought I'd never see you again," said Pilot. "Our ships were damaged. We only now got them running." They continued to hug and embrace on the monitor until the image was replaced with the President as he began his speech.

Pilot turned and listened, holding Preena close to his side.

"These are the brave, the few," said the President. "Those who risked their lives against the fearsome creatures of the dinosaur planet are now reunited with us. What tales they must have to tell! For that reason, I will keep my words brief, even though it was I who warned you about these creatures. But you know that already. We have been victorious in our first attack. Soon they will be a threat no more. Now I will let you hear it from the lips of one who has been there personally."

He motioned to Pilot to join him, stepping aside so he could take the podium.

Pilot thought about what must be said. This was the moment he had both feared and anticipated. He had given a lot of thought to these words. The time was now. He stepped up to the podium and smiled.

"Noble citizens," he began. His words were carried through loudspeakers and through video feeds to the large monitors and out to the masses. "I have returned with one message. We have nothing to fear."

The President nodded his head in approval. To him, the words reinforced the victory he sought. The enemy was defeated, there was nothing to fear.

Pilot continued speaking. "The fighting was fierce. Many ships were downed. We were forced to land on the dinosaur planet and fix them. We feared that the monsters would destroy us while we made our repairs, but it was not so. Instead they helped us."

At these words, the President began to frown. It was not what he wanted to hear. The crowd became quiet, but there were murmurs of doubt.

"Yes," continued Pilot, reassuring them that he spoke the truth. "As fantastic as it sounds, they helped us. In our moment of weakness, stranded with no way to return home, I am here to say that they helped us."

"This can't be," interrupted the President.

"But it's true," said Pilot. "Without their help I would not be here today before you. Without their help I would not be here, reunited with my wife, Preena. Nor would I see my children again. I was wounded, blood oozing from my gut. They found me in the wreckage and pulled me free. They put plants on me, one of the miracles of their planet. Plants that heal! Some of the creatures are healers themselves. I saw them lick wounds and they got better."

"You lie," said the President.

"I don't lie," said Pilot. "Why would I lie?"

"The others who returned before you did not report these things," said the President.

"They were not on the surface with the creatures," said Pilot. "They flew in, kidnapped their children, and left."

The crowd grew agitated upon hearing those words. They sounded like accusations more than comments. There were some shouts of disapproval from the crowd.

Pilot felt the growing hostility and tried to continue explaining. "Yes. Yes," he said. "We kidnapped their children. The small ones we brought back. We must return them."

"Impossible," said the President.

"What we did was wrong," said Pilot. "We have the opportunity to make it right. We can avoid further bloodshed and make peace with these wonderful creatures. There is much we can learn from them, and much we can teach them."

"What can we learn from monsters?" asked the President.

"The monsters, as you call them, are not monsters at all," explained Pilot. "They have families like us. And like us, they miss their children. We should stop the fighting and return them in good faith."

"It's a trick," shouted the President. "Don't listen to him."

"It's no trick," said Pilot calmly. "I have no reason to trick my own people, and I can't lie to my wife."

He motioned to her and she joined him on the podium. He hugged her again. She looked into his eyes for a moment and turned toward the crowd.

"I believe him," she said.

"Thank you," he said, kissing her. He turned towards the crowd. "I have a surprise for you all. But you must not be afraid. An emissary of peace has come with me to offer words of encouragement to us all. We must stop fighting."

"What?" declared the President. "Impossible. If we don't fight them now, they will grow strong and destroy us all."

"But they don't want to destroy us," said Pilot. "I told you they want to help us. They helped me."

"I don't believe you," said the President. "Prove it to me."

Pilot saw this as the critical moment. He signaled his men stationed on the top of the ramp near the entrance to the flagship. The live feed ended abruptly as the giant monitors went dark. Pilot saw this in the periphery of his vision. Whatever was about to happen, it would confined to the crowd at the starport. Preena smiled up at him, her face scrunching slightly as she saw the worry in his eyes. Pilot wondered if Penelope was also having strange feelings deep in her gut, or was he the only one who suspected that something was terribly wrong.

Chapter 22: The Arrival of King Rex

Inside the flagship Rex saw the signal and spoke to his Elite Guard.

"Wait here," he said. "There's no need to startle them. If we all go out at once we will increase the chance that they will panic."

"I don't like it," said Cassius. "You'll be unprotected."

"Then stand ready, my friend," said Rex. "Just stay here out of sight."

Rex emerged from the ship. He raised his hand in greeting, roaring hello.

The aliens became frightened. To them, it sounded like the roar of a beast. Pilot tried to explain.

"He's just saying hello," said Pilot. He roared in dinosaur language. Pilot translated Rex's words into the speaker, but spectators began to run and scream. Everywhere aliens were panicking. Preena gripped Pilot tighter, pulling him closer, fearful yet trusting. The General spoke into a hand held communicator, barking out orders. Guards rushed forward, ready to protect the crowd. They looked towards the President.

"It's a trick," yelled the President. "They're attacking. Do your duty and defend your planet."

Guards moved into position around Rex, brandishing painsticks. Cassius saw them threatening his monarch, just what he had feared. He rushed from the flagship followed by several of the Elite Guard.

"How dare you attack our King," he yelled. Once again it sounded like ferocious roaring to the aliens.

Cassius bit one of the guards and stepped on another. More guards appeared with more powerful weapons. Crowds continued to panic and flee. Screams and shouts were everywhere.

A starport guard carefully aimed a weapon at Pilot and fired. "Traitor," he yelled. "You dare bring these beasts to our world."

A blast shot out. Pilot collapsed, Preena dropping to his side. He died looking up into her face, trying to say something she would never hear. She kneeled beside him, cradling his head in her arms as alien blood spread across her dress.

There was pandemonium everywhere around her. Fleeing aliens stepped on each other in panic, crushing them underfoot. Most of the guards were shooting randomly, more out of fright than with careful aim. They seemed to be doing more harm than good. Dinosaurs and aliens were both shot indiscriminately by the guards. Rex roared in pain as he took many hits but he did not collapse.

"Get back in the ship," he said. "We have to get out of here."

The Elite Guard obeyed reluctantly, laying in a retreating pattern. Rex turned toward a group of aliens that had taken cover behind a barricade. They were wearing red arm sashes. He motioned to them.

"You, too, if you want to go with us," he said.

Some had their families gathered near them, others stood alone or in small groups. They began to talk among each other. Rex could see some saying farewell, wishing each other luck and safety.

"We want to stay with you," said one of them. Rex recognized him as the one called Navigator, a close friend of Pilot's.

"That may not be wise," cautioned Rex. "You saw what happened to Pilot and the others."

"Still, we'd like to stay," said Navigator. "I owe you my life. If not for you I would be dead on your planet right now."

"Besides, there still may be a chance for peace," said one of the aliens beside Navigator. "There are many who disagree with the President. They may be sympathetic to our cause. You will need our help to contact and organize them."

"I can't argue with that," said Rex.

A number of them moved towards the ship while the rest turned and disappeared into fleeing crowds with their families. One of them was Cedric. Dinosaurs and aliens continued to board the flagship at Rex's orders. Cassius was slow to retreat and Rex had to forcefully order him to comply.

Rex took a moment to bow towards Preena, a gesture that was not lost upon her. Rex extended a hand and nodded his head, offering her safe passage with him. She shook her head, holding her hand out to indicate little ones. Then she looked down again at her dead husband. Cassius gave Rex a tap on his side, urging the King to comply with his own orders. They stepped aboard. The doors shut and the ship hummed in preparation for lift off.

"Other ships are being attacked," said Penelope as Rex entered the ship. "My sisters are ready to convey your orders to the fleet."

"Where to?" asked Navigator as he took up Pilot's old position at the helm.

Rex looked out the window at the mayhem outside. "Take us up," he said to Navigator. "I need aerial reconnaissance."

Navigator skillfully manipulated the controls. He was every bit as good as Pilot. The ship lifted into the air and banked over the crowd, giving Rex a view of the chaos below.

Despite the departure of the peace envoy, aliens were still killing each other. Guards shot without aiming. A short distance away, Rex could see guards closing in on the larger dinosaurs near the grounded transports. This was a disaster, not what he or Pilot had wanted. He wondered how he could have prevented all this. If there was any chance for peace, it probably was with the allies who remained loyal beside him. He found himself missing Pilot's company.

"Thank you for staying," he said to Navigator.

"I intend to take you up on your offer to live back on your planet," said Navigator, speaking the dinosaur language. "Is the offer still good?"

"Of course," said Rex.

"Where to?" asked Navigator again.

"To the starport," said Rex. "We should rendezvous with our remaining troops." He spoke to all the aliens on the ship. "Once there, you are free to leave us and go to your homes, or you can stay with us and return to Earth."

"What will you do?" asked Navigator.

Before he could answer, Penelope opened her eyes from a trance. "Your Majesty," she said. "They attack our ships on the ground at the starport. The large dinosaurs are in danger and many of the alliance are wounded. What should we do?"

"Spread the word about what has happened," said Rex. "My hopes for peace may be broken. If at all possible, do not harm the people. They are just confused. Focus instead on our mission."

Penelope closed her eyes, sending the message to the other ships.

"And what is our mission?" asked Navigator.

"What it has always been," said Rex. "Rescue the children."

Chapter 23: The Battle of Starport Prime

Navigator punched the controls and maneuvered the alliance flagship over the crowd, gracefully turning the ship to head towards the large dinosaurs at the other end of the starport. Cassius turned his attention to the King. They had narrowly escaped being overtaken by the guards. Rex was wounded, dripping blood from an open wound near his leg. One of the Elite Guard was down on his side, exposing a burn scar that ran the length of his body. Cassius called for a medical dino. The ankylosaurus went right for the King but Rex waved him off.

"Attend to him first," he said, indicating the fallen soldier.

"No," said the burned dinosaur.

"What's your name?" demanded the King.

"Gwangi," said the Elite Guardsman, nervous at having the King's attention.

"Attend to Gwangi," he ordered. The Ankylosaurus instantly obeyed, licking the burn gently.

Rex looked out of a porthole at the pandemonium below. The welcome podium was on fire, dark smoke spiraling into the air. Somewhere down there was the lifeless body of Pilot, a friend he had come to love and accept as one of his own tribe. His hopes for peace lay down there too, as lifeless and as lost to him as Pilot.

"We were lucky to get away," said Cassius. "No hands were lost."

"What about Pilot?" said Rex. He looked over at Gwangi, who was being soothed by the Ankylosaurus. A compy was assisting, crumbling a small amount of dry leaf and dusting it gently over the burned area. Gwangi smiled and looked at the King.

"Heal well, my friend," said Rex. "I will need you in the battle to come."

Gwangi nodded and widened his smile, honored to be fighting with his King. The scar on his side was better than any medal that could be awarded by any alien general. He could not wait to tell his children the tale of how he fought with the King to rescue them.

Rex turned back towards the porthole. They were a short distance from the landing field where many of the alliance saucers had landed. Rex saw aliens and dinosaurs disembarking from the parked fleet. The large dinosaurs had been freed and were busy knocking down walls and piling up debris to create makeshift fortifications. They had claimed their first piece of alien ground and were readying to defend it. Rex could not help but admire a million years of territorial instinct coming to life before his eyes.

He spotted a convoy of alien gun trucks moving along a road and taking up defensive positions near the landing field. Some guns pointed skyward and began firing upon the flagship. The ship teetered from the explosions.

"Evasive maneuvers," said Navigator. He frantically pushed buttons and pulled levers. "It's a shame they killed Pilot," he said. "He was the best flyer in the fleet."

There were more explosions. Rex steadied himself, continuing to survey the events below. He saw a small party of dinosaurs moving down the road towards the gun trucks. A triceratops charged one of them, knocking it on its side. Aliens spilled out on the ground like rocks scattering in a landslide. A stegosaurus rushed forward, using his tail to swipe at them. One of the aliens got stuck, impaled on a horn on his tail. The pinned alien shuddered like a large leaf trapped in a windstorm. The stegosaurus continued to swing at the fleeing aliens. Rex watched the impaled body break in two as it fell loose from the tail horn.

Two of the gun trucks stopped shooting at the flagship and turned their weapons on the stegosaurus. Explosions flared around him and he turned and retreated towards the fortifications. The trucks started moving to pursue him, firing wildly. Other trucks stopped shooting at the flagship and joined the barrage, pointing their powerful guns at the beast. With all odds against him, one of the explosions finally hit too close and the stegosaurus went down, collapsing in a heap.

Rex could see them cheer on the gun truck, raising their arms in victory. He could almost hear the cheers taunting him, even from this far away. The victory was short lived, and Rex smiled as he watched a pack of angry raptors descend upon the trucks. They were all teeth and claws. They knocked aliens off the turrets and sides of the trucks. One of the trucks turned around, speeding to get away from them. A raptor leaped onto the door and latched on. The driver opened it, thinking he could shake the animal loose. Instead of falling off, the raptor reached in and extracted the driver with his powerful claws. He held the body up for display, letting out a series of high pitched war cries. The truck began to careen without a driver, swaying slightly on the road. The raptor yelped in surprise, tossing the body aside as he leaped to safety.

Spurred by momentum, the truck continued down the road. A column of alien vehicles approached; too late to see that there was no driver. The truck came right at them. The first car avoided it by pulling off the road and running into a fence. The driverless truck collided with a troop transport and the ammunition on the gun truck exploded. Alien soldiers ran everywhere trying to escape the flames. Some were already on fire. They ran aimlessly for a short while until they fell, wiggling as they melted into a mass of charred flesh.

From the flagship Rex could almost hear the screams. He saw a compy run up the hood of another speeding truck and climb into an open window. The truck began to move erratically, veering from side to side. The door flew open and an alien jumped out, desperately trying to knock the compy off his back. He fell to the ground rolling. A pack of compys descended upon him, gnawing at him ruthlessly. The truck continued forward until it crashed into a building and exploded.

From the air Rex noticed a ravine running parallel to the road, a strategic advantage he noted. The road was narrow compared to the open land, but the trucks seemed to be limited to moving along the road. His dinosaurs didn't need the road and Rex saw the possibilities in this mind. On a field near the starport he saw loyal aliens and dinosaurs still emerging from the saucers. The giant supply ships had landed behind the fortifications and all the large dinosaurs had been released from their transport bags.

The battle was fierce. Attacking gun trucks pummeled the field. There were so many of them and they just kept coming. A parked ship exploded and Rex saw aliens and dinosaurs trapped inside the burning wreckage.

"We have to get down there," said Rex. "My men need my leadership."

An explosion rocked the flagship.

"It may be sooner than you think," said Navigator. "We're losing power."

The flagship wobbled. The floor shifted underneath and everyone slid to one side. Rex tried to claw his way uphill. "Try to balance it out with your weight," he said to his men, but they were all struggling uphill.

The ship started to stabilize, but it was too late.

"I can't hold it steady," shouted Navigator. "Brace yourself."

The ship pancaked down and skidded to a halt, crashing into an empty parked spaceship. "Everyone out!" yelled Cassius. Aliens ran to the exit door but it was jammed.

Rex looked out the viewport and saw a charging triceratops.

"Everyone hold tight," he yelled.

A triceratops horn came through the side of the flagship, tearing a hole in it. Members of the Elite Guard rushed forward to try to widen the hole. There was an explosion from the command console and sparks flew all around them. Flames broke out and smoke began to fill the ship. Rex heard coughing as it thickened, filling the space around him. Aliens pulled at the door while the Elite Guard tried to widen the hole that the triceratops had begun.

"Get out," yelled Rex. "Some of you can make it."

Aliens and small dinosaurs scurried through the hole. Navigator was about to exit when everyone heard him yell, "Watch it! Everyone back."

Rex stepped back just in time to see a triceratops horn rip through the side again. It lifted upward, tearing a gash close to the existing hole. A small unbroken strip of metal now hung between two long gashes. Rex punched the metal with his foot, creating one big hole.

"Everybody out," he yelled. "Now."

The other dinosaurs and the Elite Guard ran through the hole, all except Rex and Cassius. Rex searched the ship, trying to see if anyone was left behind. Cassius knew what he was doing and helped.

"I told you to get out of here," said Rex.

"I can't leave until I know you are safe," said Cassius. "Let's go. There's no one here."

Rex jumped through the hole followed by Cassius. The fire spread and the ship exploded behind them.

"That was close," said Cassius.

"Did everybody make it?" asked Rex.

"No hands lost," said Navigator.

"Good," said Rex.

Rex saw a band of dinosaurs fighting with some alien foot soldiers nearby. He took command of his troops.

"Over there," he said, rallying the aliens and dinosaurs who had just escaped. "Let's help them."

The Elite Guard and a few others struck with unparalleled fury. A Dimetrodon, a low, four legged dinosaur with a large fin on his back, came out of nowhere and bit a hostile alien in half. The fin quivered for a moment, drawing everyone's attention. Then he spit a piece of uneaten alien into the dust below him.

"They do taste bad your majesty," he said.

The aliens became terrified at the sight of the broken body lying in the dirt. They stopped advancing and turned and ran. Raptors set after them as they fled, bringing some to the ground. Rex smiled, but stayed focused. He continued to assess the situation and order his troops about. He noticed some bold guards terrorizing a group of aliens wearing red sashes. One of them was Navigator.

"Protect our allies," said Rex.

A group formed a protective cover around Navigator and the huddled band of loyal aliens. The guards retreated instead of facing of a wall of dinosaurs.

Rex continued to scan the battle. Another line of gun trucks was fast approaching them, rushing down the road towards the starport. The cannons on them riveted about, taking aim at the alliance. "Get that brontosaurus down in that gully," demanded Rex. "He's a sitting target for those gun trucks."

Rex was proven correct as gun trucks closed in on the brontosaurus and fired away. One hit the massive beast solidly in the side and he screamed in rage. He charged the nearest truck and swatted it with his tail, sending it flying into another truck. They both burst into flames and the ammunition exploded in a shower of sparks.

"Medical dinos to the Brontosaurus," said Rex.

An ankylosaurus lumbered forward and licked the wounded brontosaurus. A corythosaurus appeared with a mouth full of healing leaves which he quickly applied to the wound. The brontosaurus was instantly soothed.

Rex spotted dust on the horizon. He narrowed his eyes and saw more gun trucks filled with aliens heading their way.

"Regroup at the ravine over there," he ordered.

They moved out of sight of the trucks and into the ravine that paralleled the road. The trucks continued to advance towards the starport while Rex and his troops worked their way down the ravine. They silently positioned themselves for an ambush. High overhead, a pterodactyl flew reconnaissance for the King. He let out a screech.

"Now!" yelled Rex.

The dinosaurs sprang up from the ravine and attacked the gun trucks from the side. The trucks were quickly overturned and crushed under the feet of the Elite Guard. Aliens fled in all directions and Raptors and Compys descend on them. Two aliens came up behind Rex. The Elite Guard turned as if to attack them, but Rex stopped them.

"Wait," said Rex. "They're with us." He turned towards the aliens. "Where are your red sashes?" asked Rex. The aliens looked mystified. "The sign of the alliance," he said.

The aliens couldn't understand him.

Navigator rushed down the ravine to join them, signaling to Rex.

"I recruited them," he explained. "These are my friends. They want to fight with you."

"This is a problem," said the Stegosaurus. "How can we tell the good guys from the bad guys?"

"Spread the word," said Rex. "All who fight with us wear the color red. The color of our blood. The color of our children's blood." He let out a roar. "Let it be a sign that we are willing to spill our last drop of blood to free our children."

"Yes, sire," said the Navigator. "I have good news about that. We located the facility where your children are being held. It is nearby. We can take you there."

"Captain of the Guard!" yelled Rex.

Cassius stood at attention beside him. "Yes, sir," he said.

"I want you and some of your best men to come with me on a mission to rescue the children," he said. "Appoint a team to defend the starport. We will need these ships to return home. Without an escape route we will be stranded here."

"I will round up the rest of our pilots and get the crews to make emergency repairs to as many ships as we can," said the Navigator.

"Good," said Rex.

"These two have volunteered to escort you to the children."

"We know exactly where they were taken," said the first alien.

"Thank you," said Rex. He had seen one of them back on Earth, remembering his face but not his name. He spoke excellent dinosaur, and Rex signaled that he was pleased.

"Where is Gwangi?" he asked, turning his attention elsewhere.

The wounded dinosaur stepped forward. "Yes sire," he said. "I'm ready to fight."

"I need your brains more than your body," he said to the Elite Guardsman. "I want you and Navigator to be in charge while I'm gone."

Gwangi snapped to attention, as did Navigator. "Yes, sire."

"Get the Brontosaurus to clear the debris from the airfield. Have the pterodactyl fly patrol. They will warn you of trouble approaching. Protect the pilots at all costs."

He turned to Navigator and the loyal aliens.

"My friends," he said. "You will be killed as traitors if you are captured by your people. This I have witnessed with my own eyes. I would welcome you on Earth. It is a large planet with enough room and shelter for us all. Bring your families and tell them we are not hostile. One day soon, your children will play beside my children when the threat of this war is behind us."

Chapter 24: The President's Treachery

The presidential palace was large and overly ornate, a tall building with white walls, flying buttresses and external supports. From a high room, The President looked out of an open window over the city. There was smoke rising from the distant starport. A general stood beside him looking out at the destruction.

"We have sent gun trucks to engage them but the battle does not go well," reported the General.

"Traitors!" said the President. "Betrayed by my own people."

"Don't be hard on them," said the General. "They were under the control of the creatures, Excellency. They were forced to lie. They had no choice."

"Yes they did," said the President. "They should have chosen death over this. And the lies they repeat! Swearing that the monsters helped them."

He walked away from the window and towards a video monitor where a technician was busy working at a nearby console. The monitor was showing scenes from the welcome celebration at the starport. There were crowds looking up at the arriving fleet, quick shots of the damaged ships, and loved ones looking up with hopeful faces. Pilot's perfect landing was seen.

"Is this what we released as the official story?" asked the President.

"Yes, sir," said the Technician.

The President, General and his Advisors watched the monitor. It was a carefully edited version of what really happened at the starport when the flagship landed. The monitor showed Pilot, but his voice did not sound like him. Anyone who knew Pilot personally would know it wasn't his words.

"The mission was a success, but the monsters fought back," said Pilot, his voice coming from the monitor. "There were casualties and many of our ships were damaged. We had to land to make repairs and treat our wounded. That's when they came. The monsters attacked us when we were at our weakest."

On the monitor they watched Rex and a barrage of dinosaurs come out of the ships. Rex roared, and the scene cut to dinosaurs trampling and fighting. There were video shots of aliens firing weapons, and finally a horrific scene depicting Pilot killed by Rex. Citizens on the monitor pointed and yelled in amazement.

"How could they have stowed away on our ships!" said one of the citizens.

"I don't know," said another citizen. "But our President was right. They're out to kill us."

There were many scenes of aliens bitten and trampled by dinosaurs. There were close shots of aliens being hit by gunfire.

"Look, they have guns and weapons," said another citizen on the monitor.

Valiant aliens shot back at the dinosaurs, but by and large the monitor showed carefully edited battle scenes that made the dinosaurs appear to have perpetrated all the violence. An announcer's voice spoke over the monitor. "Triumph turned to tragedy at the welcome reception for the returning heroes today, proving our President was right about the creatures from the dinosaur planet..." It droned on. An Aide entered with a message for the General. The President turned towards them.

"What is it?" said the President.

The General looked empty and horrified.

"Well?" demanded the President.

"They hold the starport," said the General. "I have word they ambushed a convoy of gun trucks. Some of the trucks have been turned around and are pointed towards the road. They are being helped by some of our people who are manning the guns and shooting everything that approaches the starport."

The President became enraged. "How is this possible?" he demanded. He turned to an advisor. "I told you they would do this. I warned you. It's the end of us all if we don't nip this problem now."

"They appear to be guarding the ships," said an advisor. "They obviously hope to retreat back to their planet."

"I have reports that some of them are headed towards the prison laboratory," said the General.

"Good," said the President. "We can use the hostages for bait. Get the Warden and the Garrison Commander on the communicator for me."

"Sir," reported an Aide. "They're both dead."

The President was angry. "Dead!" he said. "How is this possible?"

"They were reported killed in the escape," said the Aide.

"Escape?" said the President. "What escape?"

"We were about to tell you, sir," said the General. "There's been some kind of trouble at the prison. Just before the ceremony there were reports of an escape. It must have been part of a coordinated attack. While we were distracted with the ceremony, some of them must have landed near the prison and engineered an escape."

"This can't be!" said the President. "I'll have everyone responsible for this brought before me."

"It's too late," said the General. "As you've heard, the Garrison Commander is confirmed dead. We're not sure about the Warden. We're assuming he's dead. Either way, nobody has heard from him or anyone at the prison."

"And the laboratory?" asked the President.

"Half destroyed in an explosion, or so the reports say," said the General.

"I'll get them for this," said the President angrily. "The graviton ray! Activate the graviton ray!"

"What's the graviton ray?" asked the Aide.

"It's an experimental device that can be aimed at large bodies in space," explained the advisor. "Comets and meteors, but nothing as big as a planet.

"For what purpose?" asked the Aide.

"It can alter gravity," said the advisor. "Change the course of small objects, cause them to fall from orbit or even collapse within their own gravity well.

A second advisor spoke up. "But sir, we can't use that," he said. "That weapon could upset the balance of the solar system."

"I don't care," said the President. "The beasts hope to rescue their young and escape back to their planet. But there will be no planet there when they return. Activate the graviton ray."

"And do what?" asked the General.

The President walked over to the window and pointed skyward. "See that large comet up there?" he asked. "The one passing between our planet and theirs?"

The advisors and the general moved closer so they could see what he was pointing at. They nodded, beginning to understand the President's plan.

"Alter its course slightly using the graviton ray. I want it to collide with their planet. I want it to rain fire and death on that planet, destroying all life there once and for all."

He stared off into the distance, becoming almost maniacal in his vision of what would happen. "The seas will boil, the mountains tremble, perhaps the planet's magnetism will even be upset. Either way, every living thing on that planet will know death and destruction at our hands." He smiled wickedly. "They will die out slowly, I hope. And we'll be rid of the threat forever."

When he finished, he waited for sounds of approval, but everyone remained silent. Some thought him mad, but knew better than to react. Silence was the better part of valor.

"Well?" demanded the President in a shrill voice. They sprang to life as if suddenly dropped onto hot coals.

The general turned to an aide. "Make it happen," he said.

"Yes, Sir," replied the aide. As he left the room, the President motioned for the general to move closer.

"Assemble a small force of soldiers and arrange transport," he whispered to the General. "I want to go to the prison laboratory immediately. I want to oversee the destruction of the rest of the dinosaur creatures personally."

The General sensed something sinister. "You're not thinking of using the doomsday weapon?" he asked nervously.

"We can control its power," said the President.

"Can you be sure?" asked the General.

The President became angry. "Why are you questioning me? You should be busy mounting a counter attack," he screamed. "The beasts hold the starport, General. Launch a second force to deal with them. Call out the reserves. We'll need air support as well. With a coordinated attack we can retake the starport. It's crucial to my plan. Now get moving."

Chapter 25: The Sphere

Nothing prepared Natalie and the dinosaurs for what they saw as they entered the light. It was the largest cavern they had ever seen, stretching for what seemed like miles above their heads. It was like being outside again. The air was fresh and clean. The walls were pasted with life, growing on tiers that hung along the sides, vines lush with ripe fruit. High overhead there were glowing spheres of light as bright as any sunlight. Natalie swore she could see clouds moving in front of them.

Below this underground canopy of sky was a fantastic city. It beckoned to her between trees that shaded her from the light of the spheres, allowing her vision to adjust after days of lantern light and darkness. The city itself was bright, with white buildings layered upon each other as they spread across the uneven floor of the cavern. They were separated by wide promenades with interlaced alleys and walkways. There were stairs leading upward, mixed with gentle paths, providing scenic routes about the city.

The most dominating features of the city were a series of mountains, rising like giant stalagmites in the proportions of this cavern. Atop the largest and highest of these massive rock pillars was a fantastic structure, a temple sitting in a high place called an acropolis. Stairs led to the temple, winding up and over hills until they climbed the pillar, sometimes circling around it, sometimes in delicate switchbacks. Eventually it led to a plateau that itself had pillars, jutting from the top like spikes on a thorn bush. Between the pillars set the temple, a building created from an alien mind, designed to touch something deep in the soul. It had the power to create a sense of presence, a structure that both inspired and humbled the individual. Was it a place of worship? A seat of government? These were the mysteries that called to Gaff and Gorka and now tugged at Natalie.

She caught glimpses of the city as she walked beneath the trees. The stone beneath her feet gradually transitioned to a smooth path set with tile in an intricate pattern. They emerged from the forest into an open area ringed with fruit trees and exotic plants.

"Finally," said the Pterodactyl. "I can stretch my wings." He ran up an embankment, flattening his body until he glided forward, tipping his wings ever so slightly until he rose in the currents of air. They watched him become a speck in the distance. He let out a screech of happiness, calling back to them as he flapped his wings and pulled himself higher.

"How did you find this place?" asked Natalie.

"I didn't find it," answered Gorka. "It found me."

"I don't understand," said Natalie.

Gaff explained. "Gorka was one of the original scientists who mapped these caves," he said. "The President made the scientisis search underground in hopes they would find hidden treasure. Something made him certain that there were riches to be found down here."

"We were not successful," said Gorka. "The President became enraged when we did not produce any treasure. He suspected we had found some and were secretly hiding it from him. He's very suspicious."

"In his anger the President converted our research facility into a prison," said Gaff. "The place we just escaped from."

"That prison?" said Natalie, astonished.

"Yes. It was a research facility, a laboratory," said Gorka. "We were studying ancient civilizations, trying to learn about the past. It was a staging area for our underground expeditions. That's why we had an equipment room."

"What happened?" asked Natalie.

"I was on an expedition when I heard the news," said Gorka.

"The President took the scientists captive one day," said Gaff. "He tried to get them to reveal where they had hidden all the treasure they had discovered. Of course, they had no idea what he was talking about."

Gorka looked shaken. "One by one they were sacrificed until only a few were left," he said sadly. "I think the President grew bored with the same results. He kept expecting one of them to crack and spill the secrets he longed to hear. I suspect they would tell him anything to stop the pain and the torture.

"Once I heard what he had done I knew there was no returning home. We wandered for weeks in these caves, always deeper, until we ran out of food. People went mad. I am ashamed to tell you what my fellow scientists did. I have seen learned men revert to savagery. They did things..."

Gaff interrupted the bad memory. "Only Gorka kept his calm," he said, putting his hand on his friend's shoulder.

"What about the food we ate on our way here?" asked Natalie. "The bioluminescence?"

"We didn't know about it," said Gorka. "It had not been discovered yet. I set out and searched for food. I couldn't stand being around my fellows anymore. They were beginning to talk about eating their own."

Natalie looked ashamed. "There are some on my world who do that regularly, even without the motive of starvation."

There was an uneasy moment before the conversation began again. "I went back to the surface to collect some of my friends, hoping to bring them here, but the President had other plans for us."

Gaff decided to change the subject. "You should explore the city," he suggested. "There is a temple here filled with many strange objects. There are floating stones hovering without wires or support. We have found mysterious pieces of glass with no purpose we can decipher. Most recently we have discovered a strange sphere that cannot be penetrated."

The pterodactyl fluttered down beside them. "He's right. You should see this place," he said. "Especially that temple at the top of the hill." He pointed a leathery wing towards the building atop the acropolis.

"You've been there already?" asked Gorka.

"It's easy when you can fly," said the pterodactyl. He turned and offered his back to Gorka. "Come on, hop aboard," he said.

Gorka was amazed. "You mean..." he began.

"Look," said the pterodactyl. "I've been cooped up in a tiny cage for a long time. This is what I do best. Now are you coming or not?"

Gorka hesitated but he climbed on the pterodactyl's back and they took off. Gaff was feeling rejected.

"Do you want to see the temple?" he asked Natalie.

"Of course," she answered. Dozer and Closer and some of the others were nodding in agreement.

"Well, our journey will at least be more dignified," said Gaff.

"Don't worry," said Natalie. "I'll ask him to give you a ride later. So, where are we headed?"

"Up these steps," said Gaff. "All the way to the top. Way up there." He pointed up to the top, his finger following what seemed to be an endless staircase leading to the temple at the pinnacle of the mountain. They could almost see the pterodactyl and Gorka, who had become distant shadows in the clear sky.

They climbed slowly, and despite her tiredness, Natalie felt refreshed. She was energized, excited at where she was headed. The temple called to her as it did to Gorka and Gaff.

Not all the dinosaurs followed. Some wandered off to explore streets and alleys or to lounge in warm, grassy plazas where a fat meal of fruit and a nap sounded better than a long climb. It seemed like they had all the time in the world to explore this paradise. Natalie had different concerns. Above all she wanted to contact her father. Something told her that she would be able to do that once she reached the temple.

In the end it was Natalie, Dozer, Closer, Gaff, and a few other hardy ones that met the pterodactyl and Gorka at the top. They were patiently waiting for them at the temple gates.

"What took you so long?" asked the pterodactyl.

Natalie looked out over the city. The light still shined from above and the whiteness of the city made it look clean and new despite its age. She could see dinosaurs roaming around through the streets below. Some were exploring buildings, poking their necks into doorways. Some were feeding off fruit growing from trees in park areas. Others were playing dinosaur games. None of them were fighting. There were steep cavern walls in the distance and from this vantage point it almost appeared like the city was in a giant circular cave and this was the exact center.

"Nice view," remarked Natalie. A breeze blew through the cave and she inhaled deeply. "Mmmmm. Smells sweet."

"What's it like to fly over the city?" Gaff asked Gorka.

"Hop on," said the pterodactyl. "I'll show you."

"I don't want to hurt you," said Gaff.

"You won't," said the pterodactyl. "I'll just drop off this cliff and we'll glide down in big circles."

"Sounds like fun," said Gaff. He climbed onto the pterodactyl's back and they took off.

"Well, guess it's left up to me to give you the temple tour," said Gorka.

As they stepped inside the temple, Natalie was overcome with the beauty of the place. The walls were covered with an intricate frieze, three dimensional pictures coming right out of the stone. She walked over to one frieze of an ancient alien teacher surrounded by students. She assumed he was a teacher because of his posture. He was an older alien surrounded by young ones who were looking up at him. It reminded her of the stenonychosaurus conducting classes at the palace back on Earth. The teacher had his hand outstretched. A suspended sphere levitated slightly above the hand.

"I like that one," said Gorka. "Go ahead and touch it."

Natalie complied, grasping the sphere with her claw.

"The sphere does not move," said Gorka, noting with delight the surprise on her face. "It's as solid and as unyielding as the rock from which it is carved, yet it is not attached."

They moved on to another frieze. This one was of an ancient alien holy man. An aura glowed from his head, a bright rainbow of colors. Natalie tried to see where the light came from but there was no apparent source. She stretched out her arm and the colors passed right through it.

"It comes from within the statue itself," explained Gorka. "At first I thought it was a trick of light, but after examining it many times I believe it comes from within the statue. Look into the eyes. There is a depth, a reflection like a living creature. They follow you everywhere."

"There are mysteries here that I could spend a lifetime trying to understand," said Natalie.

"You may well do that," said Gorka. "I doubt you can return to the surface without endangering your life."

Natalie looked out and into the city. She saw the baby dinosaurs playing. She smiled sadly.

"Nate and I used to play like that when we were young," she said.

"The young one we left behind on the table?" asked Gorka.

"How did you know?" asked Natalie.

"I feel you grieving inside," said Gorka. "I see an image in your heart of him."

Natalie was surprised. "You see images?" she asked. "You're psychic?"

"Yes," said Gorka. "A gift given to me by the city. It gave me the ability to pierce the heart and see true intentions."

"My mother called it the gift," she said. "My powers, I mean. Her powers."

Gorka nodded. "Let me show you something," he said.

They climbed up a set of stairs leading to the roof of the temple. When they walked out onto the roof, there was a black sphere there. It rested on the gound, but it was a sphere. It did not roll or move as she would have suspected. At first Natalie thought it small, maybe a meter or two in diameter, but as she approached it she could tell it was much larger. It hummed a soothing sound as they got closer. Natalie reacted, smiling, and it suddenly came to life.

"Oh!" she said, startled.

"It's okay," said Gorka. "Don't be afraid of it. The sphere has a life of its own."

They watched as the sphere reshaped itself into a chair that seemed molded to Natalie's shape.

"It looks as if it is offering you a meeting," said Gorka.

"What?" asked Natalie.

"Go ahead and sit," said Gorka. "It is trying to get to know you."

Natalie was hesitant.

"It's safe," assured Gorka. "You'll see."

She looked nervously at the dark chair for a moment. There was a soothing, humming sound that felt like it ended in a question mark. Natalie took a deep breath and sat down.

She could feel the sphere making further adjustments to her shape. The chair shaped itself into something deep and comfortable, reminding her of her bed nest back home. It almost smelled like it too. She took another deep breath and slipped into a trance. She felt powerful, like her psychic powers had grown to new proportions. She decided to see if it was true.

She took another deep breath and cleared her mind of all obstructions. "Mother," she whispered.

Her mind filled with an image of her mother. Almost instantly, she sailed across space and connected with the Queen.

"Mother!" she said elatedly.

"You are safe, my child," answered the Queen.

"I'm safe mother," she said. "The children are safe."

"Yet you are pensive and sad," said the Queen.

She started to cry. "It's Nate," she said. "He's dead."

"I know," replied the Queen.

"He died protecting me," she said.

"Natalie, you must be strong," said the Queen. "Remember who you are. Think of your father."

"Father!" she said.

"He is there, trying to find you," said the Queen.

"I have heard reports but I cannot contact him," she said.

"You must," said the Queen. "He has come to rescue you. Reach out to him. Feel his presence."

"I've tried, but..."

"Try again," commanded the Queen.

She closed her eyes and smiled, thinking of her father in a tender moment. There was a time when they were all together as a family. Father was not so busy. He was younger, and mother, as always, was beautiful. He took them on a journey, across many rivers and through jungles with mountains that spit fire. At the end of their journey they met a tribe of dinosaurs, Labocanias, distant relatives of the Tyrannosaurs. Father hunted with them while mother and Natalie met with the rest of the tribe. Father was so proud of her that day. So was Mother. They slept together that night under the stars, surrounded by relatives, sharing their warmth and their friendship. They had never been closer. It tugged at her heart, a tender chord that defined what family meant to her. She breathed in and she could smell his scent, the raw reptilian manhood that defined her father's pheromones. She breathed in again, the breath swirling into her brain, forming the image of her father.

"I see him," she said.

On the surface of the alien planet, Rex suddenly stopped a short distance from the prison and stared blankly ahead. The band of soldiers with him also stopped. Cassius, Captain of the Guard, looked at him, his face scrunched in curiosity. Others, including loyal aliens, also turned to look at the King. They could all tell something was different in him, something had happened.

"Your majesty?" asked Cassius, concerned.

Rex spoke slowly, as if from a great depth. "Strange," he said. "I see my wife."

Cassius looked around, thinking she was nearby. "The Queen?" he asked, continuing to scan the area.

Rex shook his head. "Not here," he said. He pointed to his heart. "But here."

There was suddenly a glow on Rex's chest, barely visible at first, but it grew stronger. Cassius and the others noticed it right away.

"I see my daughter as well," said Rex. "Natalie."

He heard her reply as if she were right beside him. "Father," she said. "I'm safe."

"I'm coming to rescue you," said Rex. "Where are you? I can't find you."

"You're not psychic," said Cassius. This was very strange behavior for the King.

"No. I'm not, yet I feel their presence," said Rex. It appeared that he was in a trance just like the Queen when she had these moments of psychic contact. Cassius could see the faraway look in his eye, the blurred vision.

In Rex's eyes and in his heart, he, Natalie, and the Queen all reached out at once and embraced each other, as if reunited as a family again. He saw visions of them snuggling in a nest, playing in the jungle again, eating together. They were happy days, memories long gone since this war began. He breathed deep, relishing the details of a life he could barely remember.

As he looked into his past, the tender scene was suddenly ripped in the center by a comet plunging towards them. There was fear and terror. Dinosaurs on Earth looked up at the sky, aware of the comet. They were plunged into darkness. With the visions momentarily gone, Rex opened his eyes and saw the same comet in the sky above the Alien Planet. Cassius and his troops saw the comet as well. It was real and it was heading towards the Earth.

Natalie also felt it, even though she was underground in the City of the Ancients. The same thing had happened to her visions. One moment she was soothed by memories of her early life with her mother and father, the next moment the fabric of her vision was torn by a plummeting comet. She drew the air in around her with an audible gasp that made Gorka take a step backwards.

On Earth, the Queen was interrupted by her handmaiden.

"Your Majesty," she said softly. "It approaches."

The Queen awoke from her trance, having established contact with her husband and her daughter. She rose quietly and moved out onto a balcony. Looking up, she could see the comet clearly now, huge, dominating the sky with fire.

"I love you all," she said. Her words were felt by everyone: Natalie, Rex, Cassius, dinosaurs on Earth and the Alien Planet. She sent her love to them all.

Chapter 26: A Past Revealed

In the Warden's office, the President looked out at the landscape surrounding the prison. Above, he could see the Earth hanging like a blue-green moon in the evening sky. The fiery comet with its long tail was closer to it now. From the alien planet it looked like an arrow pointed towards a small, round target.

He looked away and began to pace nervously. The Warden sat silently nearby, afraid to say or do anything. Anytime the President came for a visit it was always unpleasant, and this occasion was no different. At first, the President was glad to see him, grateful that the Warden had not been killed as reported, but soon after his demeanor changed. It had not been a pleasant visit.

In mid stride, the President suddenly stopped. He grabbed at his heart, as if to rip at something painful attached to his chest, but whatever he felt, it would not budge. He walked back to the window and looked up at the sky.

Something tugged at his heart again. For a moment he could have sworn that he saw a large dinosaur in front of him. He shook his head and rubbed his eyes and it was gone. Then he thought he saw it again, this time as a reflection in the window, as if the dinosaur was standing behind him. He turned around and saw nothing. He turned back and looked out the window again, scanning the periphery of his vision for another reflection.

"I love you all," he heard a voice say.

"Who said that?" he asked out loud. He turned and looked at the Warden who stared back at him. "Did you hear that?" he asked.

The Warden observed this strange behavior and was about to say something, but then he thought the better of it. Who was he to question the inner workings of his leader's great mind?

The President looked into the glass and saw the dinosaur again. "You feel it, don't you," she said. "The weight of your decision." Her eye looked right into his heart and he could not help but see what she saw. There was a stone in his heart called remorse. He could feel it rising up and blocking his throat. There were tears in his eyes from the weight of the sadness.

In the distant underground City of the Ancients, Natalie sat in the chair, melting into the soothing sound and shape of the sphere. She was so happy to have seen her mother again. She thought that this was a good sign and that things were going to get better now. Tears began to form in her eyes. The humming increased, a vibration that seemed to come from deep within the sphere. It made her to relax even more.

In the Warden's office the President heard the humming sound of the sphere. He thought he was going mad. First he was seeing things, now he was hearing them. He tried to focus on the sound, a strange melody that sounded like a lullaby his mother used to sing to him when he was a child. He started humming the tune out loud. The stone in his heart seemed to move.

The Warden looked at him again but the President did not acknowledge him. The President was overcome with strange emotions. He stopped humming and buried his head in his hands. The Warden again noticed this odd behavior but did not say anything.

"Mother," said the President. "What have I done?"

He pressed his face deeper into his hands, deep into self-imposed darkness. In the comfort of that darkness he saw an image of the day his mother died. He was very young, barely at an age he could remember. His father was wrapped in grief and anger, but he had his own childish fears. With his mother gone, he wondered who would be with him and take care of him. His father never had time for him, he barely knew his father. Even at his young age he realized that without his mother there could be no family, no sense of completeness for either him or his father. He was alone suddenly, his heart on fire with the injustice.

He remembered standing beside his father at his mother's grave. He was holding on tightly to his father's hand. Then, for reasons unknown, his father pried his small hand from his own and put it into another person's hand that gripped it just as tightly. He heard his father's words in his mind, as clear as he had heard them that day.

"You must live with them, now, son," he had said. "They will take care of you."

These were strangers, he thought, his young mind trying to comprehend why his father would abandon him. Was it something he did? He remembered the hand gripping his own tiny hand even tighter. He struggled to get free but could not. He watched his father walk away, not even turning for a last look at his son. He suddenly spoke out loud, the same words he had uttered as a child bursting from his lips.

"Dad! Don't leave me with these strangers," he said. "I'll be good. I promise."

The Warden again kept quiet, wondering what was going on in his leader's mind.

The President pulled his hands away from his face and looked up at the sky. The Warden had never seen anyone look so sad and forlorn. He went to the window and looked up to see what the President was staring at. There was a fiery ball, a bright comet trailing gas, ice and space debris, headed directly towards the planet of the dinosaurs.

With victory at hand, he wondered how the President could look so defeated.

Chapter 27: Death of a Planet

Most of the inhabitants of Earth could see it. The comet loomed in the sky, dominating it as it grew ever larger. Weather patterns were affected by the massive gravity of the thing. A storm began to blow, hot winds carrying the scent of death. Dinosaurs stampeded, running everywhere in a panic. This was something new, something more sinister than the attack of the alien space ships.

On the balcony the Queen stood, her heart glowing. She saw the catastrophe and knew the truth. She had no control over the impending doom. It was unavoidable. All that was left was to face death with dignity. She knew time would stop for a moment, allowing her to escape the shell of her body and travel to a place without pain. There she would wait for Rex, an eternity if necessary, knowing that the reward would be another eternity with him.

"You will be safe, my daughter," she said reassuringly.

On the temple rooftop in the City of the Ancients Natalie heard her. She sat in the sphere-chair, her eyes closed. She sighed deeply. Her heart began to glow just as the Queen's glowed on Earth.

Natalie wasn't the only one to hear her. Outside the Prison Rex stood with his team waiting. He felt something deep inside. His heart began to glow as well. It was not as bright as Natalie's or the Queen's, but it glowed.

He understood what was happening, he knew of the President's treachery. This terrible knowledge was somehow being shown to him. He heard his wife's voice.

"I love you, husband," she said.

Cassius pointed to the sky where the comet was about to collide with Earth.

"What is that?" he asked.

"The end of us all," said Rex.

On the balcony of the Palace, the handmaiden was concerned about the Queen. "Please come inside where you will be safe, mistress."

The Queen knew better, and so did the handmaiden as she looked into the sky and saw the giant ball of flaming rock and gas directly overhead.

The comet struck the Earth in fury. The Palace shook, and the dinosaurs that were not instantly cooked in the inferno were crushed by rock when the walls fell in upon them. The jungles erupted with fire. Pterodactyl dropped out of the sky in mid flight. The seas and rivers boiled, spewing steam and debris skyward. Brontosauri standing in the water were cooked instantly as were many of the marine animals. The wind blew with tornado force. Tsunamis pelted the shores of the great seas. Mountains that had once spit fire grew angry again, adding to the cataclysm. A haze began to blot out the sun, plunging the world into darkness.

And from the alien planet the Earth seemed to bleed into space.

The glow on Rex's chest turned to pain and he grabbed at it, his knees weakening. Cassius came to his side to support him.

At the top of the temple in the City of the Ancients, the chair became a sphere again, Natalie disappearing within its dark folds. Gorka rushed forward, slamming into solid dark matter as the sphere assumed its old, familiar shape. The surface became obsidian black, reflecting the surroundings back like a negative. Gorka stared at his distorted image in the bright, polished surface. The sphere began to hum gently, a comforting sound he seemed to remember from somewhere in his past.

Above, on the surface of the alien planet, beyond the artificial sky of the giant cavern, the dinosaurs looked up at the end of their world. Flames shot outward and the formerly blue and green sphere grew bright with fire then dark with smoke.

"Why?" asked Rex.

Chapter 28: For the Children

At the starport they all saw it. They felt it. Who can say what the destruction of a homeworld feels like, or what feelings dinosaurs or aliens have, but nonetheless there was a great emptiness after that. They were all left with that, except the President, who felt satisfaction.

At an alien military compound, the scientist who turned on the graviton ray and made the comet plummet into the Earth looked up and felt the emptiness. "What have I done," he said. A strange sadness overcame him making him swoon. "They struggled for millions of years to attain life, and I destroyed it in less than a day." He collapsed to the floor, his knees weak with the will to remain standing.

King Rex felt it too, a loss far greater than any King should have to bear. "Why?" he asked again. They all looked at him. There was no answer to that question.

Across the plain, enemy ships approached the starport. Rex saw them coming, heading directly for the landing field. The group crouched low and watched them fly past the prison and over the dinosaur fortifications. They hovered and began blasting everything in sight. The ground shook from the force. Rex instantly became animated, his body charged with purpose. He started to turn, feeling like he should be there, leading the battle.

Cassius stopped him. "Trust Gwangi and Navigator," he said. "We have our own part to play in this drama."

"My sisters send their assurance," said Penelope. "The troops have rallied."

Rex thought about it for a moment, an indulgence he felt guilty about. There was a tug at his heart, and he remembered the many times the Queen would help him control his impulsiveness. She would be the first one to tell him to think before acting. The dreams he had for his kingdom were gone forever, just as she was. Natalie was all he had left. She was worth fighting for.

"You're right, Cassius," he said. "Let's go get our children."

An alien with a red sash pointed the way to the prison. "Over here," he said.

At the starport, explosions rocked the area. The alliance pilots sprang into action, running for the parked ships. Some did not make it. They were cut down by yellow rays from the attacking ships. The few that did manage to get their ships off the ground mounted a vicious counterattack.

On the ground, the captured gun trucks manned by the alliance turned from the road to point upwards. The sky grew bright with explosions and smoke. The attacking saucers flew in a steady formation, secure and arrogant in their purpose. They did not fear counterattack. They continued to pummel the starport and the surrounding area with blasts from their rays.

One battered ship from the Earth fleet flew high over the airfield. It glowed red for a moment, the color of the Alien-Dinosaur Alliance. Then it plummeted into the center of the attacking formation. It gyrated, knocking ships aside like stones. As it crashed into the formation, it caused a cascade effect. An explosion lit the sky, expanding gas throwing out waves of fire. One of the saucers was in the process of firing yellow rays. As it tilted, the yellow ray sliced back through its own ranks, taking out a few more of the enemy ships. The sky rained debris over the starport and dinosaurs and aliens alike squinted with the brightness of the explosions. On the ground, parked space ships were crushed under the hail of falling metal.

"There goes our escape route," said Navigator.

A dinosaur beside him looked up. Above the explosions and fire he could see the burning Earth. "You forget," he said. "We have no place to escape to."

Gun trucks were approaching down the road, the ground force sent by the President as part of the coordinated attack with the flying saucers.

Gwangi roared, crying out a cheer that rallied the dinosaurs. "For the homeworld!" he yelled. "For Earth and for our children!"

A brontosaurus led the charge, slamming through a barricade of vehicles and trash that was blocking the road. "For the homeworld" he yelled. On the other side of the barricade there stood a line of enemy gun trucks pointed at him. As he crashed through the barricade debris flew everywhere, some of it arcing forward to hit the gun trucks. One of the trucks exploded, bursting into a pillar of fire. It rolled onto its side, pushing another gun truck off the road and into the gully.

The brontosaurus continued to charge, crushing a third truck under his massive foot as he roared past the flames. "For the children," he screamed.

He thought about what he was saying. He thought about his children. Tears poured out of his eyes, agony ripping at his heart. He looked up at the burning Earth. Something had snapped inside him. He had grieved for family and friends before, but not for everyone, not for an entire world. Not for everything he knew.

He thought about his mate, the scars the aliens had burned into her skin when she tried to protect the children. For all his love, she still felt ugly with those scars. Those scars were not as deep as the ones she hid from him, scars the aliens had made when they tore the children out of her life. Could she still be alive? How could she have survived the destruction of their homeworld? He thought about his children left behind on Earth, of all the good things in life he wanted to teach them. He thought of the one he came to rescue, his daughter, packaged in a little red bag and stolen from him, presumably somewhere on this planet.

"I'm coming," he yelled. He opened his throat to roar. A sound came out of him, something that was neither anger nor pain, a horrible cry that carried all the broken parts of him, a message to his comrades, a warning to his enemies.

Dinosaurs began to pour through the hole in the barricade, following the Brontosaurus' charge: Gwangi with his horrible, body length scar, now a badge of honor; Tyrannosaurus Rex, followed by a Stegosaurus and Triceratops, Raptors and Compys, Pachycephalosaurus and Spinosaurus, and the rest of the force. Even the old planners and advisors, dinosaurs once prized for their brains, reverted to savagery as they rushed forward. They tore at everything in their path. Trucks were already crushed to the thickness of leaves underfoot as the dinosaurs trampled everything.

Another convoy of gun trucks approached from the city. The guns swiveled to point ahead. They began to open fire on the brontosaurus, pummeling the ground around him. He kept charging, meeting the first truck in the convoy head on and running over it as if it were nothing. His massive foot kicked the second truck sending it crashing into the third truck in the line. Aliens scrambled from the wreckage but were quickly overtaken by the charging dinosaurs. Raptors clawed at them and angry T-Rexes snapped them in half with their powerful jaws. Some of the trucks drove off the road and into the ravine to avoid the brontosaurus, as if crashing into rocks was an easier choice. Even the medical dinos joined the fight as ankylosaurus worked their way up the ditch crushing the heads of fallen aliens with the heavy club-like protuberance on their tails. One of them had a piece of an alien impaled on the spikes that jutted sideways from his shell. He was still alive and though he struggled he could not pull himself free from the trap.

Overhead, enemy ships descended upon the fray firing lightning bolts at the charging beasts in an attempt to slow them. As the ships moved in low over the herd, there were explosions in the air around them. Captured gun trucks manned by loyal members of the alliance had opened fire at them from behind the barricades. A team of Stenonychosaurus, intelligent dinosaurs with useful claws, were doing a keen job of keeping the gun trucks supplied with ammunition by looting the smashed enemy trucks. Aliens wearing red sashes spoke in the language of the palace explaining how to operate the guns.

The alliance gun trucks caused a distraction, giving the alien ships another nuisance to deal with. They managed to bring a few down but the numbers were insurmountable. Some broke off from the main force and hovered over the charging dinosaurs. They concentrated on the brontosaurus, firing yellow rays again and again at the beast. The brontosaurus continued to charge, scattering the approaching convoy.

The enemy ships continued to pound the brontosaurus with rays. They didn't care that some of the blasts were hitting their own men. Trucks exploded as ammunition ignited from the spark of the lightning. The brontosaurus felt the heat of the blasts, his skin seared with burns. A piece of flying metal cut his side but he continued to charge, still scattering the convoy. The ships were merciless, focusing blasts again and again on the brontosaurus. Several pterodactyls opposed them, swooping down to pick up rocks and debris in their claws, flying over the ships to drop them on top. Sometimes they were successful but more often the debris would roll off the rounded shapes of the stone like flying machines.

"Over here," shouted some of the raptors. The pterodactyls knew the drill, a strategy that had been successful at downing enemy ships when they attacked Earth. The pterodactyls picked up the raptors and dropped them on the ships. One raptor was so angry that he managed to find a fissure in the seam of a ship. He ripped it open with his claws and wiggled inside. The ship wobbled for a moment and screams came from inside. It finally fell from the sky, crashing into the ground. The raptor emerged from the wreckage smiling, signaling a pterodactyl for another pickup.

Red rays shot out from one of the ships. It formed a catch bag around one of the pterodactyls. Before he could fly free, the bag closed around him. Instead of keeping its shape, it shrank, the walls growing tighter and tighter around the trapped dinosaur. He squawked and another pterodactyl crashed against it in an attempt to free him. There was another squawk and the bag turned into a small red globe containing nothing recognizable. The globe disappeared and blood fell in its place, landing on a patch of dry alien soil.

Rays continued to blast the brontosaurus. Nothing seemed to bring him down. Finally, an alien magazine truck filled with ammunition drove under him. The driver ignited an incendiary device and the truck exploded. The driver burst into flames and jumped out of the truck, running around screaming while he burned. He finally fell to the ground, laying still and silent.

He had been successful. His tactic worked. The brontosaurus was damaged, a hole in his stomach where the explosion had torn some of his guts out. Still he continued to lumber forward, the effort becoming more difficult with every step. His head lowered slowly, his body twisted sideways as he fell onto several trucks and a column of men, crushing them underneath. He let out a death wail, a thunderous bray of pain, and then his head dropped to the ground. A medical dino ran to his side but it was too late. The beast was silent, his heaving breath rising one last time before expiring in a last blast of air.

"For the homeworld! For the children!" yelled a Tyrannosaurus Rex, taking up the battle cry, charging forward with fury.

"Destroy the city!" yelled Gwangi, pointing to the distant spires of the capital. The dinosaurs became filled with purpose, setting their sights on the huge buildings in the distance.

"Let's destroy their world," yelled a triceratops, rushing down the road.

They trampled the convoy, letting nothing stand in their way. Some aliens turned and ran rather than be destroyed by the charging dinosaurs. Trucks tried to outrun them, but were chased down by other T-rexes and Triceratops. "Let none escape!" yelled a Stegosaurus.

Meanwhile the enemy ships were dropping out of the sky. They were so focused on killing the brontosaurus that they did not pay attention to the alliance gun trucks. The alliance gunners had time to take careful aim, shooting many of them out of the sky. The ones that exploded in the sky were lucky. Anything that hit the ground was fair game for the compys and raptors who would squeeze through narrow holes and cracks in the downed ships, feasting on the survivors of the crashes.

The alien ground force was broken, scattered in all directions. The fearsome charge of the brontosaurus had not been in vain. What he had not crushed underfoot was stepped on by a Tyrannosaurus Rex or toppled by the horns of a Triceratops or even impaled on the tail of a Stegosaurus. Other dinosaurs made sure the destruction was complete, stopping only to silence the moans of any wounded aliens remaining behind the path of carnage.

"Don't chase them down," ordered Gwangi. "Let the cowards run. Stay together. Regroup. Our target is the city."

A lumbering brachiosaurus followed at the rear of the dinosaur force. The dinosaurs stopped on the outskirts of the city, pausing for a moment. They parted, allowing the brachiosaurus to take up the lead position. Raising his head high he began to emit a long, deep note. The sound was deafening. A second brachiosaurus caught up with him and joined in, the low note shaking the dust on the ground. The spires of the city began to shake, resonating with the bass sound coming from their throats. Cracks could be seen in the stone walls.

"Charge!" yelled Gwangi. They all roared, terrible dinosaur screams and growls. Thunderous hooves and claws shook the ground, making the already unstable buildings shake and collapse. In the city, aliens cringed in fear, but there was no place to hide. The walls were cracking, crumbling to reveal cowering aliens inside their apartments.

"For the homeworld!" yelled a dinosaur.

"For Earth," yelled a second.

"For the children," yelled a third.

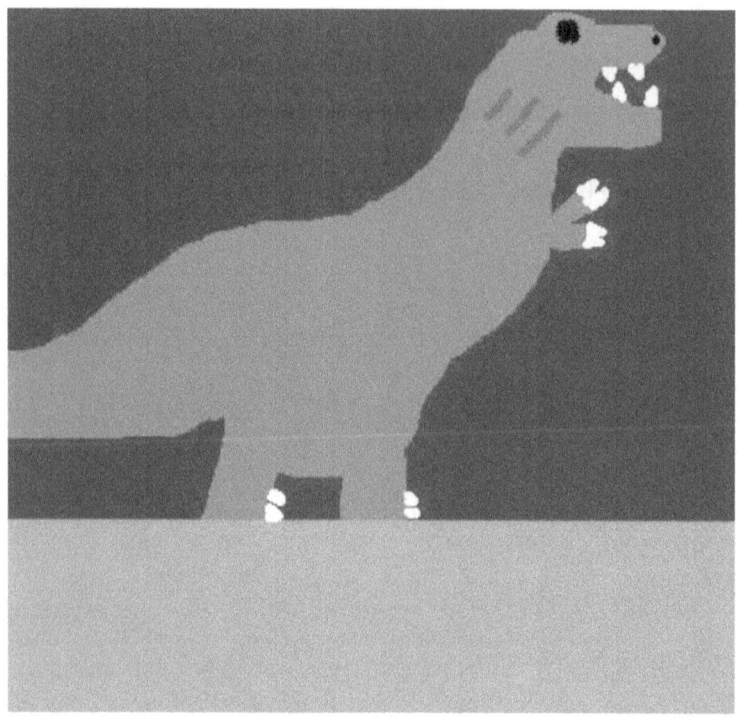

Chapter 29: The Rescue

Rex studied the low, flat building.

"What do you think?" he asked his team.

Cocotele, one of the friendly aliens, was the guide appointed by Navigator. He pointed to a bay door on the side of the building, gibbering to Rex.

Penelope listened and translated for them. "He says there is a big door over there."

The dinosaurs turned and looked at where he pointed. "We see it," said Rex.

"He thinks it would be the best way inside considering our size," said Penelope

Cassius sniffed the air. "I smell them, Sire. I smell the children," he said.

Rex cautioned him. "Patience," he said. "Let's study the situation. I smell a trap."

Cocotele discussed more of his plan with Penelope, who explained it to the dinosaurs.

"He wants to go in alone and open that large door for us. Then we can charge in."

"What's preventing us from just smashing the door down now," said Cassius.

The alien drew diagrams on the ground and spoke to Penelope. He moved his body up and down, his arms flat. "It is level inside," said Penelope. "But it is also deep inside, below ground level. He says it is like a small canyon in there." Cocotele squatted and extended his arms, gibbering and using his hands to draw things in the air.

"A ramp leads down just inside and to the left, but he says we are too big to fit on that ramp," said Penelope. "There are overhead walkways at the same level, but again he says we are too big to fit. He also says there may be guards with weapons in these locations."

Cocotele was nodding his head, as if agreeing with Penelope. He gibbered and bounced around some more.

Rex shook his head. Once again, communication baffled him. He thought of the Queen and how his wife could patiently explain it to him if she were here. He started to wander, to think about her and how much he missed her. He felt something in his heart, like the glow he had experienced earlier. He looked down at his chest and saw nothing. Somehow he knew Natalie was alive and he must go on. She needed him. She needed her father as much as he needed her.

He became aware of Penelope talking, as if he had been away somewhere for a moment. "Cocotele will go in the small door to activate a moving platform that will take us to the bottom of the canyon," she said. "A guard has to apply a key, but once the key is turned, it activates everything in that area including the big door."

"He knows a lot about that place," said Rex.

Penelope conversed with Cocotele. The alien was not as animated now. He looked more somber and sincere.

"He used to work here," she said.

Rex took a hard look at him. Rex had seen a lot of aliens up close and under all conditions: in the infirmary, at rest, at battle, working hard to make repairs. Cocotele did not look healthy for an alien. He smelled different to Rex, there was something more than fear, a slight smell of sickness. His face was long and sad, making Rex wonder what Cocotele had seen inside that building. He would soon know.

Cocotele continued to speak to Penelope. "Once the key is turned, he will throw the switch and open the big door." He interrupted Penelope to tell her something else. "It's very important. Be ready to rush in as soon as it opens. We may not get much time."

"Any discussion?" asked Rex, turning to his team.

"What's preventing us from smashing the door down right now," said Cassius again.

"Nothing," said Rex. "But it would be easier going through an open door, that way we could save our strength for battle."

Cassius perked up at the thought of battle. "What can we expect inside?"

Penelope spoke to Cocotele and he crouched down beside his diagram again. He modified the floor plan, drawing X's and lines in the dirt.

"He says there will be guards and soldiers. We will probably be outnumbered."

"We could take them by surprise," said Cassius to Rex. "You go one way, I'll go the other."

The King nodded approval. Cocotele circled the room of cages in his diagram, drawing lines towards it from the door, past the X's that represented guards and into the heart of the prison. He circled the room of cages again and stabbed at it several times with his pointer.

"Our children are there," said Penelope. Cocotele nodded with her in agreement. There was a smile on his face. Not of smugness or of vengeance, but of heartfelt love, a smile knowing that families would be reunited, that happiness was attainable, that penance was possible.

Rex asked what lay beyond that, and how big was that building. Cocotele didn't know how large, but he knew what lay behind the ominous doors, an area left blank in his crude drawing. That's when the King smelled the fear. Like a spurt it erupted from the alien, a scent of overpowering fear.

In that moment, Rex knew he must go there and see with his own eyes what put the fear into Cocotele.

"Any more discussion?" asked Rex.

Cassius remained silent, as did the rest of the team.

"Penelope, you'll deal with the children when we release them, correct?" asked Rex.

"Of course, your Majesty," she said.

"I know you will," he said. "I had to ask. It is your part in this operation, one best suited to your talents. The children will need comfort and direction. That said, I want you to stay outside until we've cleared the area. Guard our backs. Signal us if there is danger. We don't want to get trapped in there."

"Of course," she said again.

"And you," he said, looking at Cassius' handpicked men. "Brutus, Antilles, Sampson, are you with me?"

"Yes, sire," they said in unison.

Cocotele gibbered, and Rex somehow knew what it was about.

"No, my little friend," said Rex. "I can't forget you. We all know what risks you take. Your people will kill you when they find out you helped us."

Rex looked around the group and nodded to each of them individually, taking in their faces and acknowledging their contributions. "Sounds like we have a good plan, then. Let's make it happen. If we move quickly, we can take them by surprise."

"That's what I said," said Cassius.

The small band moved closer to the building, crouching behind a pile of supplies and boxes that kept them out of view. Cocotele motioned for them to wait. He pointed towards the large door and nodded, walking quickly towards a smaller door beside it.

"Why should we trust him?" asked Cassius. "He could be leading us into a trap."

"Navigator trusted him," said Rex.

"Why trust Navigator?" asked Cassius.

"Pilot trusted him," said Rex.

"And you trust Pilot. I know. Where does it all end?" asked Cassius.

"It ends here," said Rex. "Inside this building. We will confront whatever is in there together."

Cassius smiled. "I enjoy hunting with you."

Rex laughed. "I know. This is what it's all about. There's something about the hunt that compels me to it. I don't know what it is. I know that it makes my senses keen and it sharpens my wit. Look at our friend over there," said Rex, indicating Cocotele. "He's hunting as well."

"What do you mean?" asked Cassius.

"A moment ago he was sickly. He was sad, looking lost and full of fear. But look at him now. He walks with confidence and his eyes seem clear with purpose. He goes to confront his fear and test himself."

"Yes," said Cassius. "I see it."

"He fights another war, one just as personal as ours, but personal in a different way," said Rex. "It is easy to underestimate these people, Cassius, but don't fall into that trap. We have a lot in common."

"Like what?" asked Cassius. "We're as different as we can get," he said. "On our planet we live outside, with nothing to separate us from the heavens when we sleep at night. When we do go inside, it's for protection. It's odd for me to think of living like they do. Not just living inside, but walled up in separate little rooms. I can see it with a friend or a family, like a nest, but I don't understand. How can they interact as a tribe like that?"

"I don't know, Cassius" said Rex. "But you bring up some good points. The way they live probably has a great bearing on the way they interact with each other."

Cassius made an acute observation, but as usual, he tempered his observations with caution. "They have honor, yet not all of them are honorable," he said.

"You're right," said Rex. "That's the answer, my friend. We must seek out the honorable ones. We can't hold them all responsible for the actions of their leaders." Rex became excited as he continued. "My dream of peace is possible, Cassius. You've given it back to me. Peace may not be possible between governments, but it is possible between individuals. We will win our peace one person at a time."

Cocotele turned and looked back towards Rex and Cassius, then continued towards the door. Cocotele stood proudly at the door, speaking into a wall communicator, requesting access to the prison.

"I still think we should have smashed the door down," said Cassius.

Chapter 30: Surprise Attack

The prison laboratory was in ruins from the escape. Nate's body was still strapped to an exam table. A nearby table held a half dissected compsognathus lying open on it. There were dinosaur parts and jars of fluid spewed everywhere. Some were broken open, lying mixed with broken pieces of laboratory furniture. The room looked like it was decorated by some kind of ghoulish madman.

Cleanup was not a concern for now, pursuing the escapees was. Workers had opened the door jammed shut by the pachycephalosaurus. Behind that they found a rockslide. Gorka had placed his charges very effectively along weak fissures in the rock, causing the explosion to do more damage than normal. Now the work crews had to deal with the rocks and debris, moving it slowly using digging equipment and machinery.

"I don't know if we're going to get through this mess," said one of the workers. "It's unstable and every place we clear seems to collapse right after that."

"We're not really making any progress," said another.

"We better," said the first. "The Warden seems to be watching this job personally."

"It's not the Warden," said someone else on the work crew. He pointed towards the doors. "I heard that the President is here."

At the other end of the room near the ominous doors, Guards stood with painsticks. The doors looked battered. One door was slightly askew; hanging by a single hinge, the other lay open and stuck. In the room of cages, two guards were busy setting up explosives and rigging charges.

The President walked into the room of cages with one of his aides. They went past the guards and through the broken doors into the laboratory. They didn't say a word and the men volunteered nothing. The whole compound was on eggshells, and the guards thought they had the easier job. If these explosives went off, they would do less damage than the President's temper going off.

A General who was supervising the men saw the President arrive. He followed the President, caught up in the wake of his leader's greatness. In the laboratory, the President stopped and stood over Nate's body, staring at it. Nate's leg had been severed from the body. The distinctive markings caught his attention. He looked at them and saw not the badge of honor that Nate did, but a deformed and savage scar.

"Beasts," he muttered to himself. "Primitive animals. Soon you'll threaten us no more."

The General interrupted him to give a report.

"My men have made progress," said the General. "We have excavated most of the rockslide caused by the explosions. Soon it will be wide enough for the vehicles to pass through. We'll deploy the light pods and track the escapees down with trucks and special teams."

"And the explosive charges?" asked the President.

"As you can see," said the General. "They are being set as I speak."

"See to it personally," said the President. "We must be prepared to barricade ourselves in here should the need arise. My intelligence tells us they will try to come here to rescue the prisoners."

"But there are no prisoners," said the General.

The President frowned. "Don't remind me of that fact again," he said.

The President stared at the dinosaur parts for a moment.

"They are stupid animals," said the President. "They probably don't know that there has been an escape. We've kept it a secret, even from our own people."

The President continued to stare at the dinosaur parts.

The General wondered what he was contemplating, but he didn't say anything. Finally, the President turned and walked away to the other end of the laboratory. The General stood for a moment, wondering if he was dismissed, decided he was and went back to work directing his men.

At the other end of the laboratory in a small niche there was a bank of switches and buttons set beside a large monitor. A scientist busied himself calibrating knobs and reading gauges. He made notes with a stylus on a small board. There were a series of strange beeps and whirs and new lights flashed on and off. The monitor blurred in and out of focus and a red crosshair appeared in the center. The President watched him carefully until he grew impatient.

"Now. You," he said. "Explain this device to me."

The scientist was startled, but when he saw it was the President, he apologized. "The device is activated by this switch, Excellency," he said. "You push this round lever like this."

He reached out and adjusted a lever and threw a small switch. A low humming noise began. The scientist continued. "The device is now armed. You aim it with this scope."

He walked over to another panel near the monitor and fiddled with a knob. The image on the monitor changed but the crosshair remained stationary. The scientist used an electronic pointer to focus the screen on the starport. He rotated a trackball in front of the monitor.

"By rotating this ball you can change the view on the screen which also changes the detonation point for the device," he explained. The monitor changed, moving towards an overhead view of the capital city. The humming noise got slightly louder.

"What's that?" asked the President.

"The device is building up charge," explained the scientist. "The longer you wait before throwing the final lever, the stronger the device will become. Right now it probably has the power to destroy a small animal, maybe a person. In a while it will be strong enough to destroy a gun truck. Soon after that, a spacecraft the size of one of our small ships."

"What's the maximum potential?" asked the President.

"We don't really know," said the scientist. "We never let it build up that much. It's still untested and very dangerous. Be careful using it."

The President grabbed the trackball and began manipulating the controls, moving the scope and searching for something. "Where are they? Where are the crafty monsters?" he asked. "I don't see them at the starport anymore."

They heard garbled noises and shouting, echoing from the room of cages through the open doors. Both the President and the scientist turned and looked.

"What is that?" asked the President.

"I'll go see," volunteered the scientist.

The President went back to looking at the screen and playing with the trackball. The scientist went into the next room, following the noise to the source. Past all the cages at the other end of the room he found a group of guards assembled near the service entrance.

"What's going on?" asked the scientist.

"Someone here to see the President," said the guard. The other guards continued to shout. The room had a bad echo and the scientist could barely understand them. The guard shouted, "He says the city is in danger and the citizens need the President."

The President, hearing his name above the noise, decided to investigate personally. Like the scientist, he followed the noise to the source.

"Send up the elevator," demanded Cocotele, standing above them, close to the entrance.

"What for?" asked a suspicious guard. "Just come down the ramp."

Before he could react, however, one of the other guards slipped a key into a slot and activated the elevator. A mechanism clinked and a platform began to rise from the floor towards the top of the stairs.

Cocotele's heart quickened. His head pounded. His plan just might work.

"Come down here now," yelled the suspicious guard.

"Who is that man," demanded the President. "Bring him to me."

The guards snapped to attention upon hearing the President's voice, eager to follow his orders. Two of them took off immediately, going up a metal ramp attached to the wall.

"You there," shouted the President, pointing at Cocotele. "Get down here." He stared at Cocotele, recognition triggering in his brain. "Don't I know you?" he asked.

As the platform neared half way, Cocotele quickly hit a button on the wall. The bay door opened and the sound of thunder came in from outside. It got louder, becoming more distinguishable, the sound of massive footsteps. Any one of the thunder lizards would shake the ground, but this was the sound of a herd of full grown tyrannosaurus rexes on the run. Cocotele flattened against the wall, standing back from the entrance.

One of the guards sensed what was happening. "Traitor," he yelled, pointing at Cocotele.

"I thought so," yelled the suspicious guard. "It's a trick."

Cassius was the first to breach the door. He had wanted to smash something and the first thing he saw was two guards coming up a metal ramp. It had supports coming down from above, attaching it to the ceiling. He lowered his head and pushed forward with his huge legs. The metal bent easily and he quickly shoved it out of the way. It smashed into a corner of a support that held the elevator. The platform stopped moving half way from the top, the grinding sound of a motor coming to a halt. Cassius saw the ramp as a stepping stone to the ground floor. The canyon was not that deep for someone his size. He broke through the flimsy railings, leaving it hanging in barely attached pieces. Guards clung to the metal, but Cassius leaped past them onto the platform, continuing in a second bound to the main floor.

Rex came through right behind Cassius, following his comrade's path of destruction. He kicked a piece of metal out of the way and crushed a piece of railing underfoot. He took a swipe at a guard hanging on to a broken piece of railing that was hanging from the ceiling.

The guard pulled back, screaming, trying to scramble to safety. Rex moved on, leaping towards the platform behind Cassius, stepping stone to the ground floor. Another tyrannosaurus rex whizzed past the guard, barely missing him, followed by another. It was the last one that got him, Brutus, stopping on the platform for a moment to roar, announcing the presence of the King and his Elite Guard in the building. Other members of the Elite Guard joined him. It was a dinosaur war cry that echoed through all the rooms in the prison. It even shook dust and turned heads in the far corners of the equipment room where workers were clearing debris. Then Brutus bit the hanging guard, picking him up in his razor sharp teeth and closing his jaws over and over until the guard became a wad of unrecognizable green pulp in his mouth. He spit it against the wall and it dripped into a puddle on the floor.

"Protect the President," yelled the suspicious guard. "Fall back to the laboratory." Several of the guards advanced to face the dinosaurs while the remaining ones formed a protective cover in front of the President. They quickly retreated to the laboratory. Above on the catwalks, more guards appeared. One aimed a gun at Rex and fired.

Rex dodged the ray as a piece of broken metal burst into flames beside him. Cassius advanced, stepping on one of the puny guards while standing above the other. He opened his jaws over him. Spittle from his mouth dripped on the guard as the alien screamed in terror. His strange, high pitched voice squealed. Cassius brought his head down, muffling the scream in his mouth, then he silenced it with a final, crunchy chomp.

The lower half of the body fell to the floor. He spit the other half up at the catwalk, denting the catwalk and hitting the guard who was aiming the gun. The sheer mass of being hit with something half his size knocked him off balance and caused him to drop the ray gun. He screamed when the body hit him. It landed on top of him, alien blood dripping and smearing across his clean uniform. It was the look in the dead alien's face that made him scream, the still alien face with that frozen look of terror. It stared at him, a message of fear. He screamed again, trapped under the body, held in place by a twisted piece of railing. He screamed again but nobody came to his aid, the frozen face staring at him.

The President retreated to the other room. "Detonate the charges," he ordered.

"But sir, some of our own men are out there," protested the guard.

"Do it," commanded the President. "Detonate the charges. It's our only hope of stopping them."

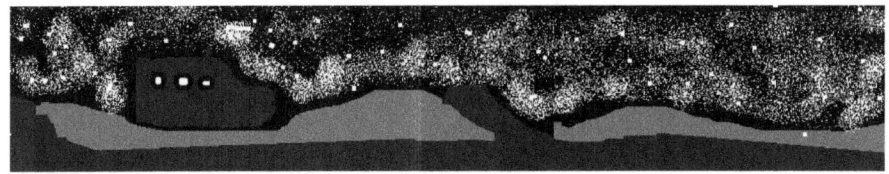

Chapter 31: I Smell Them

The guard went to a portable panel and began pushing buttons. Explosions rocked the room. The elevator platform under Brutus exploded, throwing him across the room where he struck a wall. The war cry of the Elite Guard was silenced. He fell to the floor unconscious, debris falling on top of him. The metal supports that held the elevator in place buckled and the platform fell. It struck the ground and a crack formed in the wall where the supports had pulled away. The crack spread up the side of the building until it reached the frame above the large door.

A second explosion blasted the area near the ramp. A piece of flying debris hit Cocotele and he fell to the ground unconscious. The catwalk was struck as well, knocking a guard over the side as it came loose and collapsed to the floor below. Flying debris from the explosion hit the doorway and the door frame gave way. The crack opened wider and the wall collapsed, followed by a section of the roof, burying Cocotele in a grave of rubble and debris. Daylight streamed in through the massive hole, illuminating the artificial canyon. Penelope looked in from outside.

A guard saw her through the hole. "Fall back," he yelled. "There are more of them coming."

"These are the monsters the President warned us about," said another.

They retreated into the laboratory in fear.

Cassius started to pursue but paused to sniff the air. "I smell him," he said. "I smell my son."

Rex was in front of the cage that held Natalie. He sniffed it, inhaling deeply. "I smell my daughter as well," he said. "They were here, all of them, in these small cages."

Cassius roared again, his anger boiling into rage. He stepped towards the broken doors of the laboratory as the Guards continued to back away.

He spoke to the retreating guards, even though they couldn't understand him. "Is this where you kept him?" he asked. Rex moved forward with him.

More charges were detonated behind Cassius and Rex. One exploded between Cassius and the doors, directly underneath some of the guards. They screamed as they flew in the air landing a short distance away. Cassius ducked under a flying piece of metal, barely missing an injury.

In the confusion, guards, scientists and technicians rushed forward to close and secure the massive doors. The doors creaked with strain. The aliens used one of their digging machines to upright and hold the loose doors in place. The sound of stressed metal filled the air as they closed with a thud. They left the digging machine parked behind the doors as a barricade. Working quickly, they pumped emergency sealant over the doors, using it to putty cracks and sure up the barrier between them and the rampaging dinosaurs. More workers placed angled braces and massive metal beams against the doors and secured them in place. They continued to hear explosions on the other side of the door. There were sounds of guards screaming. The aliens knew their comrades were buying them precious time with their lives.

Rex, Cassius and Antilles retreated to huddle in a corner of the room of cages.

"This place seems safe," said Cassius. "But those volcano blasts took out two of our team."

"Three," corrected Rex. "Don't forget Cocotele." Rex pointed with his head to the fallen alien. His body lay in the rubble, partially covered, but broken at such an odd angle that they knew he could never be repaired.

"They want to keep us away from those doors," said Rex.

"The children aren't here, sire," said Antilles.

"They're behind those doors," said Rex. "That's where the scent leads."

"I know," said Cassius. "I smelled it too."

"Looks like the small volcano blasts have stopped," said Antilles. "I'll make sure." He moved off cautiously, scouting the area for guards.

"I don't think we can trick them into opening up this door," said Rex.

"Nope," said Cassius. "Doubt it."

"What do you say we try smashing it down," said Rex.

"You want to smash the door down?" said Cassius.

"Yes," said Rex. "Smash it down. That's what you wanted to do originally, isn't it?"

"Yes. It's just good to hear you say that," said Cassius. "I love smashing through their little barricades. Let's go."

Rex and Cassius threw themselves against the door. Nothing happened. It stood as firm as a rock wall.

Antilles heard the noise and joined Rex and Cassius. The three of them charged the weakened door. It started to buckle but it would not give. They smashed at it again. There were groans and creaking sounds but still the doors would not give way.

On the other side, aliens continued to secure the doors using anything they could find. They debated bringing the other digging machine out of the tunnel. Guards discussed what they would do if the doors gave. The pounding was terrifying. The sound of the dinosaurs hitting the door became rhythmic, like the ticking of a doomsday clock. The sound continued for a while, then suddenly stopped.

"We have to get in there," said Rex, taking a breath.

"We need to synchronize our thrusts," said Antilles.

"All together," said Rex.

"For the children," yelled Cassius

They threw themselves at the door together creating one mighty force. A dent formed in the doors. Encouraged, they hit it again. They stepped back, preparing to strike again. As they slammed into the doors, there were suddenly four dinosaurs heaving together. Brutus had recovered from the explosion and joined them.

Antilles was happy to see him. "Glad you're okay," he said. "What were you doing, napping?"

"I woke up hungry," he said, indicating a few guards he had just neutralized. "You didn't see these guys behind you, did you?"

"I thought we got them all," said Cassius.

"The doors," said Rex. "Let's give it another try. Together now."

They slammed into it together, getting a slow, steady rhythm to it. Behind the doors the floor shuddered. Technicians cowered, unsure if their temporary fortifications would hold. The digging machine being used as a barricade jumped backward, moving in tiny bumps towards the guards.

Workers went back to removing debris and tunneling in the equipment room, the only other exit. The aliens realized they had barricaded themselves into a trap. The digging machine in the tunnel sputtered to life, grabbing and chopping rock into tiny bits. The crew worked feverishly to move the cut rock out of the way to build an escape route.

The dinosaurs rammed the doors again. They stepped back, roared "For the children!" and slammed into the doors again. This time it felt different, not quite solid rock, more like soft dirt. The doors cracked, and they could see inside the room through a hole that appeared.

They hit it again, this time something seemed to give. There was more force.

"Did you miss me boys," said Penelope, joining them.

Antilles and Brutus laughed.

"Keep at it," yelled Cassius.

They rammed into it again, working together. The doors gave, one jamming outward while the other fell flat. Rubble flew from underneath and bits of hardened sealant shattered against the walls. A piece of shrapnel hit an alien killing him instantly. The digging machine rolled over on its side crushing two more.

Terrified aliens took off running. Antilles and Brutus were the first through the door, squeezing their way through the tight opening. They pushed the digging machine out of the way and the leaning door with no hinges fell flat. They began to pursue the fleeing aliens but were blocked by a line of guards holding painsticks.

The guards stood, defiant and defensive, protected behind armor and shields. Brutus snapped at them and one jutted forward and jabbed Antilles in the leg with a painstick. He screamed, horrible dinosaur screams. Brutus lunged forward in retaliation, trying to bite the guard, but he ducked behind his shield. He tried snapping at him again, and the guard used the shield to keep his jaws away. It was like fighting a triceratops.

Behind the guards and hidden around a corner, the President stood before the monitor twisting the trackball fanatically. Through all this he remained focused, scanning constantly with the targeting device. "Where are they?" he asked himself, searching for dinosaurs to destroy. The alien scientist tried to help him but the President shrugged him off. The scientist stepped back and stood aside respectfully.

The President scanned through scenes of destruction at the starport, once a magnificent achievement of the alien civilization. There were holes and cracks in the landing fields. Crashed and damaged spaceships lay in piles and pieces. There were fallen gun trucks, broken buildings, and wreckage everywhere. Bodies of aliens and dinosaurs littered the ground.

He twisted the trackball, stopping to stare at the dead brontosaurus lying on its side, spilled intestines oozing from the open wound in his underbelly. A fallen pterodactyl laid still and silent beside him.

"Where are they?" asked the President. "They've left the starport." He continued twisting the trackball. The machine hummed louder, continuing to build charge as the President searched.

When the door fell, Cassius charged through the opening and went left, following a scent into a long room full of broken laboratory equipment. Rex was close behind. The Captain bounded over debris, shoving things aside as he sniffed the air. He suddenly stopped, then slowly used his head to nudge a pile of junk aside. There on the floor was a small leg, bloody on one side where it had been ripped from the body. There were three distinctive gashes on it, deep and red, overshadowed by a burn mark.

Cassius was in shock. "His badge of courage," he said sadly, staring down at the leg. "He got those... I was teaching him to hunt."

He sniffed, looking up and following his nose to where he found Nate's body strapped to the nearby table. The leg was missing and his chest was sawed open, revealing his insides. His face was frozen in pain, yet somehow peaceful, as if death had been welcome after so much suffering. There was a defiant smirk on his face.

"Rebellious to the end," muttered Cassius. He sniffed again, but this time it was to suppress a tear from forming in his eye. He looked mournfully at the corpse. Thank goodness his mother wasn't here to see him like this. Then he realized his homeworld had been destroyed and his wife was probably dead as well.

Rex came up beside him and stared down at Nate. He started to say something, but somehow could not find the words.

Cassius stewed, a sea of torrid emotions. Anger grew in his heart. How could they do this to a child? Nature was cruel, but this was sadistic. This was evil visited upon them from other living things. Didn't the aliens realize what they were doing? It didn't make sense. Cassius looked over at the guards. Antilles and Brutus were snapping ineffectively at them. The Captain of the Guard thought about what they did to his son, about his son's body lying nearby, open on a table, vivisected as if gored by a raptor. Nate had been restrained. The cowards didn't even give him a fighting chance.

He couldn't take it any longer. With surprising speed, he pivoted on his powerful legs and bounded towards the guards.

"For the children," he yelled, attacking the guards with renewed vengeance. "Move aside, he said to Brutus and Antilles. "I'll show you how to handle these guys." He raised his head high, as if to bite down on them. As the guards raised their shields above their heads, he spun in a circle, swinging at their feet with his tail. They fell like rotten trees in a windstorm. Brutus lunged forward, stepping on two of the fallen guards before they could react. Their bodies were crushed under his huge feet.

Some of the fallen guards managed to roll out of the way and run for the escape tunnel. Antilles took up the chase, pushing past Cassius and Brutus. As he broke through the lines a brave alien stepped forward and jabbed him with a painstick.

"Ahhh, now that hurt!" yelled Antilles.

Cassius lunged forward and crushed the brave alien. He stepped on his arm and broke it against some rock debris on the floor. The painstick snapped in half and clunked to the ground, breaking into a sharp point that exposed the inner mechanism. It fell among the debris, activated, ready to inflict pain, but useless with no hand to wield it.

Two guards slipped past Rex and back into the room of cages. Penelope took off after them. Rex heard high pitched squeals and screams from the room. He turned around in time to see Brutus and Antilles disappear into the equipment room towards the escape tunnel.

Cassius started to run after them, but stopped to coordinate with Rex. The room had emptied of all but a few guards. Some had run back towards the room of cages, but most went towards the tunnel. The remaining few stood near the President, defending their leader. Rex and Cassius looked down the long end of the room towards the President, busy at his monitor. Between them were three guards trying to look defiant, but the smell of fear told the dinosaurs they felt otherwise. The alien technician beside the President didn't look like much of a threat.

"Let me deal with this lot," said Rex. "Go join the hunt."

Cassius started to take off after Brutus and Antilles, but instead stopped for a moment. In one swift movement he lunged towards the frozen guards. He pushed one out of the way with his tail, tossing him against the wall. The guard struck with a thud, then collapsed in a heap at the bottom of the wall. Then he clamped his jaws down over the other guard's head. He shook his mouth, and the weight of the body ripped free from the head and dropped to the floor beside the alien technician.

The third guard stood rooted in fear. He made a strange, sudden gesture, pointing towards the other side of the room. Rex and Cassius followed his movement, looking away for a moment. The guard was swift. Running for all he could, he darted past the dinosaurs and into the room of cages.

Rex laughed, the sight was almost comical.

"We won't have any more trouble from him," said Cassius.

"Thanks for the help," said Rex, turning his attention back towards the President and the technician. "I think I can handle these two."

Cassius nodded and went off to join his men.

The President had his full attention on the monitor and the trackball. The alien technician, still shaking from the sight of the headless guard on the floor at his feet, saw Rex advance. He tried to warn the President, but Rex reached out with his claw and grabbed him by the leg, holding him upside down and dangling him like a twisted puppet. He screamed and fainted.

The machine suddenly hummed louder, catching Rex's attention. He looked about the room, spying Nate's leg in the debris on the floor. He, too, recognized the leg with its distinctive scars. He stared at the President in disbelief.

"How could you do this to children?" he asked the President. "Innocent children? Why would you possibly want to bring them here for this?"

Again he looked at Nate's body across the room, then back at the President who was still focused on the monitor and ignoring him. Rex swung the alien scientist like a club, hitting the President on the shoulder.

"Hey, I'm talking to you," he screamed.

The President was stunned, he backed away, rubbing his shoulder. Rex ranted on, as if the President could understand him, but to the alien it only sounded like the angry roars of a dinosaur.

"Don't you have children of your own?" asked Rex. "At least show some respect for the son of my Captain."

As he talked, he gesticulated with his hands, trying to be expressive. The alien scientist's body dangled in his claw like a limp rag. It made Rex look even more menacing as he spoke, a jerking body thrashing in his grasp.

"Nate was my daughter's best friend, and Cassius wanted more for his son than this," said Rex. He threw his claws outward and he alien scientist hit his head on the wall. Blood gushed from a crack in his skull. Rex held the limp body up and looked at what he had done.

The President had been studying the beast, waiting for just such a moment. He looked down and spied the broken painstick on the floor. He had an evil thought. Using a piece of cloth from a fallen guard, he reached out and picked it up, aimed the pointed end at Rex and lunged forward with all his body weight behind it. The stick connected with Rex at a soft spot on his thigh. It went in deep, then snapped off, leaving only a small piece of it sticking out. The nub of the painstick hummed and throbbed, activating as it sensed flesh.

Rex screamed in agony as he railed back and dropped to the floor. The dead alien scientist fell from his grasp, dropping beside him. Rex thrashed about, trying to shake the stick out. He tried to bite it out with his teeth but it was just out of reach. He squirmed on the ground beating his leg against the floor, trying to knock the stick loose, but it would not come free.

Chapter 32: Descent into Madness

The President laughed while Rex thrashed on the ground in agony. The pain was incredible, like nothing the King had ever felt before. It blinded him, his eyes watered and they became red with pain. He lay in the rubble on the floor, unable to focus, knocking objects about as he squirmed. He roared as he tried to shake the stick loose, but it was jammed. He could see it in his thigh. There was a small light flashing rhythmically in an exposed part of the stick, and with each flash of the light he felt pain.

The humming grew louder.

The President gloated over the fallen King. It didn't matter that Rex couldn't understand a word he was saying. But gloating is like that; the words are really for the speaker's benefit. "Thought you could take us, did you?" he said, taunting the fallen King. "We showed you. We destroyed your planet! It was I who caused the comet to crash into your world. You were fools to come here and confront us. You should have stayed on your own planet where you belonged." In anger, he went over to Rex and stepped on the wound with the painstick, kicking it and running away before Rex could react.

The humming in the room became louder as the machine built more potential energy.

"I was right about you all along," said the President. He continued to speak, but Rex could no longer hear the words. He thought about chewing his leg off. Would it stop the pain that was slowly spreading across his body? Every throb of the painstick drilled deeper into his core. It spread like fire across his flesh, burning him with pain.

The President finished gloating and moved away from Rex, returning to the monitor. He stepped over the broken body of the alien scientist, pausing for a moment before taking up the trackball. He manipulated the controls franticly. "Where are they?" he yelled, looking for the dinosaur army.

The machine hummed louder.

"What do I do now?" The President looked over at the broken alien scientist. "Fool. You went and got yourself killed," he said. "Now who's going to explain this machine to me?"

The President heard Rex scream, a horrible moan of agony. It was the cry of a wounded animal. It sent shivers down his spine. He looked at Rex and saw the agony he had caused. He was no longer afraid of the dinosaurs. With the help of this machine, it would all be over soon. He turned back to the monitor.

He found them in the capitol city. The dinosaurs were going berserk, pushing over buildings and stepping on fleeing aliens. Two of the larger beasts were attacking the Presidential Mansion. A triceratops beat his head against the doors, eventually smashing them down. Angry raptors ran through the open door.

"My home," yelled the President. "They are invading my home."

The guards at the mansion looked scared. On the monitor the President could see them running from the dinosaurs. "The cowards," he yelled out loud. "You deserve to die."

He moved towards the switch that would activate the machine. "I wonder if it has enough charge," he said. He looked at the dead alien scientist again, as if expecting an answer. "Maybe I should wait a little longer."

Nearby, King Rex lay on the floor in searing pain. He had never felt anything like this. The painstick kept sending impulses to his brain, causing his nerves to tremble in agony. He tried desperately to reach down and remove the stick, but his short arms could not reach it. He began to go mad with the pain, screaming and roaring.

His mind snapped. No one could take that much pain. Traveling up his leg, up his backbone and into his brain were a million impulses with one message. They throbbed to the beat of a small light flashing on his thigh: Pain. Pain. Pain!

Adrenaline poured into his body. The overload on his nerves had an odd effect, it drove him insane. He twitched and his body quivered uncontrollably. He entered a state of shock where he did not feel the pain any longer. He found a place beyond pain. The redness before his eyes cleared. The image of his wife called to him in a cloud.

Chapter 33: Cassius' Revenge

The equipment room that led to the escape tunnel was the focus of intense fighting. Brutus and Antilles faced devious aliens who had planted explosive traps to try to kill the dinosaurs as they advanced. One had exploded right under Brutus, delivering a fatal wound. The aliens retreated deeper into the room through the tunnel they had been digging. Antilles started to attack, but Cassius arrived just in time to stop him.

"Use your senses," he said to Antilles. "Show some restraint. Don't you smell a trap?"

Brutus sighed, lying on the floor. He was covered with bits of rock and dust and there was a large boulder pinning his leg. "It was foolish, Captain," he said. "I was overconfident."

Antilles looked at the wound in his friend's side. It was grave, a large amount of Brutus' insides were exposed. There were jagged pieces of metal wedged under his arm, puncturing his lung. Breathing was difficult for him.

"Even if we did have an ankylosaurus, I don't know if you're going to make it, old friend," he said. "You look a lot worse than you did after the first battle for the homeworld."

"You saved a lot of kids that day," said Cassius.

"You're right," coughed Brutus, trying to laugh. He tried to talk, his words coming out broken. "I got... pretty tore up... in that one."

They all laughed, recalling a good moment shared in battle. Then things got serious. "The hunt is over for you," said Cassius. "Death is often sudden, with no time to plan. You have been given these precious minutes. Let me take your memory and your spirit with me."

Brutus was weak. "I know it is your right, Captain, but I would rather pass to Antilles. We served together too long."

"A good choice, soldier," said Cassius. "I am burdened by too many honors already. May you find rich game and good friends in the great hunt which lies beyond." He stepped away, turning to study the aliens down the dark tunnel while Antilles comforted his friend.

"It doesn't end, Brutus," said Antilles, bending over his friend. "The great hunt awaits you. You will know all life's answers. As usual, you are going first to lead the way for the rest of us."

Brutus looked as if he was trying to speak. He breathed deep, as painful as it was, the hole in his lungs making it feel as if they would never be full. He heaved and whispered, "Friend," exhaled on a long, raspy breath. Antilles hovered over him and closed his eyes, sniffing deeply, as if inhaling the essence of Brutus and making it a part of him.

"I will honor your memory, and pass your name down in my oral history. I will tell your children about your bravery here at this evil place. My children shall know of my friend, Brutus, and of the adventures we shared. The King will praise your deeds." He went on talking, not realizing Brutus had expired.

"It is over," said Cassius. There was a thump ahead from down in the dark hole where the aliens retreated, drawing their attention away from their deceased friend. "Let's honor his memory. He sacrificed so we could learn of the enemy's cleverness. Don't be in such a hurry to run down there. Let's think it through."

There was a roar and a wail from the other room. "The King," said Cassius, snapping to attention.

"Go," said Antilles. "I'll hold this position until I hear from you."

Cassius was off. The Captain of the Guard ran through the equipment room towards the exit. He heard Rex scream through the open portal, but before he could pass, a metal door slipped out of place, falling down to block his way. He cursed his heavy footsteps and the unstable rock in the room. He again flung himself at a metal door, pounding against it with all his might. He laughed to himself, thinking about how he had wanted to smash doors all day. Now he was getting his wish. "What I wouldn't give for a good Triceratops or a few Pachycephalosaurus," he said to himself.

He heard a muffled scream from the other side of the door. He threw himself against it with all his might. Rex was silent on the other side. Cassius imagined the worst. He began to batter the door, throwing himself against it over and over.

On the other side of the door, Rex was growing more insane by the moment. It didn't matter anymore. Rex knew what it meant to be numb with pain. He stood up, suddenly feeling strong. He heard someone pounding at the door, but he didn't care. The President heard the sound as well and turned away from the monitor, surprised to see the dinosaur king looming over him. He looked up and saw the empty look in Rex's eyes. The dinosaur's jaws were open, dripping spit like a waterfall. The sharp teeth glistened. Rex turned and looked across the room at Nate lying on the slab. The President followed his eyes across the room to see what he was looking at, then he became afraid. Really afraid.

The humming became louder. The pounding at the door continued as Cassius became more desperate. The President started to run. Rex swooped down, turning his body to block the alien with his powerful tail. In his madness, he smiled at the President, picking him up between his teeth. The President screamed, the sharp teeth cut his skin. Rex tasted the blood, his jaws trembled but he fought the impulse to bite down and snap the President in two. He had something else in mind.

The door shuddered again. The President squirmed, but being in the jaws of King Rex was like resting on top of a row of knives. Any wrong movement would cause the dinosaur's teeth to sink deeper. Rex bent his head down and nuzzled the lifeless body of the young t-Rex laying on a slab. He gently pushed it off the table, a hint of sadness in his eyes. The President looked on in terror. Rex opened his jaws, dropping him onto the empty table. It activated something which caused straps to snap up from the sides, trapping the President in place.

The door shuddered again, the humming grew even louder, but Rex did not notice. He hung his head over the table, dripping spit on the President again. He looked beside the table at the young T-rex. He nuzzled the body again, half expecting it to come to life, so strong was his insanity. He went over to the wall where the leg laid. He picked it up in his teeth and set it down beside the body. He pushed it gently with his nose, expecting it to somehow reattach itself. Then he thought about what he was doing and stopped. He had the thought that he must be going mad. He noticed the body was cut open, the insides had fallen out. Why hadn't he noticed that before? Then he felt the pain again and he screamed.

The Captain of the Guard heard the scream and put all his might behind the next blow. The door gave way slightly, he could feel it. He stepped back, taking another run at it. The door shuddered and fell forward. He saw Rex standing over the President, the President strapped firmly to the table. Beside the table on the floor was his son, the leg put back in place where it had once been. He looked over at the King and saw the wound in his leg, the protruding painstick broken off, the flashing light. "Your majesty," he said. "You've been hurt."

Rex turned calmly towards him, talking in a spooky voice. "It's all right, Captain," he said. "Everything's under control." He grimaced, feeling the painstick send a jolt up his leg. His mind clouded again. "Your son is all right. He's just resting."

The Captain was afraid. He had never seen the King like this. He recognized the device stuck in the King's thigh. He noticed that Rex grimaced every time the light on the painstick flashed. "Are you all right?" he asked.

"Just fine," said Rex. "Just fine. Look at what I have here," he said, indicating the President strapped to the table. "I was just about to have a little fun."

The humming grew louder. The Captain of the Guard and the King turned to look at the monitor. They saw the dinosaurs fighting the aliens in the capitol city. A brontosaurus was picking up vehicles in his mouth and heaving them across the field in front of the Presidential Mansion, piling them up like broken boulders. The triceratops pounded buttresses that were holding up the sides of the building. The structure was weakening. They watched it crumble and suddenly a whole side wall of the mansion fell, exposing the insides. They could see aliens running and screaming, cowering in terror before the wrath of the dinosaurs.

A pterodactyl swooped down over an alien that had fallen to the ground. He picked him up in his claws, flapping his strong, leathery wings to gain altitude quickly. He flew off the monitor until seconds later they saw the body pass down across the screen as it fell to the ground.

Through the open building raptors had already breached the first floor of the mansion, making their way quickly through the inner corridors and silencing the screams one by one. On the highest floor a band of alien children huddled, cowering in the corner. A female struggled with the door, trying to open it. A brontosaurus craned his head into the room and snatched her up, tossing her a long way into the air before she fell onto the pile of cars he had been making. The children screamed.

There were a few alien spaceships trying to fight off the dinosaur attack, but they were ineffective. They were doing more damage to the city than the attackers. A ray shot out from one ship, aimed at a raptor, but he was quick. The ray missed and instead started a fire in the mansion. The pterodactyl swooped down, picking up another alien. He dropped him into the center of the fire.

Everywhere aliens fled in terror. The brontosaurus continues to fling cars, aiming at the ships and at crowds of running aliens. Many of them missed their targets and collided into buildings, ripping huge gashes in them and raining debris on the fleeing aliens. As one crowd turned a corner, they ran into a pack of dilophosaurus who spit venom on them. The aliens grabbed their faces and screamed as the poison made them tremble and die.

Rex turned to the President, helplessly strapped to the table. "How does it feel to see your world collapsing," he said, his voice again sounding spooky and weird.

It scared the Captain of the Guard. "Your majesty, are you all right?" he asked again.

"I'm all right, Captain," he said calmly, his eyes hollow. The way he moved was weird, too, slow and controlled, like each motion was purposeful. "I have everything in control. You can go now, if you'd like. Take your son home."

Now that really scared the Captain. He knew something was wrong. "I think I'll stay, if it's all right with you," he said. He looked down at the Kings leg. The wound was bleeding and he again recognized the painstick as a weapon the guards had used in battle. His hide still stung where he had felt it touch him. "Sire, you're wounded," he said.

"Yeah, I know," he replied in a matter of fact voice. The Captain might as well have told him that it was raining outside, or that the walls were brown. He didn't seem to care. Then the Captain understood. He imagined what it would be like with one of those stuck in your leg. He remembered hearing the horrifying roars of his king through the door. That seemed so long ago, long before the death of Brutus, before he battered the door down to get in here. What pain it must have been. What pain it must still be causing, he couldn't imagine. He knew what must be done.

"Your Majesty," he said, calmly as if he were talking to a child. "Excuse me, but you have a thorn in your leg."

The King looked down at his bleeding leg. The flashing light beat rhythmically. "Ah, so I have," he said calmly. "I had some trouble with that earlier. Couldn't seem to get it out."

"Let me," began the Captain, lowering his head. The King stuck out his leg. "This may hurt a bit," he said, summoning all his strength. He stuck out his teeth, slowly clenching the end of the painstick in his mouth. The pain was incredible, more than he had imagined when he'd thought about the King's pain. It shot up his lips and tunneled deep between his eyes, striking at the very center of his brain. The King roared a terrifying roar. The President quivered in fear, the sound shaking him to the core.

The Captain resisted the urge to let go, but the pain was overwhelming. Instead he clenched tighter, he thought of a time long ago when he had been hurt defending the King. It had been why he was made Captain of the Guard and why he now bore the mark of three red slashes on his neck. He remembered staving off an attack from Roughstone. Cassius had been wounded in the fight, bleeding at the neck. The King had watched over him until the medical dinosaurs could be summoned and leaves could be gathered to ease the pain. During that time the King had put a stick into his mouth and told him to bite down, that it would ease the pain. He did so without questioning, and it did seem to ease the pain. He thought of all these things, as if time stood still while he clenched that awful painstick in his jaws. The stick refused to move, and the Captain thought again of the Kings words that day, and he bit down hard and tugged with all his might.

The King screamed again and the building shook with the roar of his voice. Dust fell from the ceiling and fell into the President's eyes. Rex pulled his leg back and the stick came loose, held tight between the Captain's teeth.

Cassius turned to spit it out, but as he looked down he saw his son's body on the floor. He suddenly felt the pain of that stick, the full knowledge of what he had in his mouth. He also felt a different pain. The pain of losing a son, the pain of losing his planet, the pain of never seeing home again. He looked down at the President and thrust the sharpened painstick deep into the President's leg.

He came down with such force that it stuck all the way through his leg and into the table, pinning him the way he had seen big leaves pinned on the horns of stegosaurus when they emerged from the jungle. The President screamed. The table fell over on its side. Rex smiled, still in a state of madness and shock. When the President's scream had faded, they all heard the hum of the machine suddenly get louder.

The President laughed. "Soon you will all be dead," he said.

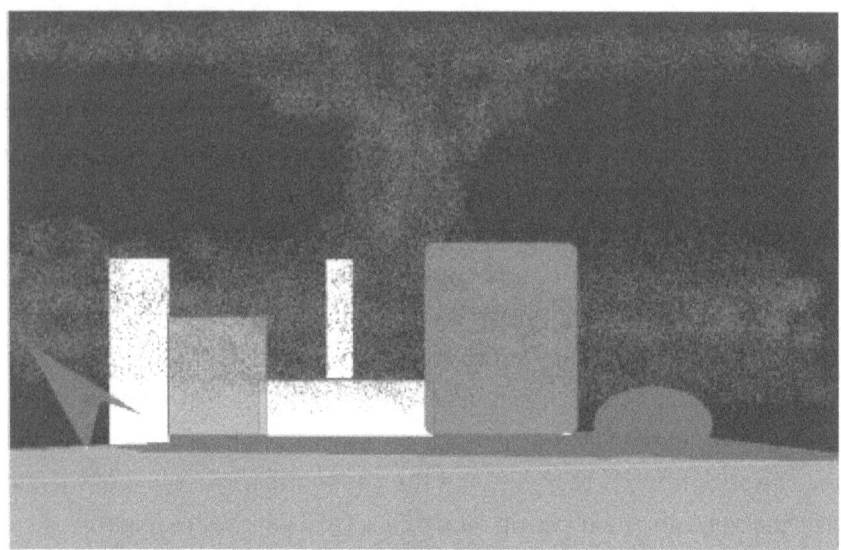

Chapter 34: The City of Death

The Captain regained his composure, understanding what was at stake. He had felt the intense pain, but his mind was coming back to him now. "What do you mean?" he said.

The President could not understand him. He twitched in pain, his leg still speared with the painstick. He screamed.

The Captain grew angry with him. "Does it hurt?" he yelled. "Here, let me help." He reached down and bit the offending leg off, severing the President's leg and the painstick from his body. "Is that better?" he mocked, watching the President squirm beneath the bonds that still held him firmly to the table. Blood poured from the stump. He thought of how his son must have struggled in much the same matter when these barbarians cut off his leg. He felt a strange satisfaction, but somehow it left a bad taste in his mouth, like he had gotten hold of some rotten meat. He spit, but the taste did not go away.

Rex turned and looked at the target monitor. The presidential mansion was crumbling; the fire consuming what little was left. The fighting had slowed a bit. He could see aliens fleeing in the distance, chased by dinosaurs.

"You think that you have won," said the President. "You think that this is over."

They both turned to look at him, and again the sound of the machine got louder.

There was a noise across the room. Several alien guards came through the doorway from the room of cages. They saw the President strapped to the table and the two dinosaurs hovering over him.

They screamed, like they had entered the wrong room or interrupted something important. They ran past the dinosaurs and into the equipment room, heading towards the escape tunnel they had heard about. Penelope was right behind them.

The Captain of the Guard lunged forward instinctively, chasing after the aliens as they ran. He disappeared through the door. Rex and the President heard explosions come from that direction.

The sound of the weapon got louder.

Rex followed the Captain of the Guard. The President saw a chance to escape, he twisted slightly and was able to free an arm enough to hit the release button on the side of the table. The bonds snapped back into the table, freeing him. He fell to the ground, struggling with the pain of his lost limb. He looked down where he had once had a leg and he cursed the dinosaurs. He looked up at the monitor and saw the battle in the city. It was not looking good for the aliens. His men were retreating and his mansion was in ruins. He grew determined to strike the last blow. Slowly he crawled forward, pulling himself along with his arms, making his way towards the console.

The machine got louder. Another explosion thundered in the corridor. He crawled another meter, pulling himself along again, getting closer to the console that controlled the weapon. It got louder again.

Roars echoed from the corridor and then alien screams. The screams ended one by one as the fighting dinosaurs made quick work of the aliens.

"Go back and check on him," came the Captain's voice from the corridor. "Keep an eye on the evil one."

"No," returned the King. Let's finish these together," he said. "It's good for the hunt, my kinsman."

The Captain recognized the spooky voice again. The madness had not yet ended.

The President got closer, finding new strength and purpose as he heard the sounds of his guards dying. "I must reach the console," he said, pulling himself forward with tremendous effort. Behind him lay a trail of green blood oozing from his open leg wound. He saw the controls now, close at reach, just a bit farther.

The sounds of the battle slowed in the adjacent room. The screams came less often. Rex and Cassius were deep in blood fever. The President could only imagine what the dinosaurs were doing. He heard the sounds of crunching bones and tearing flesh. He heard the machine get louder.

It was quiet, except for the humming of the machine, which Rex, Cassius, Penelope, and Antilles could hear even though they were in the far end of the equipment room. Crushed aliens were everywhere, broken into pieces under their feet. The floor was like a sticky bog. Rex sniffed the air.

"They went this way," he said to Cassius, indicating the hole the aliens had dug to escape.

"It's dangerous down there," said Cassius. "They have more volcano blasts. That's what killed Brutus."

Rex sniffed again, and Cassius as well. "I smell it too," he said. "Young dinosaur flesh, and waste."

"They went down this hole," said Penelope.

Rex sniffed again. His instinct began to tingle. The taste of battle faded and he sniffed the air for messages. He smelled the sweat in the laboratory, the overpowering smell of alien blood, now so familiar to him. He did not smell the fear anymore, no this was something different. He ran towards the laboratory in time to see the President propped next to the console, his hand on a strange lever.

Penelope followed him. "I have searched everywhere in this covered canyon. There are no children here."

"I suspected as much," he said. "But they were here at one time. We have a scent on their trail. Cassius and Antilles need your help getting past the traps our enemies have set."

"What about you?" she asked.

"Go," said Rex. "Follow the trail. I have something to do before I join you."

He looked at Nate's body again, the tiny leg beside it that he had set so carefully in place. The marks of his manhood stood out prominently. He thought of his world, of Natalie, of the Queen. He thought of the kidnapped children, the death of Pilot, the sacrifice of the brave Sergeant. He thought of the time he had senselessly killed an alien, and how the Queen had helped him come to terms with his conflicting emotions.

"Helena," he sighed, his heart aching. He loved her and he missed her so much. In his life he had felt the pain from harsh wounds, pain from burns of lightning bolts, even the pain of a deadly painstick. But there was no pain like the loss of a loved one. "Give me back the physical pain," he said. "I can't take this weight on my heart."

Penelope touched him, sending waves of comfort through the King.

"I'm sorry," he said. "I am weak."

"Love does not make you weak," said Penelope. "Just as you were able to endure the pain of open wounds, so you will also survive this new pain you feel now." She sent healing energy into his body, comfort and reassurance.

"We were building a life together. No, an empire," said Rex.

"All that was ever built, will crumble," she said, quoting the wisdom of the dinosaur masters. "Live as if all you will ever own are memories."

"They were good memories," said Rex.

"They are good memories," she said, correcting him. "When we hold our loved ones in memory, it is the present, not the past. By that magic, they are always with us."

Rex understood.

The machine hummed louder.

"Go to Cassius and Antilles. They need your help," said Rex. "I'll finish up here and join you."

Penelope left. Rex turned his attention to the President. He hummed gently to the President, trying to imitate sounds he heard his wife make often when she soothed the aliens. Penelope was right, love was stronger. Love overcomes even fear. He felt sad for the President.

"You must not have had a lot of love in your life," he said to the President.

The President didn't understand him. It just sounded like sad growls to him. "Don't come any closer," he shouted at Rex.

Rex took another step, looking at the monitor where dinosaurs and aliens fought each other. Ships from the other side of the planet had joined the fight. The weapons they used were doing more damage to the city than the dinosaurs were doing. One of them crashed into a building. Bodies were everywhere. A singed dinosaur was on its side smoking. Broken vehicles cluttered the streets. Half gutted buildings spewed contents everywhere.

"We could have done so much more than this together," said Rex to the President. He stepped forward.

"I warned you," said the President. "Stay back! I'll kill them all."

Rex didn't understand him. He couldn't understand any of this.

Once more, the hum got louder. Rex moved closer. The President wondered why he hadn't pulled the lever already. His mansion was already destroyed. Sadly, that had been his main concern. "I have nothing to lose anymore," he said. He looked at Rex and laughed. "You're too late," he said, pulling the lever.

The hum started to resonate, the sound of a giant switch activating, then a massive rush, like giant waves crashing against a rock beach, loud and pervasive. The room seemed to empty of all air, their ears popped like they do in high altitude. And then silence, except for what they saw on the monitor for the brief seconds that were the last moments of their lives.

Next to the palace where the targeting device had been pointed a tiny cloud formed, a dust devil that began to swirl and grow bigger. It rotated, this cloudy mass, stretching red tendrils of wind outward as it grew. The rotating wind, swirling in a circle, spread wider, growing in terrible force. It slammed against the rubble of the palace, picking up large chunks of debris and slinging it about. The pile of vehicles and debris that the brontosaurus had made collapsed, stripped flat as if a giant foot had kicked it and scattered it in a burst. Dinosaurs and aliens began to get caught up in it as it continued to grow, a red cloud of dust, like a tornado pressing down upon the surface. The dust blasted against the buildings, crushing them in rubble and breaking off pieces of wall and ceiling and turning them into flying debris to smash against the next thing in its path.

And the cloud grew to giant proportions, somehow fueled by the disaster it was causing. The shape of the alien planet began to change. The green gardens were ripped from the soil, exposing the rock beneath. The buildings were hammered into tiny pieces. The aliens and dinosaurs suffered the same fate as their bodies were sandblasted by the dust.

The cloud grew, expanding outward, a terrible wind beginning to blow across the plains. It was huge now, reaching high into the atmosphere, forming a spout that spit out a stream of red dust that rained down on the planet. What did not die from being blasted, suffocated in that dense air of pulverized rock and flesh. Behind the moving cloud was nothing, a desert of red rock and dust in its wake.

They watched the monitor until they themselves were engulfed in the cataclysm. The walls of the prison began to tremble, shaking dust free from cracks that got larger and larger. The metal doors trembled and all at once the full force of the wind ripped the top of the building off. The terrifying sound of the wind was everywhere. It swirled in the room, blowing things around and around with more and more strength. Jars of dinosaur parts on shelves began to shake, some of them falling, some of them getting caught in the wind and disappearing into the storm. Debris on the floor began to vanish, pulled into the whirling red wind. Nate's body shuddered on the floor beside the dissecting table. The table broke free of the floor mounts and disappeared, giving the wind an open path to take Nate's body away.

Rex and the President looked helplessly on. The lifeless body of the technician rolled over, pulled into a seated position by the wind just before it vanished into the maelstrom. The President was next, his hand slipping from the control bar as his grip faded in the force of the wind. His face contorted with the effort, he finally screamed in terror as he was pulled upward. Rex watched as he hung there in mid air, suspended for a moment until a piece of flying metal sliced him in half. The two parts danced like tree limbs until they were pushed aside by the curtain of red dust.

Rex's eyes watered, he squinted to keep the dust away. He tried to roar, defying the storm to take him, but his lungs were empty. The pressure of the wind took the last breath from him. "Mrrrrr," was the last sound he made. He lost his balance and fell, never touching the floor as he was sucked into a river of dust that sandblasted his body into tiny bits. The wind continued to lift everything up and out as if through a drain hole in the sky, pulling everything up into a red funnel of death. King Rex and the President joined together in a cloud of doom.

It was clearly visible from space. The storm spread across the surface raking it bare. A dark red spot formed, growing until it engulfed the entire planet. Wind funnels extended high into the planet's atmosphere spewing red rock that rained back down to the surface. In the distance, a burning Earth continued to bleed into space.

The surface of the alien planet cracked that day, huge volcanoes erupted and spewed poisonous gas into the once blue sky. Earthquakes shook the land and the seas choked under the rain of red dust.

Beneath the surface of the alien planet, in a hidden city of the ancients, Natalie rested safely inside the strange sphere. She stirred for a moment, thinking she heard her mother say, "You will be safe, my daughter."

Epilog

Sixty five million years passed. Life never returned to the surface of the alien planet. The red dust covered everything with a fine powder that kept the sunlight and the air away from anything that had a chance to survive.

Eons passed while the planet slept.

Earth, meanwhile, recovered.

In the last part of the last million years, a new species of life emerged on Earth, different, yet just as intelligent as the dinosaurs and the aliens. They studied the sky. The alien planet captivated their interest, as if beckoning them to uncover some mystery, as if somehow the destinies of these two worlds were interrelated.

The new life would be called Man. They would grow clever enough to send spacecraft of their own to investigate the alien planet. They would dig in the dirt, take rock samples, and analyze them. Then they would announce with pride in their scientific methods that one day, in the far distant past, there was possibly life on The Red Planet. That perhaps, Mars was very similar to Earth at one time. Perhaps it even held life that was intelligent.

THE END

Aliens vs. Dinosaurs – Behind the Story

Aliens vs Dinosaurs is really about a father and son inventing bedtime stories. In 1995 the family watched a hurricane take everything they had as they hid in a closet through the night. Windows smashed, tornados shook the floor, and wind pushed rain sideways against the walls. In the aftermath came the cleanup and the recovery. The power was out for months. With no television and no books they started to make up bedtime stories. It began with mom telling a story about how good king Elvis saved the dinosaurs. Suddenly the demand for dinosaur stories went up, especially since one of the few things left behind by the storm were plastic dinosaurs.

It followed with discussions of what would happen. What if dinosaurs were intelligent? How would they fight against aliens with superior technology? At night by lantern light they would draw pictures and imagine ways the dinosaurs would repel aliens. As the story was told and retold it got more elaborate. After three years of oral storytelling they started writing it all down.

The first version of Aliens vs Dinosaurs at the Beginning of Time was published as an eBook in 2001. It was about a team of explorers who find a mysterious sphere on Mars. Inside is a dinosaur princess who tells a fantastic tale about a battle far in the past. She talks about dinosaur children kidnapped and taken away for heinous experiments, aliens and dinosaurs locked in combat, and the fate of two worlds intertwined forever.

Chad Barbour did the exciting cover art and engineered the audio book version of that first story. The younger Delmedico illustrated the insides with pictures drawn in Microsoft Paint. It was a story within a story where explorers make an incredible find. Nick and his father heard on the radio one day how the children who are going to Mars are already born today. That was long before war and economic strain took their toll on mankind's vision to visit other worlds. In retrospect the story was almost prophetic as it weaved a tale of fear and misunderstanding across a backdrop of war.

In the years that followed the publishing of that story, the team presented it to the traditional publishing world. Now the novel really began to evolve as they received artistic feedback from professionals who took the time to hear and read their story. They were worried about the violence but one editor said it was fantasy and that no humans were harmed in the writing of this book, so don't worry about it. She also said they had a great story, but it was buried inside the construct of this modern Martian space thing. Why not just rip the essential story out of it and focus on that. It was a great idea, and so began the rewrite.

Nick, now a sophomore in high school, wrote Chapter One, The Beginning of Time, which officially began the rewriting. He read it at Hugo House, a Seattle landmark for emerging writers, where he received encouragement and education. He and his Dad tag teamed as they wrote and wrote and rewrote. Together they drafted new plot lines. A nameless dinosaur strapped to a table became a major character. The princess had a name change. The dinosaur world took on new dimensions as they built palaces among thick jungles. Likewise the alien world took on proportions that stretched the limits of their imaginations.

One agent told them it wasn't long enough, so they added details and character development. They went to writing classes, joined the Pacific

Northwest Writers and went to their conference every year where they met more agents and editors (as well as some of their favorite authors). A Hollywood agent loved it, agreed that it was high concept and offered more comment. He said the story needed more time in the dinosaur world in the beginning. So now you know where the prologue came from as they added Chapter zero to the tale. It seems that the details had always been in the back of their minds. They just needed someone prodding it out of the muck.

There was more prodding and even some Rick Rolling as agents and editors continued to provide input. Someone said it was silly that the aliens and dinosaurs could talk and it wasn't realistic. Now communication and culture became part of the story. Another said the ending was implausible, but then reversed that decision after reading the story. Finally in 2009 they had a good draft of the second version. The older Nick even wrote the story as a screen play and entered it in a contest, helping the team visualize it from a new perspective. Tweaks and changes, but through all this time the draft incubated until it emerged in late 2011 in the final version. Well, not quite final. When they made it into an audio book they really trashed chapter 10 which resulted in a reissue of the book. E-publishing is very forgiving. But other than that it was deemed complete, bringing an end to seventeen years of telling and retelling a story, orally and in writing, until it emerged like a diamond from years of prehistoric pressure.

Is there more to the story? Of course! The team imagined this as a trilogy. The second and third books are already plotted out. The oral history of telling and retelling has already started. Stories on par with the original, in a world based on seventeen years of history. Working titles at this point are Aliens vs. Dinosaurs, the Battle of Zinthar and Aliens vs. Dinosaurs, Escape from Disaster.

Before beginning another novel they want to gauge the success of this story. Hopefully it won't be another seventeen years! Thanks for supporting this lifetime of work.

*Rod Gonzales, friend and artist
(1948-2012)*

Rod drew the fantastic pictures of aliens and dinosaurs fighting on pages 12, 19, 61, 163, and 185. He helped visualize our project and contributed to the rewrite with ideas that brought it to life. He described these pictures with such depth. The one below, for example. The brontosaurus are sacrificing themselves so the raptors can climb up and bring down the alien ships. In the background left, a baby dinosaur is abducted in an organic bag. The skies are filled with fighting ships and flying dinosaurs.

Rod lives on, and not just in the art he left behind. He loved Mt. Denali, and I believe his restless, artistic spirit lives somewhere up there with Mary, his wife of many years, where he paints the mountain with color for the tourists in the summer. The rest of the time he's playing hockey on the mountain glaciers, competing for the Stanley Cup which he always thought belonged in Alaska. God Bless Ya, Rod.

www.ingramcontent.com/pod-product-compliance
Lightning Source LLC
Chambersburg PA
CBHW070833120626
46556CB00002B/747